W9-BDQ-804

SEXUAL STRATEGIES

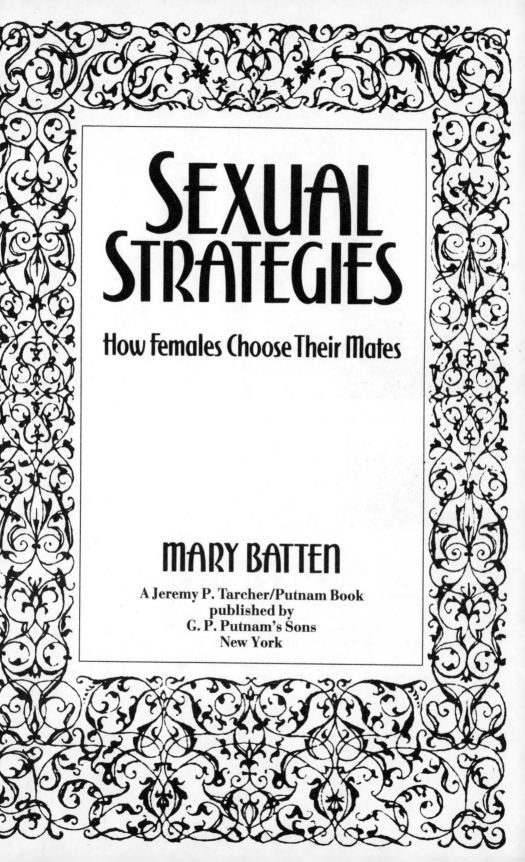

SEXUAL STRATEGIES

How Females Choose Their Mates

MARY BATTEN

A Jeremy P. Tarcher/Putnam Book
published by
G. P. Putnam's Sons
New York

A Jeremy P. Tarcher/Putnam Book
Published by G. P. Putnam's Sons
Publishers Since 1838
200 Madison Avenue
New York, NY 10016

Copyright © 1992 by Mary Batten

All rights reserved. This book, or parts thereof, may not be reproduced in any form without permission. Requests for such permissions should be addressed to:

Jeremy P. Tarcher, Inc.
5858 Wilshire Blvd., Suite 200
Los Angeles, CA 90036

Published simultaneously in Canada

Library of Congress Cataloging-in-Publication Data

Batten, Mary.
    Sexual strategies : how females choose their mates / Mary Batten.—
1st ed.
        p.   cm.
    "A Jeremy P. Tarcher/Putnam book."
    Includes bibliographical references and index.
    ISBN 0-87477-705-4
    1. Women—Psychology.   2. Mate selection.   3. Courtship of
animals.   I. Title.
HQ1206.B295   1992   92-16962 CIP
646.7′7—dc20

Design by Susan Shankin
Printed in the United States of America
1   2   3   4   5   6   7   8   9   10
This book is printed on acid-free paper.
                    ∞

To
Mother
for her unbounded love
and
to the memory of
my father
for his strength of character
and
my grandmother,
Emma Maud Scott Jones,
who encouraged my individualism

ACKNOWLEDGMENTS

IN WRITING THIS BOOK, I have called on many for their time and expertise, and all have generously answered my questions and provided me with reprints or manuscripts. I am particularly indebted to Meredith Small, Mollie Gregory, Doris Gwaltney, Judith Rosenthal, and Geraldine Schlein, who read the entire manuscript and gave me their valuable and constructive criticism. I thank especially Mildred Dickemann, whose comments and thoughtful criticism of the first chapter in its earliest stages and of portions of later chapters helped to clarify some fundamental ideas and steer me in fruitful directions. I also thank the following, who patiently answered my questions and critiqued specific chapters: Henry Harpending, John Hartung, Donald Symons, and Frederick vom Saal. For reading and commenting on portions of chapters, I thank Bruce Beehler, Robert Bland, Nancy Burley, Napoleon Chagnon, Lee Cronk, Zelda Dana, Robert Gibson, Owen Lovejoy, Monique Borgerhoff Mulder, Michael Ryan, Pamela Stacey, and Randy Thornhill. To those who answered my questions by phone or letter, my sincerest thanks: John Alcock, Alexandra Basolo, Jack Bradbury, David Buss, Bruce Ellis, Sarah Blaffer Hrdy, Sheila Ryan Johansson, Mark Kirkpatrick, Scott Kraus, James Lloyd, John Sivinski, Dorothy Tennov, Robert Trivers, Eckart Voland,

Edward O. Wilson, and Chung I. Wu. Of course, any errors that may have crept into the text are my responsibility alone.

Special thanks to my agent, Barbara Markowitz, for her enthusiastic support and to Harvey Markowitz, for his wise counsel; to my editor, Mary Ellen Strote, for her thoughtful, sensitive reading, which curbed my polemical tendencies and helped to tighten the book's structure; and to Jeremy Tarcher for believing in this book from the beginning.

Thanks, too, to my daughter, Stefanie, for her help and understanding. Last, but certainly not least, I thank Ed Bland, who read numerous drafts, endured many conversations about female choice, and gave me his usual insightful comments. His support and encouragement were a constant source of nourishment throughout many months of intense work.

The exertion of some choice on the part of the female seems almost as general a law as the eagerness of the male. . . . The power to charm the female has been in some few instances more important than the power to conquer other males in battle.

CHARLES DARWIN
The Descent of Man, and Selection in Relation to Sex
1871

All social organization is in principle interpretable as the outcome of the sexual strategies by which animals try to reproduce themselves.

MARTIN DALY AND MARGO WILSON
Sex, Evolution, and Behavior
1983

CONTENTS

༒

PREFACE: JOURNEY TO THE LEVEL OF THE SPECIES

AT SOME LEVEL OF AWARENESS, women seem to know that one of their most crucial roles is to choose their mates—to decide who, among all their suitors, will father their children. They feel little ambiguity. Even without having studied biology, women—and men, too—seem to understand that in the mating relationship females are the decision makers. We act as if we've always known a fact of life that biology has only recently discovered.

Our awareness usually starts with natural curiosity about the act through which we were conceived. At a very early age, sex becomes life's most interesting topic. Long before we understand the general principles of reproduction, we want to know the specifics of what makes it happen. Sometimes the birth of pet kittens or guinea pigs triggers this interest. Often it is the announcement by parents that a little brother or sister will be coming along. Young children pay close attention as their mother's belly begins to swell. They feel a sense of awe and wonder when she describes the baby inside her bulging abdomen.

Questions come tumbling out as three- and four-year-olds try to grasp the concept of new life. How did Mother and Daddy make the baby? How did the baby get inside Mother? How will it get out? If parents are comfortable answering those questions, children learn their first lessons about sexual reproduction and the differences between female and male anatomy.

I was almost three years old when my brother was born, and I remember my own excitement, fascination, and insatiable curiosity about this seemingly magical event. Since I lived on a farm, I was already more aware of mating and birthing than most kids. Our cows, pigs, dogs, and cats gave birth regularly. There were always babies of one sort or another on the farm, and to me the newborns were fascinating—not just because of their mysterious origin but because they came out of females. I didn't understand how a woman became a mother or how female dogs and cats made their babies, but the fact that only females could be mothers impressed me because I sensed that one day I could do that, too.

A few years after my brother's birth, my sister came along, and I began to wonder just how my mother and father had gotten together to make us. I wanted to know how my parents met, what attracted them to each other, how long they dated, why they decided to get married. When had my father proposed? What made my mother accept? Without knowing why, I assumed the final decision on whether they would marry had been hers.

Later on I heard my aunts and older cousins talking about how they had "picked" their husbands. "I knew we were going to marry before he did" was a repeated observation. The women in my family seemed to take it for granted that an important part of being female was selecting the man you would marry—the man who would father your children. It seemed the most important choice any girl would ever make.

As I passed through puberty and started dating, my interest in this kind of conversation intensified. My friends and I talked about our choice of boyfriends and the kind of man we wanted to spend our lives with. Little did I know or even suspect that what we were talking about, and feeling on some intuitive level, was part of a much larger picture—that female choice of mates was a fundamental process in evolution.

I didn't think too much about this "girl talk" until years later when, as a science writer, I was doing research on the mating behavior of animals. In the library at the American Museum of Natural History in New York City, I happened upon an article on the subject of *female choice*. The phrase caught my eye. I was intrigued to learn that scientists were actually studying something called female choice. The article said that females choose their mates and the ways in which they do so may have played a very important part in the evolution of species.

At first, I read literature on female mate choice only as I came across it while researching other topics. As I began building up a file of material, I found the subject both exciting and maddening—exciting because it implied there was some fundamental wisdom in women's intuition of their role in choosing mates; maddening because none of my biology or psychology courses, either in high school or in college, had ever mentioned female choice. When female behavior was discussed, it was in the context of sexual reproduction and maternal-infant behavior. But female choice of mates playing an important part in evolution? I'd never heard of it.

Charles Darwin, the father of modern biology, had introduced the theory of female choice more than a century ago, but only in the late seventies and early eighties did the subject enter college texts. Unfortunately, neither the theory of evolution by natural selection nor Darwin himself had been discussed in my high-school biology class in rural Virginia. Like that of many other Americans, my science education was deficient. In my case, real education in the sciences came years later through my work.

Remembering those long-ago conversations among women in my family and more recent conversations with my female friends, it seemed to me that women certainly talk as if they understand their power of mate choice. But, I wondered, was there scientific evidence to support that intuitive knowledge? Were females of other species exercising choice? Had Darwin's theory of female choice ever been proven? Was choicemaking part of female nature? And if so, what did that mean?

Over the next couple of years, from 1980 to 1982, I began an intellectual journey into territory that was both strange and familiar—strange in that I had never before taken a close look at animal sexual behavior; familiar because I'd grown up on a farm and had a general acquaintance with many species of animals. In retrospect, I can see that our farm had functioned as my first biological field station and that many of my unanswered questions about the mating behavior of farm animals were part of my inquiry into female choice.

But it was a journey to a tropical rainforest that intensified my connection to nature, stimulated my interest in evolutionary biology, and ultimately enabled me to write this book. I was researching and writing for a television nature-science film series. Assigned to make a field survey in Panama, I took off with all the usual intellectual baggage of misconceptions about jungles—as rainforests are popularly known. I expected the rainforest to be a steamy, disease-ridden, fearsome place with all sorts of terrible spiders and snakes just waiting to inject their venom into an unsuspecting human—namely me. But none of these nightmarish visions turned out to be true. The jungle's reputation as a menacing environment is a myth.

The actual rainforest bombarded my senses with its extraordinary beauty and diversity; it was everything I loved about the farm multiplied thousands of times over. In a rainforest, all the evolutionary processes display themselves in a dazzling show of color and form—thousands of species of animals and plants growing, interacting, competing, cooperating, feeding, mating, and giving birth. The rainforest is the ultimate biological field station, the ultimate source of biodiversity, the ultimate gene pool for life on Earth. There, sex and reproduction go on all the time and—as I saw from the lush abundance of life—with evident success.

One afternoon while sitting on a mountaintop on Panama's Barro Colorado Island, where the Smithsonian Tropical Research Insitute maintains a field station, I felt strangely at home . . . free in some profound way. In this place, in the midst of such rich diversity, I sensed that the limitations of the human world and the intellectual barriers we erect between ourselves and the rest of nature were very small, almost insignificant—a humbling experience and, at the same time, quite joyful. At that moment I felt my personal identity expand beyond family, friends, nation, gender, and even species. I knew I was part of the grand continuum of life.

This experience both prepared and motivated me to look further into female choice. The fecundity of the rainforest was evidence that females and males were going about the business of mating and reproduction with great intensity. I was eager to learn about female choice not just among humans but across species, to find out whether there were patterns of female behavior among other animals that could help to explain some of human behavior.

I was not disappointed. Learning about female choice was a kind of psychological homecoming. My reading and conversations with biologists revealed an aspect of femaleness that had remained hidden and ignored but that recalled my own experience and observations. There in the pages of scientific journals were articles describing how females of many species select their mates, thereby determining which males' genes will be passed along to future generations and which males will leave no offspring at all. Female choice was shaping future generations, influencing not only how animals looked but how they behaved.

And the males? They were dancing and prancing and fighting and squawking and doing everything they could to get a female to choose them. The similarities to human behavior were inescapable. My mind leapt to singles bars, to dating customs, to hearts and flowers and wining and dining and the entire range of maneuvers that men and women use to attract, trick, and seduce each other. There seemed to be some powerful connective strands between human and nonhuman behavior.

As I read more about female choice, I learned more about evolutionary biology, a field that uses all the disciplines of biology to investigate the evolution and characteristics of animals and plants. For me, evolutionary biology was liberating because it expanded the definition of what it means to be human.

The fact that there are two sexes—male and female—became insignificant compared with the fact that we evolved at all, that given the millions of ways in which molecules could have combined, we—human beings—had appeared. Evolutionary biology provides a perspective that encompasses the entire panorama of nature, from flocks of birds and swarms of ants to human culture—all of it, past, present, and future.

As I became more and more interested in female choice, I noticed that this field of inquiry was heating up in scientific circles, too. More and more articles on the subject were appearing in scientific journals. At first the research focused on nonhuman animals, but then anthropologists started studying female choice among humans. The research stirred up controversy because many people still have difficulty accepting the fact that human beings are members of the animal kingdom and that biology influences human behavior. Yes, we are different from other animals, but it is only by understanding our kinship with them that we can appreciate and define our differences.

As research on female choice gained momentum, it opened a window on a secret world. The image of females that emerged from evolutionary biology was very different from the image that men—and women, too—had supported, and believed to be true, for so many centuries.

Historically, women have been viewed as weak and childlike, both physiologically and intellectually inferior to men, and unsuited by nature for any occupation beyond the bearing and raising of children. This attitude toward women influenced the way scientists thought about nonhuman female animals. Females of many species, from rats to chimpanzees, were presumed to be passive creatures. But reports from field biologists and other scientists studying female behavior have proven exactly the opposite. Real females are strategic, competitive, and deliberate; they make shrewd and informed choices.

By understanding female choice—how females throughout the animal kingdom choose their mates—we see our own complex species with greater clarity. We gain greater understanding of why males and females, men and women, behave as they do—why men love to look at young, voluptuous women; why so many women are attracted to wealthy, powerful men; why many men try to control women; why men and women lie to each other; why men and women have different sexual fantasies; and why some men engage in violent competition.

Above all, an understanding of female choice offers insights that can help us change some of our self-destructive ways and, in the process, become more fully human, more joyfully alive.

Mary Batten
Los Angeles, California
April 1992

ONE

෨෬

THE UNIVERSAL MATING GAME

*In looking at Nature, it is most necessary to keep the foregoing
considerations always in mind—never to forget that every single
organic being may be said to be striving to the utmost
to increase in numbers.*

CHARLES DARWIN
The Origin of Species
1859

RELATIONSHIPS BETWEEN WOMEN and men are fraught with tensions.
Virtually every woman, at some point in a relationship, fears that
her mate may be using her for sexual gratification, that he may
desert her for another woman. Men, on the other hand, fear that
women are out to manipulate and control them. When the romance of courtship and the flush of lovemaking result in babies,
when women and men are left face to face with each other without
the benefit of their fantasies, they tend to fall back on stereotypes
of femininity and masculinity that have persisted through the
ages: the competitive, dominant male; the passive, submissive female. Without even realizing what is happening, intelligent, sensitive people can slide into role-playing almost as a reflex action. But
where do these male/female stereotypes originate? Is dominance

1

an inborn male trait? Is passivity an inborn female trait? Why do we think about women and men as we do? Why do many men and women treat each other with so much callousness, injustice, and even violence?

If we were biologically literate, if we accepted ourselves as members of the animal kingdom, we could see that sexual differences lead to patterns of behavior that we share with other animals. We would also see that sexual differences are merely biological facts: Males make sperm; females make eggs. The trouble is that humans have imposed value judgments on these biological facts, and these value judgments have become part of culture, influencing courtship and marriage customs, laws, politics, and attitudes about what it means to be male or female.

But the biological record needs to be set straight. Until fairly recently, even biologists went along with the sexual stereotypes. Until the mid-twentieth century, research focused altogether on male behavior as the engine powering evolution and society. Studies showed that men, like males of other species, compete for mates, sometimes violently. The winners of these bouts were believed to control the mating process. When women and other females were taken seriously, it was only in the context of reproduction. Scientists as well as artists extolled the maternal ideal. But almost nobody looked at females, human or otherwise, as strategic, competitive animals. Nobody considered that the way in which females were choosing mates might have a powerful influence on male behavior, on social organization, and on the evolution of species. The idea that women or female animals in general might be playing a significant role in evolution didn't even seem worthy of discussion. In retrospect, it's easy to understand why. The idea of a male-directed universe had been entrenched first in theology and then in science, not out of any deliberate maliciousness or conspiracy, but simply because men controlled most governments and they tended to view the world in their own image. The average biologist—until the 1960s, they were mostly men— didn't think female choice could possibly be important. The idea that females might have control over such an important decision as choosing mates would have upset—and indeed *has* upset—a world view in which females were type-cast in a predominantly subordinate role.

But the biology texts have been rewritten during the past decade to include an updated view of females. Biologists now recognize that females across species exercise mate choice—that choice-making is part of female nature. But what does this mean for our everyday lives, for the way people treat each other, and the way societies work?

Could it be that females play a more dominant social role than anybody has given them credit for? Could it mean that males are more dependent on females than the other way around? Could sexual strategies, courtship and mate choice—fundamental reproductive behavior—influence not only intimate male-female relationships but also social relationships, political relationships, and economic relationships?

To unravel why we behave as we do, and why there is so much friction between the sexes, we must look at sexual strategies across the animal kingdom—how males compete for females, how females choose their mates. By discovering our similarities and our differences in the context of other animals, we may be able to apply wisdom rather than force to our problems and move on to the next step in our ongoing evolution as a species. But first we must be willing to see what is really going on.

Outside the opening to a bumblebee nest, dive-bombing drones tear off each other's wings as they compete for the virgin queens inside. But the young queens aren't in any hurry. They may wait three or four days before emerging to choose their mates.

Bull elephant seals slam their ponderous two-ton bulks against each other and bite each other's necks, noses, and tail flippers, often inflicting grave wounds as they fight to control the beach where females come to breed. By calling loudly and making vigorous attempts to escape the ardor of males that try to copulate, females incite them to additional competitive bouts. Usually females mate with the winner.[1] The result is a polygynous system in which only a small fraction of males actually breed.

All forms of life strive mightily to reproduce, but females and males pursue distinctly different strategies. Females are extremely selective. Males are highly competitive, sometimes fighting each other for access to females. Almost all females mate and reproduce, but many fewer males do, the percentage varying with the species. Why don't more males mate? It isn't for lack of interest. Either they are killed off or prevented from mating by their rivals or they are rejected by females.

Life is also violent for some human males. "In preliterate societies competition over women probably is the single most important cause of violence," says anthropologist Donald Symons.[2] Even among people known to be peaceable, such as the Bushmen of the Kalahari Desert, most murders are committed by men in arguments over women. Anthropologist Napoleon Chagnon points out that competition for the means and ends of reproduction probably characterized human societies long before citizens of the industrialized world began to compete for the means and ends of production.[3]

The Yânomamö Indians of Venezuela and Brazil provide a striking example of just how violent the competition for human mates can be. Yânomamö men wage bloody wars that usually begin over sexual issues such as infidelity or suspicion of infidelity, jealousy, attempts to seduce another man's wife, seizure of a married woman or a woman from a visiting group, and failure to give up a girl promised in marriage.[4] The fighting can be so intense that villages split up. When this happens, each warring group becomes a new village and often an enemy of the other.[5]

Chagnon, who has studied these Indians of the Amazon rainforest since 1965, reports that approximately 30 percent of adult male deaths are due to violence.[6] Chagnon sees Yânomamö homicide, blood revenge, and warfare as "manifestations of individual conflicts of interest over material and reproductive resources."[7]

Such competition is not confined to preliterate societies. In cultures around the world, including North American cities such as Miami, Cleveland, Philadelphia, Chicago, and Detroit—worlds apart from tribal villages—something similar may be going on.

In an international study, sociobiologists Martin Daly and Margo Wilson found that the overwhelming proportion of homicides are committed by men against men, as opposed to murders of women by men or of men by women. In some North American cities, men kill other men at rates as high as 93 to 99 percent. Male-male murders are also concentrated among *young* men, from late adolescence through early adulthood—the period of life when they are most likely to be competing for the status and re-sources that attract mates. "There is no evidence," say Daly and Wilson "that women in modern America are approaching the level of violent conflict prevailing among men. Indeed there is no evidence that women in any society have ever approached the level of violent conflict prevailing among men in the same society."[8]

In order to understand why men compete in more violent ways than women, it is necessary to understand the differences between male and female reproductive strategies. A brief excursion into some basic principles of evolutionary biology reveals why females are generally choosy and males generally competitive, sometimes violently so.

NATURAL SELECTION AND SEXUAL SELECTION

In 1859, British naturalist Charles Darwin laid the foundations of modern biology with the publication of his monumental book, *The Origin of Species.* In this work, Darwin elaborated his theory of biological evolution through natural selection.

Even then, the concept of evolution was not unknown. In the seventeenth century naturalist-philosophers had examined fossils and concluded that these traces of ancient plants and animals provided a very different view of life on Earth than that preached from pulpits. Fossils were evidence of enormous changes; they contradicted the accepted religious view of a static universe in which all living things had been created perfectly in their present forms. Fossils told a history of great geological upheavals: the rise of mountains, the disappearance of seas, and the extinction of en-tire species. The theory of evolution had taken shape over nearly two centuries preceding Darwin, but there was still no satisfactory explanation of how it worked. Darwin's great contribution was to explain the process by which species develop and change. He called this process *natural selection.*

The concept of natural selection first came to Darwin through his observation that individuals within species vary in size, fertility, strength, health, longevity, behavior, and other characteristics. In his study of domesticated animals and plants, he realized that breeders used such natural random variation to advantage by selecting and mating only individuals with the desired characteristics. In an intellectual leap, Darwin theorized that a similar process must be going on in nature, but he was hard-pressed to explain how natural selection worked.

A clue came from English clergyman T. R. Malthus's 1798 work, *An Essay on the Principle of Population.* In this essay Malthus argued that human beings can reproduce in far greater numbers than the environment can support. Population, he pointed out, increases geometrically but the food supply increases only arithmetically. Malthus predicted that population growth is checked by what he called the difficulty of subsistence, or what is now called carrying capacity—the number of people or other animals that a particular environment can support. When a population grows beyond the environment's carrying capacity, famine, starvation, and disease intervene to restore ecological balance. Today we see this happening in the vast urban slums of Mexico City, Calcutta, São Paulo, and other areas of the Third World where burgeoning populations have already outstripped local supplies of food and clean drinking water. Today some 14 million children under age five die every year in poor countries because of tainted drinking water, poor sanitation, malnutrition, common diseases, and environmental pollution.

Darwin felt that Malthus's work on population was crucial to the understanding of natural selection, not only in humans but also in plants and nonhuman animals. Taking Malthus's principle a step further, Darwin theorized that within any population, individuals with certain characteristics are better adapted to their particular environment and are more likely to survive than those without. Through the process of elimination, nature *selects* those individuals that have some advantage that helps them in the struggle to survive and reproduce.

Every environment, said Darwin, presents living things with pressures, whether extreme cold or heat, flood or drought, scarcity of food, predation, or limited space. Those that can withstand those pressures survive and reproduce, passing their genes on to future generations. Since offspring inherit their parents' genes, successive generations take on the adaptive advantages.

Losers in the struggle to survive leave few or no offspring, and eventually suffer genetic death. The unfortunate and much misused phrase *survival of the fittest* was invented by English philosopher Herbert Spencer. Darwin was persuaded to use it, but as biologists today recognize, a phrase that better describes the ultimate criterion of evolutionary success would have been *reproduction of the fittest.*[9]

Darwin theorized that a process he called *sexual selection* also influenced evolution. He spelled this out in more detail in *The Descent of Man, and Selection in Relation to Sex*, which appeared in 1871. In this book, Darwin observed that certain male physical traits that seemed largely ornamental, such as the male peacock's elaborate fantail and other birds' "combs, wattles, protuberances, horns, air-distended sacs, top knots, naked shafts, plumes and lengthened feathers gracefully springing from all parts of the body,"[10] couldn't be explained by natural selection. Some of these ornamental appendages, which Darwin called *secondary sexual characteristics*, might actually hinder survival, either by making males more conspicuous to predators or so clumsy as to impede escape. Such appendages seemed contradictory to the process of natural selection, but Darwin recognized their value for another function—courtship.

Sexual selection, wrote Darwin, "is in itself an extremely complex affair, depending, as it does, on ardour in love, courage, and the rivalry of the males, and on the powers of perception, taste, and will of the female."[11]

Darwin suggested that secondary sexual characteristics evolved because females found them attractive and repeatedly selected the males possessing them. As he described it, sexual selection comprised (1) male-male competition, or *intra*sexual selection, which favors "the power to conquer other males in battle"; and (2) female choice, or *inter*sexual selection, favoring "the male's power to charm the females."

Darwin theorized that the sole function of male ornaments is to attract females. In *The Descent of Man, and Selection in Relation to Sex,* he wrote, "So it appears that female birds in a state of nature, have by a long selection of the more attractive males, added to their beauty or other attractive qualities."[12]

In spite of his recognition that females were indeed choosing their mates, Darwin was still a product of his time. "No doubt this implies powers of discrimination and taste on the part of the female which will at first appear extremely improbable," he wrote, "but I hope hereafter to shew [*sic*] that this is not the case."[13] He saw males as the prime movers of life and attributed choice to females only with this proviso: "supposing that their mental capacity sufficed for the exertion of a choice."[14]

To understand his reluctance to ascribe the power of choice to females, one need only read a few lines of the essay "On Women," by Darwin's contemporary, German philosopher Arthur Schopenhauer:

> *Women exist in the main solely for the propagation of the species, and are not destined for anything else. . . . You need only look at the way in which she is formed, to see that woman is not meant to undergo great labor, whether of the mind or of the body. . . . She pays the debt of life not by what she does, but by what she suffers; by the pains of childbearing and care for the child, and by submission to her husband, to whom she should be a patient and cheering companion. The keenest sorrows and joys are not for her, nor is she called upon to display a great deal of strength. The current of her life should be more gentle, peaceful and trivial than man's, without being essentially happier or unhappier.[15]*

Given the prevailing attitude toward women, Darwin's belief that any females exercised mate choice was extremely controversial. He was ridiculed for suggesting that female choice was a significant evolutionary force. In spite of his ground-breaking theory, Darwin never gave up the Victorian attitude that women, as well as females of other species, were passive vessels and that they would choose only one male, presumably the best. "She generally requires to be courted," he wrote of nonhuman female behavior. "She is coy, and may often be seen endeavouring for a long time to escape from the male. . . . The female, though comparatively passive, generally exerts some choice and accepts one male in preference to others. Or she may accept, as appearances would sometimes lead us to believe, not the male which is the most attractive to her but the one which is the least distasteful."[16]

It is clear today that the submissive, yielding female was a figment of man's ancient fantasy of woman as he would like her to be—patiently waiting to serve his needs, a cheerful slave. Before the full power of female choice could be revealed, the biology establishment had to give up one of its prized myths.

DEMOLISHING THE MYTH OF THE PASSIVE FEMALE

The myth of the passive female persisted in the biological sciences well past the middle of the twentieth century, leading many researchers to deny what took place before their eyes. Their belief in the passivity of women colored scientists' perceptions of nonhuman females as well, despite contradictory field observations.

Among many species of primates, for example, including the mountain gorilla, gelada baboon, and brown capuchin monkey, females initiate the majority of copulations. Sometimes female solicitations are subtle—a gesture such as a flick of the tongue, a head shake, or a simple approach. Other solicitations may be bolder. The female chimpanzee sticks her swollen, reddened rump in the male's face to show him she is in estrus, or sexual heat—hardly a passive gesture. Nor is the female chimpanzee true to one male. She may consort for prolonged periods with one male, but she also mates promiscuously with all other males in her vicinity.

Field research among many primates, including gelada baboons, macaques, chimpanzees, brown monkeys, howler monkeys, and others, showed that females are highly competitive among themselves for status, especially when resources or the males that provide them are scarce. "The central organizing principle of primate social life is competition between females and

9

especially female lineages," writes sociobiologist Sarah Blaffer Hrdy. "Whereas males compete for transitory status and transient access to females, it is females who tend to play for more enduring stakes."[17]

Despite mounting evidence that challenged the myth of female passivity, many male biologists hewed to the image of women that had served them so well. Science—a discipline of inquiry that advances knowledge by asking questions and subsequently modifying theories—was tenaciously closed-minded on this subject. The attitude seemed rooted in the psyche as deeply as the belief in an Earth-centered universe was engraved on the medieval mind.

"The bias for passive females was so ingrained that researchers couldn't see what they were actually seeing," says biologist Frederick vom Saal. "They were looking at what women were supposed to be, not what they were really like." As a student in the mid-seventies, vom Saal reported his experimental observations that some female mice were more aggressive than others, only to be told by his male advisor that "what females are doing doesn't really matter."[18]

Vom Saal thought otherwise. Rejecting conventional wisdom, he continued investigating aggression in female mice and discovered that the relative position of a mouse fetus among its siblings in its mother's uterus—whether it develops between two males, two females, or a male and a female—determines its level of aggression as an adult. Fetuses, whether male or female, that develop between two males are the most aggressive as adults. The least aggressive are those that develop between two females.[19]

The myth of the passive female even influenced the breeding of laboratory mice. "Females were selected for passivity because aggressive females were considered abnormal," says vom Saal. When he trapped wild mice and studied them in laboratory conditions, he found that females acted as aggressively as males. Some females defended territories while the males stayed in the nest tending the babies; female siblings were even observed killing each other's babies. Such discoveries meant not only that female aggression was normal, but that it influenced and was influenced by the social pressures on the population.

Scientists are now investigating the probability that the proportion of aggressive females among rodents increases as population becomes more dense, and that aggressive females within a high-density population might lead to population crashes, or sudden declines. Such declines could happen because the presence of aggressive, dominant females in close proximity suppresses ovulation in other females. Vom Saal's experiments with wild mice show that when two aggressive females are placed in a group, neither is able to reproduce successfully. Subordinate females in the presence of dominant, aggressive females do not become pregnant.[20] The female rodent's reproductive system is extremely sensitive to stresses. "In fact, the female is determining the social structure," says vom Saal, adding that such investigations "would have been considered ridiculous twenty years ago."[21]

The male bias is still evident in studies of human populations. "Anthropologists haven't paid much attention to what women do," says anthropologist Henry Harpending, citing a lamentable lack of information about women in the ethnographic literature. Harpending's training as a biologist led him to study people the way he would have studied blackbirds, looking at the behavior of both sexes. When he investigated an African people called the Herero, he learned how little the men knew about tribal births, deaths, and their own family history. "I'd ask men how many children they had, and they didn't know. Men were tied up in ritual and social structure," he says. "Women keep track of births and other vital events. If you read African anthropology, you're reading about the male world."[22]

The viewing of females as active reproductive strategists was revolutionary. It meant that the male-biased perspective on animal social behavior, including that of the human animal, had to change. Females could no longer be viewed only as sex objects and mothers. If the role of females was much broader than anyone had acknowledged, then the view of males also had to change. Male-male competition could no longer be considered the engine running the universe. In looking at females in a larger, multidimensional context, biologists were challenged to stretch their own visions, to see that social organization was more richly complex, with more subtle interactions among individuals, than many had wanted to admit.

Women researchers, especially those who were primatologists, played a crucial role in breaking down the male bias that had dominated biology for more than a century. They were more likely to empathize with female animals, and to pay closer attention to their behavior.

Sarah Blaffer Hrdy recalls her own experience as a graduate student studying langurs in India. She identified with the problems confronted by female langurs whose infants had been killed or might be killed by infanticidal males. This led her to ask different questions about female behavior than she had been taught to ask as a student at Harvard:

> If it was really true that females did not benefit from additional matings, why were female langurs taking such risks to solicit males outside their troop? Why would pregnant females solicit and mate with males? What influence might such behavior have for the eventual fate of a female's offspring? What were the main sources of variance in female reproductive success and what role did nonreproductive sexuality play in all this? . . . Where did the idea of the coy female ever come from anyway? These are questions that preoccupied me since 1977 and all of them grow out of an ability to imagine females as active strategists.[23]

Examples from numerous species have now disproved the image of the passive female, a fantasy imposed on biology because men wanted to see females as subordinate. Alas, most women accepted that role; many even believed there was a social advantage to female passivity.

Thanks to a large, continually growing body of research, the myth is at last dead—in biology if not in romance novels. Biologists have taken a fresh look at sexual selection and in the process given us new insights into the female's role in evolution.

FEMALE FRUIT FLIES AND FEMALE CHOICE

Serious work on female choice got under way in 1948 when British geneticist A. J. Bateman began his study of the fruit-fly species *Drosophila melanogaster.* Bateman is credited with starting a new era of interest in sexual selection. His research demonstrated that female fruit flies, when allowed to choose, did indeed select certain males over others. Using genetic markers, Bateman found that the majority of the females copulated with only one or two of the available males. Although all of the males showed a readiness to court, many failed to mate even once.

Bateman's work was important for establishing the sexual differences in reproductive success—the number of offspring an individual produces. In his experiments with fruit flies, Bateman observed that because females were selective, only a few males produced most of the offspring. He described three important sexual differences.

13

1. Male reproductive success varied much more widely than the female's; some males produced almost three times as many offspring as the most successful female.

2. Female reproductive success was not limited by the female's ability to attract males but by her ability to produce eggs. The number of offspring a male could sire, however, was not limited by his biology but by his ability to attract females.

3. A female's reproductive success increased only minimally after the first copulation, and not at all after the second.

In Bateman's experiments, most female fruit flies seemed uninterested in copulating more than once or twice, while males tended not to mate with the same female twice.[24] Similar results have been confirmed by many other researchers working with other species of animals.

Bateman's demonstration of the dramatic difference between male and female reproductive success proved important to developments in evolutionary biology that came in the 1970s.

A NEW LOOK AT OLD BEHAVIOR

Darwin's work focused on individual behavior; he showed that physical adaptations that enabled animals to survive and reproduce were *selected*. But what about societies? How was evolution by natural selection operating with regard to social behavior?

During the 1960s and '70s, scientists who called themselves sociobiologists began applying Darwin's theory of natural selection to the social behavior of animals, including human beings. This meant looking at the dynamics of reproduction that underlie behavior, whether in chimpanzee society or human culture.

One of sociobiology's major ideas, known as *inclusive fitness*, was developed by British biologist W. D. Hamilton. In 1964, Hamilton pointed out that natural selection acts on the smallest unit of reproduction—the gene—rather than on individuals, groups, or species. Because offspring carry the parents' genes, Hamilton argued, parents are protective of their young. Other genetic relatives also carry the same genes. Altruistic behavior in those cases in which the altruist is related genetically to the beneficiary is explained by Hamilton's theory of kin selection, or inclusive fitness. Why, for example, do men in some societies act as guardians for their sisters' children? Although a man may not be certain that his wife's children are his own, he can be sure that his sister, with whom he shares genes, will have offspring that also carry some of his genes. Kin selection helped to explain why people everywhere generally organize their social life around systems of kinship. By protecting one's kin, one is protecting the long-term survival of one's genes,[25] although not necessarily with any conscious awareness of genetic inheritance.

Biologist Richard Alexander summed up the concept: "We . . . learn to love and assist our own offspring, and often help other relatives even in the face of powerful resistance and high risk to our own status or well-being. In other words, we act as though we know about inclusive fitness."[26]

The key question sociobiology asks is, How does a behavior contribute to an animal's fitness—its ability to produce offspring that will themselves survive and reproduce? In the evolutionary sweepstakes, individuals that produce the most surviving offspring are the winners. They leave more descendants to transmit more of their genes to future generations, and this genetic inheritance affects everything from the shape of a nose and the color of one's eyes to mate choice.

According to sociobiology, natural selection favors any behavior that maximizes an individual's fitness, or reproductive success. The male bowerbird that builds the most ornate bower, the elephant-seal bull that overpowers his rivals, and the man who drives a Porsche increase their chances of attracting mates and siring offspring. And females' choice of mates determines which males will have any reproductive success at all.

Evolutionary biologists first used the insights of sociobiology to explain behavior in nonhuman animals, but anthropologists slowly began climbing on board, a trend that continues. By the late 1980s, many biologists, psychologists, and anthropologists were applying the perspective of evolutionary biology to human mating patterns, marriage customs, sex differences in mate preference, and even sex differences in psychology.

Sociobiology's focus on the smallest unit of reproduction—the gene—helped update the nineteenth-century British novelist and essayist Samuel Butler's famous aphorism: "A hen is only an egg's way of making another egg." In sociobiologist Edward O. Wilson's words, "The organism is only DNA's way of making more DNA."[27]

Talk of genes, however, can be troublesome. Genetic theories have been used to justify the horrors of racism and Nazism and to perpetuate the repression of women. But genes do exist; they determine the way we look and they influence the way we act and even, perhaps, the way we feel. The trouble lies not with the genes but with eugenic interpretations when they are used to degrade or

15

enslave any group of human beings. While one must ever be wary of the misuses of any genetic theory, denying the existence of genetic influence prevents a fuller understanding of how life has evolved.

Sociobiology, like the theory of evolution itself, has been badly misinterpreted by scientists and nonscientists alike. Feminists, in particular, have attacked sociobiology as a kind of genetic determinism that might legitimize sexual discrimination. The reality, however, is that a scientific discipline attaches no value judgments to the subject it studies. Sociobiology seeks to *explain* behavior patterns, not to *justify* them.

16

For example, in explaining why females are the choosier sex and why males sometimes compete violently, sociobiologists do not argue that choosiness is better than competitiveness, or vice versa. Trouble arises when sexual differences are used as justification for limiting human development. Sexism is based on just this kind of mind manipulation. The biological fact that women give birth and provide the primary nurturing for infants has been used to keep women in subordinate, servile roles—to promote motherhood as the only proper role for women. But women can obviously function in many other capacities. The biological fact that men are larger and physically stronger than women has been used to justify male dominance and aggression—to promote the hunter/warrior/soldier image. But men are capable of far more than combat. Both sexes suffer from these restrictive definitions of womanhood and manhood. Unfortunately, some people all too easily assume that biological differences make one sex or race superior or inferior to another. But such conclusions are totally illogical; they are value judgments that certain groups try to impose on others. And in the absence of critical thinking, many people become victims of such propaganda.

Of all the intellectual skills, critical thinking is the most important for recognizing deception, for distinguishing between facts and value judgments, and for maintaining sexual and political freedom. One must always be ready to question, to doubt, and to challenge, now more than ever in our age of global electronic communications media.

Some scientists avoid using the term *sociobiology* because of its controversial reputation. Many biologists prefer to use the older terms for their field of study—*animal behavior* or *ethology*. Those who wish to emphasize the environmental aspect of their work use the term *behavioral ecology*. Anthropologists who look at human cultures through the perspective of sociobiology have recently begun to call themselves *human ethologists* or *evolutionary ethologists*.

Whatever it is called, the study of behavior in the context of evolutionary biology focuses on reproduction. Although sex usually gets most of the attention, the less glamorous, more arduous process of reproduction underlies every sexual act, every courtship and marriage ritual, and many political, legal, educational, religious, and economic systems.

As anthropologist Mildred Dickemann has noted: "Human cultural history . . . is by no means independent of, but closely bound to, the biological history of human reproduction.[28]

Many seemingly inexplicable sexual differences in behavior, including female choosiness in mate selection and male-male competition, begin to make sense when seen in terms of reproduction.

FEMALE CHOICE AND PARENTAL INVESTMENT

In 1972, American sociobiologist Robert Trivers published his theory of parental investment and its implications for sexual selection. Trivers's work is considered one of the most significant advances in evolutionary theory since Darwin.

Parental investment, which is now a key theory in evolutionary biology, refers to the total contribution that each sex makes to its offspring. The biological contribution consists of sperm, eggs, and, in the case of mammals, pregnancy and lactation. Parental investment also includes nest building, incubation of eggs, nourishment of young, and protection. For most species of animals, male and female parental investments are not equal; this inequality determines which sex is choosier.

Trivers hypothesized that "the relative parental investment of the sexes in their offspring" governed the operation of sexual selection.[29] "The sex whose typical parental investment is greater than that of the opposite sex will become a limiting resource for that sex. Individuals of the sex investing less will compete among themselves to breed with members of the sex investing more, since an individual of the former can increase its reproductive success by investing successively in the offspring of several members of the limiting sex."[30]

This means that the sex making the greatest investment in offspring—usually the female—controls the reproductive success of the sex investing less—usually the male. The reason for this is found in the difference between the sex cells themselves—the egg and the sperm.

The biological definitions of male and female derive from the sex cells, or gametes. The female is the sex that produces the larger gamete—the egg. The male produces the smaller gamete—the sperm. In all animals, the egg is many thousands of times larger than the tiny, mobile sperm. Even before conception, the female invests more metabolic energy merely in the production of eggs.

Trivers observed that by producing eggs, females invest more of themselves in parenthood than a male, who contributes sperm, an easily renewable resource. In humans, one ejaculate contains between 300 million and 400 million sperm, and a man can produce sperm throughout his lifetime. Theoretically, a man could produce thousands of offspring. He is limited not by his sperm but by the number of eggs he can fertilize. His reproductive success thus depends on how many females he can inseminate.

Not so for the female. In most species, a female's reproductive success is unaffected by the number of males with whom she mates. Her biology limits the number of her offspring. A female mammal, for example, is born with more eggs than she will ever ovulate—about 400 for a human female. A female's reproductive success is limited not only by the number of eggs she can ovulate, but also, in the case of a mammal, by the amount of time and energy it takes to gestate a fertilized egg, give birth, nurse, and rear an offspring.

Whatever choice of mate a female mammal, especially a

woman, makes, she still will carry the overwhelming reproductive burden. The mammalian female's parental investment is so great that males can be said to enjoy a free ride. Her investment consists of the pregnancy, a long gestation period during which the fetus is nurtured through a placenta, and the production of milk to feed the infant. The length of gestation varies with the species: sixteen days for a hamster; nine months for human and gorilla babies; eleven months for a dolphin; twenty-two months for an elephant. At every step of the nurturing process, during which females provide more and more care, the difference between male and female parental investment increases. In human terms, a one-night stand for a man can result in a twenty-year investment for a woman. No amount of romance, intellectualizing, or high-powered marketing of cute and appealing baby products can hide this fact.

The reproductive demands on a female mammal are so heavy that she may take up a solitary life-style and, if she is long-lived, increase the intervals between births to give herself time to restore her depleted body systems. The female Atlantic right whale, which lives about fifty years, is so depleted by pregnancy and lactation that she doesn't mate again for two years. Short-lived females, such as rodents, usually have many pregnancies and come into estrus immediately after giving birth.

Female mammals need additional resources during pregnancy and lactation. In anticipation of the demands of reproduction, a female mammal stores more calcium and iron in her body than a male would ever need. Her kidneys, heart, intestines, and liver enlarge during pregnancy and lactation. These changes help the female use food more efficiently and provide the increased energy needed for reproduction.

"For female primates, lactation is the overwhelming factor in determining body size," writes anthropologist Jane Lancaster.[31] "The demands of lactation can be so great that females spend as much time feeding and ingest as many calories as large males even if they are only half the male size."

Trivers's theory of parental investment explained why males and females must pursue different reproductive strategies: while a male's reproductive success comes from inseminating as many

19

females as possible, a female's reproductive success depends on making shrewd choices.

In choosing which males will mate, females exert what Edward O. Wilson has called a "directive and corrective force" on the course of evolution.[32] Thanks to insights from sociobiology, the view of male-driven evolution embraced by biologists since Darwin has been expanded to include the female's role as strategist par excellence.

"As with all mammals, the breeding success of each male primate depends on extensive and long-term investment in offspring by females," writes Hrdy. "Moreover, to an extraordinary degree, the predilections of the investing sex—female—potentially determine the direction in which the species will evolve. For it is the female who is ultimate arbiter of *when* she mates and how often and with whom. This is especially true in the case of primates. . . . Females, then, are and always have been the chief custodians of the breeding potential of the species."[33] How females carry out that role and what they look for in males is the subject of the next chapter.

TWO

⁧ఞ⁩

WHAT FEMALES WANT

Choice is not just a matter of permitting sex.

ROBERT TRIVERS
Social Evolution
1985[1]

FEMALE CHOICE MEANS MORE than a female showing her preference for certain males. It means more than her selecting a male for his attractiveness, more than her being receptive to sex. For female choice to be meaningful in evolutionary terms, it must also be adaptive. Her decision must enable her to produce more offspring that are better adapted to survive than if she had mated randomly.

When it comes to reproduction, all males—human and non-human—are not equally valuable. Some have greater resources to provide for a female and her offspring. Some are more vigorous and in better health. Some are better protectors, and some have better parenting skills. Female choice functions to screen males and select those of highest mate value.[2] And females generally take their time making up their minds because reproductive success rests on the wisdom of their choice.

Courtship provides an opportunity for females—both human and nonhuman—to observe, compare, and test males. Because successful courtship is essential to male reproductive success, much male behavior—more than men might willingly admit—is

21

regulated by female preference. To some extent, males tend to be what females want them to be. This means that enormous responsibility and power reside in the preferences of females. Just how much power is a controversial issue.

Some scientists believe that female choice directs male behavior. "Males are a breeding experiment run by females—a proving ground from which females can cull winning genes," says evolutionary anthropologist John Hartung.[3] Few biologists would go this far, but most acknowledge that female choice influences male behavior.

Anything and everything that a male does in relation to a female, and in relation to other males, too, may provide a cue to his potential as a mate. And females have evolved to be highly discriminating and observant of the most subtle details that indicate male health and status.

During courtship, males—both human and nonhuman—use various displays, some quite conspicuous, to attract females. Male fireflies that live along riverbanks throughout Southeast Asia gather in trees and signal females by flashing a light pattern specific to their species. Clustered by the thousands on every leaf of trees that are thirty-five to forty feet high, these insects flash in perfect synchrony, transforming a tenth of a mile of river front into an unbroken line of flashing light. The beacon is so distinctive that it is used as a navigational aid by local sailors.

From male fireflies flashing their own natural bioluminescence to men flashing credit cards, males of most species compete among themselves to advertise their quality as mates. Being chosen by a female is crucial to their reproductive success. Rejected suitors are instant losers in the evolutionary lottery; without a female, they will never sire offspring.

Evolutionary theory predicts that: (1) a female will choose males that contribute in some way to her own reproductive success; and (2) natural selection will favor the choosy female, and the genes for her particular choicemaking behavior will be passed on to successive generations of females. Although these operating principles are the same in the human world as they are among nonhuman animals, the most abundant evidence and the clearest, most unambiguous examples come from the latter. Unless stated otherwise, this chapter will focus on female choice among non-human animals.

MALES ON REVIEW

It is, of course, crucial for a female to select a male of her own species. Mistaken identity can cancel out her entire reproductive effort, resulting in hybrid offspring that are sterile. Choosing males of the right species is the minimal level of female choice, but there are other criteria for selecting a mate.

Courtship's evolutionary function is to help females evaluate fitness differences among males. Some of the traits males display during courtship may have been selected by generations of females because they signal superior genes or resources that will contribute to the female's reproductive success.

Some traits preferred by females, however, seem to have purely aesthetic value. In these cases, the female is choosing a male simply because he is pretty or because in some way he stimulates her senses—a mating call that titillates her auditory sense, a flash of colors that excites her visual sense, or a particular penile embellishment or flutter that presumably brings on exquisite sexual pleasure.

"Any component of courtship that varies in the vigorousness with which it is performed could be the basis for female choice,"[4] write Randy Thornhill and John Alcock, biologists who have made extensive studies of insect mating systems. They point to the loudness and persistence of mating songs in crickets, the flight ability and strength in butterflies, and the wing vibrations in fly courtship.

There may be similar components in courtship displays among males of other species as well—the mating calls of frogs, the songs of birds, and the dominance displays of silverback gorillas.

In some species, the least conspicuous aspect of courtship takes place internally. In such species, female choice may have influenced the shape and size of penises. One might wonder how female choice could possibly affect the shape of a penis. But think of why penises exist: They have evolved to penetrate a female's reproductive tract and to place sperm where they are most likely to fertilize eggs.

Among animals that practice external fertilization, such as frogs, some worms, and most fish, male and female genitals are scarcely more than simple openings. But among some species with internal fertilization, especially insects, the female's reproductive passageways can be extremely intricate; and in these species, males have evolved an extraordinary diversity of genital structures. Some male nematodes and flies have penises that are longer than the rest of their bodies!

The most elaborate penises generally are found in species in which the female mates with more than one male—a common case throughout the animal kingdom. In this situation, females are choosing which sperm from among several mates will fertilize their eggs. The competition among males to ensure that their sperm are chosen can result in bizarre genital structures.

A bewildering array of microscopic plumes, barbs, scales, darts, spines, and coiled tubes embellish the genitalia of some of the tiniest male animals. Entomologist James Lloyd has noted that male insects may have "little openers, snippers, levers and syringes that put sperm in the places females have evolved for sperm with priority usage—collectively a veritable Swiss Army knife of gadgetry!"[5]

Why does a male need so much genitalic gadgetry? During the past 150 years, several explanations have been proposed, but biologist William Eberhard recently came up with the most intriguing hypothesis. Noting that in many males the genitals are the body's most structurally complex organs, Eberhard theorized that male genitalia function as "internal courtship devices" that have evolved under selection of female choice to induce the female not only to copulate with a particular male but also to accept his sperm rather than that of other males. "It is just too fantastic to believe," he says, "that such complicated machinery is necessary only to perform a mechanically simple function."[6]

Copulation is an empty gesture for a male if his sperm do not fertilize a female's eggs. And copulation does not always (or even perhaps usually) lead to fertilization of all the female's eggs. Whether a male will actually sire any of her offspring often depends on how the female behaves during and after copulation. Fertilization requires that sperm deposited during copulation move from one place to another inside the female. "In most groups, the female rather than the sperm is responsible for this movement," notes Eberhard.[7]

For example, in rabbits, cows, sheep, chimpanzees, and humans, sperm are deposited in the vagina, but fertilization occurs in the Fallopian tubes. In these animals, contractions and movements of the female's reproductive tract help to move the sperm to the critical destination. It has been suggested, without any proof, that female orgasm in humans functions to get the sperm on the fast track to the Fallopian tubes.

If a penis's job is not only to transfer sperm but also to induce a female to accept the male's sperm, then some females may be discriminating among males on the basis of their penises. This would mean that males with the best-liked penis would sire more offspring than others.[8]

Eberhard argues that the embellishments of male genitalia— structures that are never used in male-male combat—may be "unusually pure products of sexual selection by female choice."[9] If his hypothesis is correct, females of many species are choosing males that are the most sexually stimulating. These males will then be favored by natural selection, and they will pass along the genes for elaborate genital structures to their sons. Eberhard and others speculate that the daughters of these males will be genetically predisposed to prefer males endowed with the attractive trait. Among humans, female choice may explain man's distinctively large penis—the largest among primates.[10] But females also use criteria other than the size of a penis to select their mates.

How Females Choose

Females appear to evaluate their potential mates using an array of cues to male fitness, some obvious and some extremely subtle. They exercise their choice through:

1. selection of males that provide significant resources or services, such as food or protection

2. selection of genetically superior males

3. rejection of males of the wrong species, or of undesirable individuals of the same species

4. selection of males for aesthetic traits

1. CHOOSING FOR RESOURCES

The clearest form of female choice, the one for which the largest body of evidence exists, is selection for resources—material benefits above and beyond the basic biological contribution of sperm. As the sex that generally makes the greatest investment in offspring, females need resources that will help them lay more eggs or produce more offspring, nurture their young, and raise them to maturity so that they, too, can mate and reproduce.

The necessary resources differ among species—the protein-rich secretion of a male insect, the food-rich territory of a hummingbird, protection by a dominant male baboon, male assistance in parenting, or a combination of several types of resources.

Universally, females prefer males with resources, and select such males whenever they have the opportunity. Their preferences set in motion the force of sexual selection that favors resource-providing males. Female choice is probably responsible for the evolution of gift-giving males, whether the gift be an insect's offering of a tasty prey or an Adélie penguin's offering of a stone to begin building a nest.

This brings up the age-old question of whether females choose a male for himself or for his resources. For many species, the answer is unclear, but among savanna baboons, females clearly prefer to mate with their male "friends." Primatologist Barbara Smuts describes the special relationships between female baboons and certain males with whom they spend most of their time.[11] "These friendships increase the reproductive success of both females and males by facilitating reciprocal exchanges of benefits," writes Smuts.[12] One great benefit is protection. A male friend protects his female friend and her offspring from other males that might act aggressively toward her, and possibly from predators as well.

Fat Is Beautiful

The resource that is most desirable to females is usually whatever most helps the animals survive in their particular environment. Female Adélie penguins, for example, prefer fat mates. A fat male can fast longer, remaining on the nest to incubate her eggs until she returns from foraging at sea and relieves him. If a male penguin runs out of fat reserves and leaves before the female returns, her embryos will die in the freezing cold of the Antarctic. The survival of young Adélies depends absolutely on care from both parents. Each must have enough stored fat to fast throughout his or her parenting shift.

Male and female fast together during their twelve-day courtship, at the end of which the female lays a clutch of two eggs. Both the fasting and the egg production deplete the female's energy reserves, so she goes to sea to feed, leaving her mate to incubate the eggs. Her foraging trip lasts about two weeks. This means that the male must fast not only through courtship but until the female returns—a total of nearly a month before he can eat again.

As soon as the female returns, the male, now thin and exhausted, hurries to sea to replenish his energy and fat reserves. He, too, is gone for about two weeks. He must return before the chicks hatch so the female will have enough time to forage and store food to regurgitate for the chicks. The chicks hatch after an incubation period of thirty-four days, and penguin males seem to have some built-in sense of time that brings them back to the nest just before their young hatch. Then both parents take turns bringing food to their ravenous young. Because of the cold and the danger from predatory birds known as skuas, the chicks must never be left alone.

Research by biologist Lloyd Spencer Davis shows that "females choose fat males either by mating with those that have already proved their fasting abilities (males that endured their female's absence the year before will be rejoined, but deserters are unlikely to be given a second chance) or possibly by assessing males on the basis of their calls. Favored males have the deepest voices . . . probably because the pitch of the voice is influenced by the size of the bird."[13] Adélie females clearly choose a male for his reliability and fasting ability. In some other species, however, females seem to prefer the resource over the male offering it.

Choice Locations

In a number of species, females are more attracted to a particular nesting site than to the particular male that controls the site. Female sparrows and woodpeckers, for example, are more interested in a male's nest than in the male himself.

One of the most well-proven cases of choice for resources rather than for the individual male is that of the bluehead wrasse *Thalassoma bifasciatum*, a common Caribbean reef fish. In this species, males are territorial and females choose nesting site rather than any particular male. In repeated experiments, marine biologist Robert Warner removed the male from his territory. The female did not follow him, and when a different male was placed in the favored territory, the female mated with him. Her fidelity was clearly to the site, not to the male.

This type of choice is the basis of what biologists call resource-defense polygyny. Whenever a male can defend an area containing food, protected nesting sites, or other resources that females need, he can monopolize many mates. Females that come to such territories to feed and lay eggs are controlled by the male owning the resources—a situation that differs little from human societies that practice polygyny, or having more than one wife. Through competition with each other, males establish a dominance hierarchy just as men in tribal societies sort out an economic pecking order. As a result, the dominant males own the best territories, which attract the largest number of females. Several females may choose to live in a harem because it is more to their reproductive advantage to become one of several mates of a resource-rich male than to become the sole mate of one with few or no resources.

Biologists have identified the polygyny threshold as the point at which an unmated female can expect to achieve greater reproductive success by pairing with an already mated male than by doing so with any available unmated male.[14] There are many examples of resource-defense polygyny, and in most instances the desirable resource is food.

Food for Sex
The theme of food in exchange for sex is universal. It turns up in human courtship no less than among birds, insects, and fishes. Among humans, both men and women use food in courtship. The old saying "The way to a man's heart is through his stomach" expresses the belief that a woman who cooks well will attract a man. At the same time, men use wining and dining, and some have also taken to cooking, to seduce women. Today many men feel that buying a woman drinks and dinner entitles them to have sex with her; some even get violently angry if their after-dinner advances are refused.

29

Among nonhuman animals, food is used in courtship rituals to lure females. Females are attracted to food-providing males because food helps them produce eggs and nourish offspring. Males, then, fight to control a food-rich territory.

A dramatic example of the relationship between nutrition and reproductive success occurs among great gray shrikes, a family of birds that live in the Negev Desert of Israel. These birds, known by derogatory names such as butcherbird and murdering-bird, impale their prey on thorns or any other pointed projection. Male great grays begin stocking their larders three or four months before females arrive in January for the breeding season. When the males are alone on their 150-acre territories, they keep no more than fifteen to twenty items in each cache. But beginning in September, they add from 90 to 120 items, including inedible objects such as feathers, snails, and pieces of cloth.

The male does not build such a larder to satisfy his appetite alone. Suspecting that the purpose was to attract females, researcher Reuven Yosef set up an experiment. He removed caches from some males' territories and added edible items to the caches of others. Then he monitored the normal cache size of a third group. The males with the most impressive larders attracted females a full month earlier than those of the control group. Males with no cache at all got no matings and remained bachelors. Females nesting with males that afforded them better nutrition were able to raise three broods during the breeding season, as compared with only one or two broods raised by the control pairs. The female's choice of a well-provisioned male makes good reproductive sense. The more food, the more babies, and the greater the reproductive success for both male and female.[15]

Similar situations are found in the insect world. In the Sonora Desert of Arizona, the male long-jawed longhorn beetle, *Trachyderes (Dendrobias) mandibularis*, fights to control access to the fleshy red fruit of the saguaro cactus that females prefer as food. The female beetles mate in return for access to food, but saguaro fruits are scarce, and only large males with well-developed, pincerlike mandibles win control of these valuable territories. Some successful males have mandibles six times larger than those of the smallest males.

Aggressive competition among males to control resources that females need has influenced the evolution of sexual differences in body shape, size, and behavior. Males of some species have evolved an array of armaments such as horns or antlers. The male impala, an African antelope, has evolved elaborate horns that he uses to defend rich pastureland that attracts many females. A territory owner patrols his boundaries continuously, defending his mates against other males that try to rush in and sneak copulations.

In a species of bird known as the Asian honeyguide, the male controls a nest of the giant honeybee *Apis dorsata*, which produces the beeswax that honeyguides eat. In one of nature's many fascinating examples of coevolution, these birds are immune to the bee's sting and are able to feed freely on the beeswax. Male honeyguides guard their territories year-round and allow entrance only to females. Visiting females sometimes copulate with the territory owner, providing yet another example of the food-for-sex dynamic.

Red-winged blackbird females also select males on the basis of their territories. At the beginning of the breeding season, about a month before females arrive, males go into the marsh and compete for territories. Females look for high-food areas with the densest vegetation. Once a female has selected a territory and settled in, she aggressively tries to keep other females off. A male usually has five or six females on a territory, which he actively defends from intruders. Biologist Sarah Lennington reported going into the marsh with an umbrella to protect herself from dive-bombing males.[16]

Red-winged blackbirds, the most abundant bird in North America, illustrate the role of female choice in sustaining a polygynous mating system. Studies show that females can assess resources to such a fine degree that those living in a harem have the same reproductive success as a female that mates monogamously.

The "Oldest Profession" in the Nonhuman World

Throughout history, women have bartered sex to get food for themselves, a tactic not unknown on contemporary urban streets. This behavior is seen in the nonhuman world as well. During the nonbreeding season, the female purple-throated Carib hummingbird uses sex to get food, leading researcher Larry Wolf to apply the term *prostitution* to her behavior.[17]

Most hummingbirds feed on nectar, and males of many species defend groups of flowers from other hummingbirds. The males also tend to dominate females, so the latter are forced to poach on males' territories or to forage at poor, undefended sites. Female purple-throated Carib hummingbirds use mating behavior to gain entry to a male's food-rich territory. Since the male is aggressively defending his food cache, the female must enter his territory repeatedly, just as she would in the mating sequence. Again and again, the male chases her away, but she persists until she is allowed to stay and feed with no further aggression from him. Why does the male allow a female to stay when she is not ready to lay eggs and, therefore, of no immediate reproductive advantage to him? Possibly to get a head start. As the breeding season approaches, it may be to the male's advantage to mate with as many females as possible on the chance that one or more are ready to be fertilized.

Female megachilid bees exhibit the same behavior. Males of

31

this species control clumps of flowers that produce the pollen and nectar on which females feed. In order to get food, the female visits several territories within fifteen to thirty minutes and may copulate on demand with each resident male. If she doesn't copulate, the male may attack her as he would any other poacher that does not contribute to his reproductive success.[18]

Judging a Male by the Size of His Gift

In the scorpionfly, the food-for-sex pattern has been examined in minute detail. Also known as a hangingfly, this insect is no more than two centimeters (less than an inch) long, but it provides one of the best-known cases of adaptive female choice. This insect variation on dinner for two was discovered by biologist Randy Thornhill.[19] A male scorpionfly—the black-tipped hangingfly *Hylobittacus apicalis*—must come courting with a gift if he expects any attention at all from a female. And it can't be just any old gift. Females are very particular and refuse to accept gifts under a certain minimum size.

To catch the nuptial gift—a tasty insect—the tiny male scorpionfly must go hunting. This places him at risk of predation from web-building spiders. He is not hunting to feed himself, so he is highly discriminating about the prey he will use for a nuptial gift. Small prey are rejected. When he finally selects a prey insect, he kills it by driving his sharp proboscis into his victim's body. Then he releases enzymes that liquefy its body contents so they can be sucked out. He also releases a pheromone, a chemical that attracts females from as far as thirteen meters (forty-two feet) away.

Hanging from a twig with his nuptial gift grasped in his hind legs, the male scorpionfly is now subject to female choice. The female examines the prey and tastes it. All the while, the male tries to make genital contact, but the female doesn't permit mating until she has taken her time evaluating the male's gift. Some prey, such as ladybird beetles, are large enough but unacceptable because they contain nasty chemicals. Females reject undersized prey, along with the male carrying it, and fly away to respond to another male's pheromone. Only males with large prey are chosen by females. But the males with large prey aren't themselves larger in size than other males; they're simply better hunters.

Through his research, Thornhill has determined that the nuptial gift must be sixteen square millimeters or more in surface area to be accepted by a female. Then she eats throughout copulation, which lasts only as long as the nuptial gift lasts. Fast food is not to the male's advantage. A male with smaller prey may succeed in mating no more than five minutes, not enough time for any sperm to be transferred. Beyond five minutes of copulation, the amount of sperm accepted by the female increases steadily up to twenty minutes. The length of copulation determines not only how many sperm the female will take, but also whether the sperm will fertilize the female's eggs. If, for example, a female gets only a twelve-minute meal, she will leave and seek out another male with a larger nuptial gift. But if she is satisfied, she will become unreceptive to any other male and begin laying eggs.

When a female accepts a large nuptial gift, she allows the male to mate with her for twenty minutes or more. At the end of copulation, the two struggle for possession of any remaining prey. Usually the male wins. The size of the remaining prey may hold advantages for him. If it is large enough, he can use it again to attract another female. Sometimes he can gain as many as three copulations from one nuptial gift. In this courtship and mating vignette, the fundamental tension between male and female reproductive strategies is clearly dramatized. The male's success depends on mating with as many females as possible and seeing that his sperm fertilize the female's eggs; the female's reproductive success depends on getting as many resources as possible from the male.

The exercise of choice by female scorpionflies precludes reproduction in as many as 10 percent of the males. Females, however, gain a measurable fitness advantage by being choosy. A larger prey provides extra protein that goes into egg production. "Females who prefer males with big prey go off and lay more eggs per unit of time," says Thornhill.[20] If they get enough food from males, females don't have to hunt and expose themselves to predation.

The scorpionfly meets both criteria for adaptive female choice. First, the female clearly chooses certain males over others. Second, her choice provides her with the resources necessary to lay more eggs and produce more young, thereby enhancing her fitness.

This tiny insect species serves as a prototype for a dynamic

33

that turns up repeatedly—the female choosing for resources that help her to lay more eggs, produce more offspring, or raise more offspring to maturity. As fathers and mothers, insects provide an easily observable microcosm of reproductive behavior found throughout the animal kingdom. Like all other forms of life, insects are driven by the reproductive imperative. Since virtually all females reproduce, and many require protein-rich food to produce eggs, males compete to provide these nutritional supplements. Success gains them mates and ensures paternity.

Paternal Investment among Insects

The competition to sire offspring is so fierce among insects that they have evolved some unusual methods of providing nutrition as their paternal investment. The scorpionfly's nuptial gift of prey is one of three types. Other males produce nutritional products, some in the form of secretions from glands on the back or from the saliva gland. Another glandular product is a spermatophore, the sperm container that is transferred from male to female. Rich in protein, the spermatophore is usually eaten by the female after the sperm has been transferred. Some male crickets even produce two spermatophores during mating; the first is eaten by the female, and the second is used to fertilize her eggs. And in one genus of katydids, *Ephippiger,* the male's spermatophore, which reaches 30 percent of his body weight, has evolved a specialized part that seems to function purely as a food source.[21]

A third type of nutritious paternal investment is the male himself! In the ultimate sacrifice for reproductive success, some male insects, including sagebrush crickets, a carabid beetle, two species of midges, and several praying mantids, practice mating in extremis, offering themselves to be cannibalized, sometimes during the act of copulation itself.

The mantid, in particular, illustrates the extent to which life pulsates in the service of biological reproduction. Mating is fatal for some male mantids. Smaller than his mate, the male must take his chances and jump onto her at just the right moment. If his timing is off, the female may attack him, seizing him by the head before copulation takes place. In this variation of insect mating, a male may, indeed, "lose his head" over a female. But all may not be lost in reproductive terms, for a headless male mantis can mate successfully even in his death throes! If anything, the male mantis does it better without his head. The center of copulatory control in male insects is located in the ganglia of the abdomen, and the brain's role is primarily inhibitory. Decapitation merely removes the inhibitory nerves in his head. Freed from inhibition, his headless body bends in intense copulatory movements. Meanwhile, the female eats her mate, using the protein to make her egg cases. Then she, too, dies.

In female insects, control over egg laying is found in the abdominal ganglia. Researchers have observed that the severed abdomens of egg-bearing female dragonflies and moths can lay eggs in nearly normal fashion.[22] Copulation in spite of decapitation does not occur outside the insect arena. However, the fact that postmortem fertilization and egg laying can take place at all, in any species, demonstrates the extremes to which some forms of life are designed to go in order to reproduce, passing on their genes even as they pass on.

Some male mammals also give their all for reproduction. The antechinus is a small, shrewlike marsupial that lives in the wet forests and heaths of Australia. Males that manage to reach adulthood die at eleven and a half months of life, an age that coincides with the end of their first and only rut. Researchers who study these little animals, which are sometimes called marsupial mice, report finding corpses of males strewn on the forest floor at the end of the first week of a brief mating season. During this time, males run around in a frenzy, trying to locate and mate with females. They may not eat, and they can lose their hair, teeth, and one-third of their weight within a few days. Not all males will succeed in mating, so there is enormous pressure to find a female before their time is up.

Examination of the dead males reveals gastrointestinal ulcers and evidence of a suppressed immune system, both conditions commonly associated with stress. Researchers theorize that the fierce competition pushes the males' production of stress hormones (glucocorticoids) to a pathological level. While the higher

35

level of these hormones provides energy to compete for females, males pay the ultimate price for their effort. Females, on the other hand, live to reproduce for a second or third season.[23]

In the human world, we place great emphasis on the dying person's last words, but last deeds—particularly last sexual deeds—figure far more prominently in the rest of the animal kingdom. Living things strive to reproduce at all costs, pushing themselves even to the last tick of their biological clocks for the slimmest chance of producing offspring. Their last hurrah is often spent in the attempt to achieve reproductive success.

2. CHOICE BY SELECTION OF SUPERIOR GENES

One of the most controversial and hotly pursued questions in studies of female choice is whether females ever choose males for their genes alone. Some researchers argue that if female choice does play a significant role in evolution, females should be able to discriminate among males on the basis of their genetic quality.

Darwin focused on female choice as it influenced male secondary sexual characteristics—traits, such as deer antlers and the peacock's elaborate plumage, that are transmitted genetically to sons. Current research is demonstrating that some of these characteristics may have more than aesthetic value to females. The old expression "Looks are more than skin deep" gains new meaning in sociobiological terms. Researchers are discovering that in some cases, good looks can provide cues to an animal's genetic health, a trait that can be passed on to both male *and* female offspring.

"The opportunities for nonarbitrary mate choice by females are so varied and significant that purely aesthetic features rarely play a central role in female discrimination of mates,"[24] write Thornhill and Alcock with respect to insects. But females of many other animals also have a range of choice.

A number of biologists are currently conducting experiments to learn whether some females can really detect good genes. One of biology's major advances during the eighties was made in research on parasites, the hypothesis being that females, by choosing healthy, strong males, are able to get parasite-resistant genes for their offspring. A second area of research that has been building steadily over twenty years, but which intensified during the late eighties, emphasizes a genetic benefit to all of a female's offspring, most particularly her daughters. According to sociobiologist Robert Trivers, "Females will be selected to value their daughters slightly more heavily than their sons when they're choosing good genes for their offspring."[25]

To understand this concept, imagine that a female has a gene leading her to choose a male whose genes improve her daughters' chance of surviving by 10 percent, while decreasing her sons' survival by a similar amount. Over time, more generations of females would possess this gene, benefiting the males they prefer because there would be an increased number of females to mate with them. "Genes in males that increase survival in sons make life slightly more difficult for these sons (fewer females per male), while genes in males that increase survival in daughters make life slightly easier for males carrying these genes (more females per male)," writes Trivers. He adds: "Thus, female choice genes for sons inhibit their own spread, while choice genes for daughters do not."[26]

The idea that females may be able to base their selection of mates on genetic quality may seem like science fiction, but experiments show that females of some species can, indeed, discriminate good genes from bad. Female wild house mice, for example, discriminate against males carrying a lethal gene that can result in fetal death. The cue seems to be an odor given off by male carriers.

Researchers Sarah Lennington and Pat Kennedy marked large groups of mice for easy identification. They discovered that males without the lethal gene obtained the most copulations. In experiments, Lennington gave female mice a choice of going into a tube containing wood chips with the odor of a male that had no lethal gene or into a tube containing wood chips marked with the odor of a male carrying the lethal gene. Consistently females chose the odor of the normal, unaffected male.[27]

Parasite-Resistant Genes
Some biologists believe that the complexity of songs and the brightness of coloration that figure in the courtship rituals of some animals, especially birds, are cues to a male's resistance to parasites.

If so, it would help to explain why males of many species are more brightly colored than females, especially during the breeding season. First proposed by William Hamilton and Marlene Zuk in 1982,[28] the theory suggests that an animal's general good health is often indicated by the condition of plumage and fur, particularly when they are bright rather than dull. In a sense, the choice-making animal would diagnose the health of a potential mate in much the same way a doctor inspects a patient's tongue for signs of general health. "The methods used," wrote Hamilton and Zuk, "should have much in common with those of a physician checking eligibility for life insurance."[29] Females that select males for parasite-resistant genes are gaining the biological equivalent of life insurance for their offspring.

In the late 1980s, researchers began testing this theory on various animals. Some of the strongest proof that females can choose males for genetic quality has come from experiments with the red jungle fowl *Gallus gallus*, an Asian bird that is the ancestor of the domestic chicken.[30] Roosters are highly ornamented with combs, wattles, and decorative feathers. These ornaments not only are attractive to females, but also advertise the male's resistance to parasites. Roundworm, an intestinal parasite, noticeably affects the condition of the male's ornaments. "You can see marked effects on comb size; the color becomes drab, and there is retarded ornamental feather development," says Randy Thornhill, adding that these changes carry through to adulthood.[31]

To test female choice for parasite-resistant genes, Thornhill parasitized one group of male chickens and kept a control group free of parasites. He reports that the comb is so sensitive to the male's health that within a few hours of parasitization the size and color can decline. "The comb tracks the male's physiological internal state immediately, and the feathers reflect his health history,"[32] says Thornhill. Both comb and feathers are under the control of the hormone testosterone, and the infected male seems to assess his own condition, shutting down his testosterone production and shrinking his comb. Thornhill points out that it is in the male's interest to appear less conspicuous to his rivals so they won't pick fights with him while he's in a weakened condition. Females can use these same cues to avoid mating with a sick male.

When Thornhill put individual females in a pen with two males, one diseased and one healthy, he observed that the females consistently chose the healthy male. Thornhill suspects that the ability of females to choose males with good genes may exist in other species, but very little research has been done, especially in mammals.[33]

Similar research on a fish, the three-spined stickleback, turned up evidence that females of this species use the male's red coloration as a cue to his health. At the start of the breeding season, male three-spined sticklebacks develop bright red coloration due to carotenoids in their bodies. Females prefer the reddest males. The reason, discovered Manfred Milinski and Theo Bakker, is that the red color indicates health.[34] When the researchers infected bright red males with a widespread fish disease known as white-spot, their color faded. And with the fading of color, so faded their attractiveness as mates. Females that had preferred these same males when they were healthy no longer selected them. For these male fish, losing their ruddy color meant losing out in the competition to reproduce.

Do Women Choose Men for Their Health?

By 1990, the research on parasite-resistant genes was considered important enough for an entire symposium to be held on the subject, Parasites and Sexual Selection.[35] One of the more intriguing papers presented at this symposium suggested that disease also affects human mate choice.

Researcher Bobbi Low investigated marriage systems and the occurrence of diseases, including leishmaniasis (tropical sore), trypanosomes (sleeping sickness), malaria, schistosomes, leprosy, the spirochetes, and the filariae, in 186 societies. She found that societies with the highest incidence of these diseases had more polygynous marriages. Men tended not to marry the sister of a wife, and the capture of women from outside societies was more frequent. "Major pathogens may have been, during human evolutionary history, an important selective force," Low speculates.[36]

Disease would directly affect a male's physical appearance and his ability to compete with other males. Like the red jungle hens, women would not likely find diseased males attractive; they or their families might discriminate against them. Disease would have the effect of reducing the number of desirable males available as mates, making the healthiest men highly sought after by a number of women. The stage for polygyny would be set. "Thus pathogen stress may exacerbate the impact of sexual selection, and may favor increasing degrees of polygyny," says Low.[37]

The diseases that Low investigated are well documented worldwide. More of these diseases occur in the tropics than in northern and southern latitudes; and, significantly, Low points out, 78 percent of highly polygynous societies occur in the tropics. "In high pathogen areas, there are no monogamous societies," she says.[38]

Much work needs to be done to determine in which ways women are sensitive to cues of genetic health in men, and whether these cues influence mate choice. Studies already show that men prefer young, healthy females; and, not surprisingly, health and youth are correlated with female fertility. Touch, vision, hearing, and smell may help humans, as well as other animals, to select healthy mates. It is worth noting that a major purpose of cosmetics is to provide a look of glowing health.

Female Choice and the Mischievous X Chromosome

Some female fruit flies can choose males on the basis of a particular chromosome. Although they are only tiny insects—animals we don't associate with any degree of intelligence—these female fruit flies make extremely complex mate choices, demonstrating their ability to choose males for their genetic quality.

In laboratory experiments, evolutionary geneticist Chung I. Wu has shown that nonvirgin females of the species *Drosophila pseudoobscura* discriminate against males carrying the X chromosome, which is called the sex-ratio gene. "This is a special case of an ultra selfish gene," says Wu. "It is ultra selfish because it violates the very first rule of genetics that paternal and maternal copies of genes should be passed on to the next generation at an equal rate. But the sex-ratio gene refuses to do that. It decided to take over all the sperm."[39] As a consequence, males carrying the X chromosome produce only daughters, all of them genetically programmed to choose males also carrying the sex-ratio gene. Eventually a point would be reached where there would be no males, and the population would become extinct. Since this had not happened, Wu wanted to learn why.

He suspected that there must be "some counterbalancing force, some kind of policing force that holds the males carrying the sex-ratio gene in check." In Southern California and Arizona, for example, only 20 percent of *Drosophila pseudoobscura* males carry what Wu calls the "mischievous X chromosome." He suspected that the counterbalancing force might have something to do with mate choice, because it would not be in a female's interest to choose males with a gene that would produce only female offspring.

In his laboratory, Wu set up mate-choice tests with both virgin and nonvirgin females. He found that the virgin females did not discriminate against males carrying the X chromosome, but the nonvirgin females did. It's a matter of who's had the most experience. "Virgin females need to secure sperm as soon as they can, otherwise they are losing their precious time," says Wu. Nonvirgin females can afford to be much more discriminating. With sperm already stored in their sperm-storage organ, they aren't in any hurry to mate and can afford to be picky.

Wu points out that nonvirgin mating is probably the rule rather than the exception in many fruit-fly species. When a male mates with a nonvirgin female, his virility depends in part on his ability to displace sperm already stored in her reproductive tract with his own sperm. Wu's experiments have shown that the sperm displacement of males carrying the X chromosome is weaker at low temperatures, thereby reducing their ability to fertilize a female's eggs.[40]

So far, nobody knows what cue or cues nonvirgin female fruit flies use to detect males carrying the X chromosome. Wu suspects that these males are inherently weak. Perhaps, he speculates, they give off a particular odor that the female can detect; perhaps they don't beat their wings as persistently or don't clasp the female as forcefully or don't run as fast as other males.

Whatever the cue, experienced females are able to discriminate against males carrying the sex-ratio chromosome. By exercising individual choice, females have, in effect, prevented the species from being feminized to extinction.

Wu believes that female choice has been extremely important in keeping species isolated. Species remain distinct because they don't exchange genes with other species. "Female choice is actually the critical component," says Wu, pointing out that females of species with a small population adapted to a very small range are highly discriminating, much more so that females of populous, cosmopolitan species spread over a large range. The latter females can afford to be less discriminating; they may mate with males of the more narrowly adapted species as well as males of their own species. But, says Wu, females of the small population "absolutely refuse to mate with males of the wrong kind."[41]

42

Avoiding Bad Genes

Another way to keep from receiving inferior genes is to avoid mating with fathers and brothers; inbreeding can result in more congenital defects in offspring. Among human cultures, the incest taboo is universal. Copulation between parents and children is forbidden, and generally people are not permitted to marry siblings or first cousins. There also seems to be a tendency in individuals who are reared together to avoid sexual intercourse. The strongest evidence for the latter behavior comes from Joseph Shepher's study of unrelated children raised in Israeli kibbutzim. Although encouraged to marry within their kibbutz, when they reach suitable age, these people refused to marry one another and instead chose mates from another kibbutz.[42] Human beings act as evolutionary theory would predict—choosing mates outside their family group, thereby avoiding the genetic risks of inbreeding.

The universality of incest avoidance leads sociobiologists to conclude that the behavior is genetically programmed in the human brain just as it is in many nonhuman animals. For example, in the deer-mouse species *Peromyscus*, females reared with brothers or fathers delay sexual maturation and avoid being fertilized by a close relative. Among birds, female great tits choose males whose songs are similar, but not identical, to their father's courtship song. Female olive baboons avoid incest by choosing males that have transferred into the troop from other bands. Fruit-fly females select males genetically different from themselves, a phenomenon that biologists call the *rare-male advantage*. Female fruit flies inspect several courting males but are more likely to permit only those with a rare odor to copulate with them. This may be a genetically programmed mechanism for avoiding inbreeding.

Among certain species of insects, individual recognition may be far more important in female choice than anyone has suspected. Entomologist James Lloyd reports that a female firefly monitors male behavior, watching several potential mates over a period of time. "She can see that a male that she's tracked for several days doesn't have any early acting lethals, or bad genes. A male that can be around for several days or several weeks must be pretty good at getting resources and food. He must be pretty good at escaping predators," says Lloyd.[43] When female meadow katydids and female Caribbean fruit flies take a long time to "make up their minds," as Lloyd puts it, there must be something very important going on.

Leks: The Genetic Mall

In certain species in which males have no resources to attract mates, females may choose solely for genetic quality. Male fireflies, fallow deer, Uganda kob and several other African antelopes, hammerheaded bats, birds of paradise, sage grouse, ruffs, guppies, frogs, and some male crustacea provide no food or protection, nor do they help females build nests or raise the young. Indeed, the only contribution they make is their genes.

At the beginning of the mating season, these males gather in groups called leks. The word *lek*—from the Swedish word *leka*, which means "to play"—was first used by Swedish biologists to describe the childlike activity of male game birds such as the black cock and the capercaillie, members of the European grouse family. The areas on which these birds carry on their sexual displays became known as arenas, or dancing grounds. There the males compete among themselves for a small patch of ground, for dominance, and, in general, for the chance to advertise themselves to passing females.

Wings whirr and tails tremble as male European ruffs put their best feathers forward to intimidate each other and attract females. During the breeding season, the birds gather before sunup on the same plot of ground used by their ancestors. Scattered over the arena are numerous spots trampled bare by a resident male who defends his own little space. With legs flexed, heads bent low, and bodies tensed, the males feint and spar with each other, all rivals in a frenzied competition for mates.

Spreading their large pectoral ruffs like the stiff ruffled collars of Elizabethan courtiers, these feathered suitors engage in some of the animal kingdom's most colorful and spectacular behavior. Leaping into the air, they repeatedly dance around one another and peck at the wattles on each other's faces. Occasionally they crouch, spring, and buffet one another. Bodies thump, but few serious injuries are ever inflicted. The movements seem choreographed, stylized, a ritual dance repeated from one generation of ruffs to the next, all part of the male competition for females.

In effect, the lek functions as a kind of sexual mall where males gather to flaunt the only thing they have to offer a female— themselves. Females, like comparison shoppers, come to leks to select mates. It's all very businesslike. Females tend to choose only a few males, usually those with the most extreme plumage, vocalizations, and displays.[44] In certain species, the effect of such consistent female choice has been the evolution of highly exaggerated male secondary sexual characteristics such as the elaborate plumage of some birds of paradise and the weighty antlers of deer. Just why females should be so choosy when they seem to receive no tangible benefit from their choice has been called the *paradox of the lek*. There is speculation that the secondary sexual characteristics females prefer indicate high-quality genes since, in some cases, the males bearing these traits are both dominant and older. If age is indicative of proven survival skills, then it is a reliable cue to genetic quality.

From the male perspective, there is also a puzzling question: since most lekking males get no matings at all, why would a male try to attract a mate in the company of his rivals? The answer seems to be that although he is surrounded by rivals, this may be his only opportunity to meet females. The male who tries to attract a female on his own doesn't stand a chance of being noticed. His best option—usually his only option—is to shine among a group of his fellows. "The female reproductive strategy forces males [in lekking species] to assemble and compete," says Bert Hölldobler,[45] who has studied lekking in harvesting ants. The result is that some males are spectacularly more successful at mating than others. Among fallow deer, for example, biologist Tim Clutton-Brock reports that on any given day, one male may perform three-quarters of all matings. One individual buck may be responsible for as much as 12 to 18 percent of the year's total matings.[46]

Lekking males gather where there is a lot of female traffic, such as major thoroughfares between feeding locations or areas, known as *hot spots*, where males have mated successfully in the past. If it's a small area, the males tend to cluster, as if trying to maximize their chances by being in the right place at the right time, and in the company of males that are currently successful with females.

The old theory was that males got together and sorted out their pecking order, and then females chose the winners—the dominant males. But that explanation not only is simplistic, but also applies only to some species. Newer research shows that females don't always choose dominant males, unless they don't have the time or energy to resist the hassling from a dominant male.

Female choice appears to operate most freely in large, stable leks and less freely in small, unstable leks. In large leks, such as those of sage grouse, where several hundred males congregate, there are too many males for any one to dominate the others. Thus females can shop around at their leisure. In the larger leks, you see "females going where they want, mating with whom they please, and ignoring the male interactions," says biologist Jack Bradbury, who has studied lek behavior extensively in a number of different species.[47]

Among sage grouse, vocalization plays an important part in mate selection. According to Robert Gibson, who works with Bradbury in studying sage grouse, the males produce a striking display of sounds. Blowing up their esophageal pouches, males sound off, but only three notes seem to matter to females. These are "popping notes, like pulling a cork out of a bottle, and in between the pops is a whistle," says Gibson, adding, "Males who have the longer intervals between the pops and whistle get the most matings."[48]

Female sage grouse tend to prefer males chosen by other females. Gibson has observed that the more females there are on a lek, the less likely a female is to choose a different male. He believes that a kind of copying is going on. "If a female is in a male's territory, other females tend to come to that territory," he says.[49] This copying behavior occurs especially at the beginning of the season, when there is a spurt in breeding.

Among animals that form small leks with only a few males, females don't have as much freedom to choose mates. Fewer males means there is much jockeying for position, more fighting, and less stability. Not only do females have fewer mate choices, but the dominant males are more likely to badger them with persistent attempts to copulate.

The various birds of paradise, which live in the rainforested mountains of Papua New Guinea, provide spectacular examples of the complexity of both female choice and male-male competition among lek animals. In the species known as Lawes' Parotia, males clear courts, or display sites, on the ground. A male can have from one to five courts, which are located under suitable display perches where females that he attracts with his vocalizations can sit and watch him.

The entire courtship ritual of these male birds is like street theater. Once he has a female spectator, the male goes into a lengthy and complex dance. Females, in turn, inspect one male after another. And they do not make hasty choices. In their research in Mount Missim, Papua New Guinea, S. G. and M. A. Pruett-Jones observed that most females repeatedly visited the courts of some seventeen males within their home range. Some spent up to six weeks observing males before choosing a mate. When the female Lawes' Parotia has made up her mind, she solicits the male and remains faithful to him during the breeding season. The Pruett-Joneses believe that female choice is the "primary mechanism generating sexual selection" in this particular species of bird of paradise.[50]

The social life of birds of paradise may also be an important factor in their mate choices. Some species live fifteen or twenty years, and some individuals are well known to others. Biologist Bruce Beehler, who has studied these birds for many years, says, "Females actually know individual males and are able to decide which male is the top male—the hot shot." Females are not choosing males solely for their beautiful plumage, reports Beehler, because virtually all of the males are equally beautiful, yet experiments demonstrate that not all males are mating. "Instead of measuring how pretty the male is, which females can do in part, we think they're measuring instead how important or dominant he is in male society," says Beehler, adding that "a male's dominance is an instant signal to a female that he is in good physical condition and is able to produce those fancy plumes."[51] In these cases, a male's dominance might, indeed, indicate superior genes; but again, this is speculation.

It is clear that in lek situations, males have no leverage over females. Scientists speculate that males may have lost such leverage through a series of evolutionary steps that probably began with a breakdown in the male-female pair-bond that existed in the lek species' ancient ancestors. Once the pair-bond was severed, social organization changed. Males, emancipated from nesting duties, were free to become polygynous; females were left to build a nest, incubate the eggs, and defend and raise the young on their own.

There is also an economic factor in the evolution of leks. Whenever males cannot afford to defend a territory or protect a female or a group of females, they resort to lek behavior. "Everywhere you look, it seems that leks are a default system that males are forced into when other strategies don't work," says Jack Bradbury.[52]

The inability of males to defend resources plays a large role in leks of the grotesquely muzzled hammerheaded bats in West Africa. These bats feed on fruit trees that are so widely distributed and difficult to find that it would be physically impossible for any male to defend the resource. In a real economic sense, a male hammerheaded bat can't afford to feed or protect a female.

During the biannual breeding seasons, as many as 130 hammerheaded males compete for singing perches in trees along the edge of a river. There's some chasing and batting at each other with wings until the males have settled into their positions. After that, there's almost no fighting; the process becomes gentlemanly. Hanging by their feet, the males flap their wings and make a monotonous, metallic honking call. As a female comes closer to inspect, the males speed up their call. When she hovers in front of a particular male, he syncopates the call. A female bat goes to four or five males, listens to each, then returns to some individuals, making them repeat their calls again and again until she has narrowed her choice to the one with whom she finally mates.

The Disadvantage of Being Beautiful

In competing with each other, lek males engage in elaborate displays using the same secondary sexual characteristics that females prefer. The raucous honking of hammerheaded bats, the vocalizations of sage grouse, and the elaborate plumage of male birds of paradise serve dual functions—proving their mettle in competition with other males and attracting mates. For a lekking male, it's a matter of making the most of what you've got.

Highly conspicuous ornamentation may pose risks, however. Males that are conspicuous to rivals and mates are also conspicuous to predators. Excessive plumage can make it difficult for a male to escape. Israeli biologist Amotz Zahavi has suggested that secondary sexual characteristics give the male a "handicap factor," which places him at greater risk of predation.[53] Zahavi argues that such handicaps may function as a quality test imposed on the individual. A male who can survive in spite of his excess baggage demonstrates his strength and vigor. According to Zahavi's theory, the larger and more colorful the plumage, the higher the male's genetic quality. He must be giving an honest signal as to his mate quality because the costs to him are so great. If this is the case, such elaborate features could provide females with cues to individuals with the best genes for long-term survival.

The handicap theory is intriguing, but the evidence to support it is not conclusive. A parallel but different view comes from biologists Astrid Kodric-Brown and James H. Brown. They propose that while elaborate secondary sexual characteristics function as a natural form of truth in advertising, indicating the male's genetic quality to females, "the cost of honest advertisements need not always be expressed as a handicap to survival."[54] Some traits may demonstrate the male's ability to find food, avoid his enemies, successfully compete with his rivals, and survive to the proverbial ripe old age.

In lek systems, males seem to have become useless for anything except competing for mates. In the tropics, where breeding seasons may last up to eight months, lek males spend most of their lives in a state of sexual tension. On the other hand, constant sexual tension characterizes males of certain nonlekking species as well.

Males of some twenty species of insects, including cockroaches and fleas, are so primed to mate that they engage in homosexual courtship and try to copulate with each other or with inanimate things! Male insects have been observed trying to copulate with flowers, bananas, twigs, aluminum cans, and beer bottles. But the least discriminating male in the animal kingdom may be the digger bee, which sometimes copulates with dead males and females.[55] It's difficult to imagine that copulation with corpses could satisfy the bee's sexual urge; certainly the behavior does nothing for his reproductive success.

3. EXERCISING CHOICE BY REJECTION

Not all suitors are acceptable. Across species, from house flies to primates, females actively refuse the attempts of some males to copulate. The gargantuan female North Atlantic right whale simply stops calling to males and dives, which causes the courtship group of up to thirty pursuing males to disperse immediately.[56] A female insect can pursue a closed-door strategy and keep her genital opening closed; she can stay in motion, not pausing long enough for copulation to occur; or, in the human equivalent of keeping her legs crossed, she can keep her wings closed, preventing the male from mounting. Female fruit flies of the species *Drosophila primaeva* indicate rejection in no uncertain terms—by raising their abdomen in the fruit-fly version of a headstand.

Among nonhuman primates, refusal consists of walking away from a pursuing male or simply sitting down, thereby effectively blocking access.[57] Males of most species usually accept the rejection and move on to another female, but some males, unwilling to take the hint, continue to harass a female. Primatologist Barbara Smuts recalls watching a young female olive baboon rebuff forty-two sexual advances from the same male within three hours.[58]

Other males don't take no for an answer and force themselves on unwilling females. Rape has been observed in birds, squid, insects, and other animals, including human beings. Among wild nonhuman primates, however, rape has been reported only in orangutans. Rape is generally the exception rather than the rule in animal mating systems, both human and nonhuman. The fact that rape occurs relatively infrequently, even in species that are prone to the behavior, suggests that female cooperation is necessary for successful mating, and that most males generally pursue acceptable courtship routes.

When an undesirable suitor persists in harassing a female of certain species, she uses no-nonsense tactics. Some female ants and grasshoppers forcefully reject unwanted suitors with kicks or bites. Housefly females are armed with a spine on their midlegs, which they jab into the wings of undesirable males. If the male doesn't get the message and dismount, the female may tear his wings. Other insects produce their own chemical mace. Female tenebrionid beetles of the species *Pterostichus lucublandus* use their defensive chemical not only against predators but also against unwanted males. This spray is so disabling that even after the male cleans himself, he falls into a kind of coma for several hours, giving her time to get away. Of course, the female pays a price for this defense. Until she can resynthesize her supply of defensive spray, she is vulnerable to predators.[59]

Nor are female insects limited to rejecting attempts to copulate. Even after insemination, some female insects can reject certain sperm and choose others to fertilize their eggs. This aspect of female choice, which goes on inside the female's body, is extremely difficult to demonstrate, but some researchers have found evidence that it indeed occurs.[60]

The female insect's remarkable sperm-storage organ, the spermatheca, can hold a supply of sperm from several males. Some females store their lifetime supply of sperm on their nuptial flight, during which they mate with several males. This sperm supply acts somewhat like a timed-release vitamin that is under the female's control. For the rest of her life, at appropriate times, she releases the amount of sperm needed to fertilize her eggs. This convenience enables female insects to save the time, energy, and risks of further copulations.

Within a woman's body, there appears to be some kind of chemical communication between the egg and waiting sperm. Recent research indicates that a substance in the fluid surrounding a human egg incites sperm to swim up the Fallopian tubes when that egg is ready to be fertilized. The chemical attractant may stimulate some kind of sperm competition, ensuring that only the hardiest wins the race to fertilize the egg. Of nearly 400 million sperm contenders that may wait motionless for hours in a woman's reproductive tract, only about two hundred reach the site of fertilization in the Fallopian tubes. Of these, only one—if any—will actually fertilize an egg.[61]

51

4. CHOOSING MATES FOR THEIR BEAUTY

In some cases, the male trait that females prefer appears to have nothing to do with genes or resources or anything else that might contribute to a female's fitness. It just seems to push her sensory buttons. The aesthetic trait that catches a female's eyes or ears, or stimulates her erogenous zone, may have been a quirk of nature, a feature that evolved by chance mutation and then struck a chord in the female's nervous system.

Why would a female be aroused by something new rather than the tried and the true? New research suggests that females of some species may be genetically predisposed to prefer a new trait—one they have never seen or heard before. By choosing a new trait, thereby passing the preference for this trait on to their female offspring, females can actually reshape male anatomy, as the trait itself will be passed on to sons.

The imaginative research of biologist Nancy Burley has done much to increase understanding of this variant of female choice. In fact, she has been able to manipulate the process of sexual selection right in her laboratory. While working with a monogamous little Australian bird, the zebra finch *Taeniopygia guttata*, Burley discovered that colored plastic bands that she placed on the birds' legs for identification purposes were unexpectedly affecting their attractiveness to the opposite sex. Within five months, Burley noticed that most birds wearing red or pink leg bands were breeding, but that those wearing light green bands weren't. It seemed as if the plastic leg bands were affecting mate choice in the same way as plumage in pigeons and various other birds. Both females and males were showing preferences for certain colored bands—items that had nothing to do with the birds' natural physiology.

Fascinated by her observations, Burley designed a series of experiments to learn which colors were more attractive. She found that red-banded males and black-banded females were more attractive to the opposite sex than unbanded birds. But green-banded males and blue-banded females were less attractive. These results gave Burley an objective tool for studying purely aesthetic traits that had no relationship whatsoever to the animals' genetic fitness. She was able to pursue one of the most intriguing questions in evolutionary biology: how does an animal evolve a preference for a new trait that it has never seen before?

Burley hypothesizes that animals may be genetically programmed with what she calls *latent aesthetic preferences.* These hidden preferences show up in behavior when some mutation alters individuals and suddenly makes them appealing or attractive in a way that stimulates the preference, bringing it out of the closet, so to speak.[62] The colored plastic leg bands that Burley was using in her laboratory to identify the zebra finches had just that effect. They were functioning as a pseudomutation, calling into play the birds' predisposition to prefer a novel trait. This mechanism, speculated Burley, may be akin to that of the immune system, which seems designed to respond to the new and unexpected.

As she continued her experiments on zebra finches, Burley

made other surprising discoveries: traits that are attractive to the opposite sex are possibly threatening to the same sex. She found, for example, that female zebra finches preferred to perch next to blue-banded females and avoided the black-banded ones preferred by males. Similarly, males perferred the company of the green-banded males and were not attracted to the red-banded ones preferred by females.

An even more startling discovery was that within mated couples an interesting trade-off was going on. When Burley analyzed the amount of time that each partner was spending incubating, brooding, feeding, and defending the young, she discovered that the more attractive partner, as indicated by the color of its leg band, was spending less time carrying out those parental functions. If the female wore the more attractive band, she did less work; if the male wore the more attractive band, he devoted less time to parenting. These experiments showed that not only was the unattractive partner putting in more work, or greater parental investment, per offspring, but its life span was shorter and its long-term reproductive success was lower than that of same-sex attractive birds. "Results lend support to the idea that reproductive effort has a cost, a seldom-tested evolutionary principle," says Burley.[63]

When Burley set up experiments to test the reproductive success of the attractive males and females, she found that red-banded (attractive) males were twice as successful as orange-banded (neutral) or green-banded (unattractive) males. In part, this was due to the red-banded male's tendency to become polygynous. By doing less work with his mate, he had the time to acquire an additional mate. Similarly, the more attractive (black-banded) females had higher reproductive success than orange-banded (neutral) or blue-banded (unattractive) females.

Going a step further, Burley looked at the sex ratio of offspring of birds wearing the attractive color band. In experiments in which only males or females were banded, the bird wearing the most attractive leg band produced significantly more of its own sex. Red-banded males had the most sons, and black-banded females had the most daughters. The unattractive birds (blue-

53

banded females and green-banded males) experienced the highest rates of mortality, and the attractive birds the lowest.

As evolutionary biology would predict, parents manipulate the male-female sex ratio so as to produce more of the offspring with superior mate-getting traits—in this case, more offspring of the same sex as the more attractive partner.[64] The way in which zebra finches manipulate the sex ratio is by selectively rejecting the young, usually within six days of hatching.[65]

Amazingly, the zebra finches reacted to colored plastic leg bands as if they were traits that had been inherited. Through her chance discovery, Burley has been able to investigate sexual selection and sex-ratio manipulation unemcumbered by biological ambiguity. Choosing a mate on the basis of a colored leg band is clearly an aesthetic choice.

It is also clear that an aesthetic trait can benefit its bearer by enhancing his or her attractiveness as a mate, thereby increasing reproductive success. But other dynamics relating to the role of attractiveness also come into play.

Two of the most well-worn phrases regarding mate choice among humans are "Like prefers like" and "Opposites attract." Although one cannot draw direct correlations between nonhuman and human animal behavior, Burley's experiments with the zebra finches suggest a highly plausible explanation: attractive individuals have more options. "Highly preferred individuals should be more selective of mates because they can afford to be, whereas less desirable individuals must settle for inferior mates or fail to reproduce at all," writes Burley.[66]

In human terms, this may help to explain why the rich tend to marry the rich and the poor marry the poor. Most individuals prefer attractive partners—defined here as those with high socioeconomic status—whether they themselves are attractive or not. But individuals of high socioeconomic class—which in most cultures also correlates with superior mate quality—have many more mating options than poor individuals. The poor may not *prefer* to marry the poor, but they have no other mate choices. Individuals of lower mate quality simply do not have as many options as attractive individuals.

A Preference for Swordtails

Burley's work has inspired other scientists to look for preexisting preferences for novel traits. Biologist Alexandra Basolo set up experiments to learn whether the southern platyfish had a hidden preference for males with a swordtail. Males of a closely related species, the tropical green swordtail, have a long swordlike appendage extending from the rear fin. This appendage apparently has no function other than to attract females. But Basolo's research shows that females are genetically predisposed to prefer swordtails, possibly because the wagging tail resembles food or because the pattern of the sword stimulates the female's visual system.

Basolo and a colleague surgically attached tiny plastic swords to the rear fins of males of the closely related, swordless southern platyfish. Each sword was colored black and bright yellow, similar to the color pattern of the male swordtail. For the sake of comparison, another group of male platyfish were given a transparent sword, which experiments had demonstrated were invisible to females, but which was useful to Basolo as a control in the event the false tails altered the male's behavior in any way.

For the experiment, three fish—two males and a female—were placed in a tank with three equal compartments separated by Plexiglas partitions. A male with a colorful sword occupied one of the outer compartments; a male with an invisible sword swam in the other outer compartment. A female was placed in the center compartment, which was divided into three sections, one adjacent to each of the outer compartments. Consistently, the females chose the males with the colorful swordtail and spent more time in the section adjacent to them.

Basolo believes that among green swordtails, the swordlike appendage probably first appeared in much tinier form as a mutation. This chance mutation then appealed to the female's preexisting preference for this kind of novel characteristic. Over time, female preference for males with swordtails resulted in an exaggeration of that trait.[67]

There is more to the story of preexisting preferences, and this involves the female's sensory system. For a female to find a trait attractive, it must in some way excite her senses. In an effort to unravel female preference at the level of the sensory system, researchers Michael Ryan and Stanley Rand took on a subject they had been studying for several years—the tropical túngara frog, which is found throughout Central America.

The Advantage of a Deep Voice

In the blackness of the tropical night, female túngara frogs of the species *Physalaemus pustulosus* listen to males' mating calls. Around dusk males arrive at the breeding site and begin to call. Some produce more than seven thousand calls in a single night. Females come to the site only on the night they mate. Selecting a mate from the resounding din takes time. A female sometimes spends hours swimming among the males and sitting stationary in front of some. Ryan observed a female sit in front of a calling male for twenty minutes and then swim away to take up a position in front of another calling male before returning to the first and initiating mating. These female frogs choose only those males that make a particular low-pitched sound, which scientists call a *chuck*, at the end of their call. The males that make these chucks are also the largest. In trying to learn why females prefer the chuck sounds, biologists Ryan and Rand discovered a neurological basis for sexual selection in this frog; it seems the chuck is a real ear tickler for túngara females.

Ryan and Rand designed experiments to find out whether there is anything about the frog's auditory system that makes females prefer low-frequency chucks. Their starting point was the frog's unique sense of hearing. Unlike all other land-dwelling vertebrates, amphibians have two inner-ear organs—the amphibian papilla and the basilar papilla—both of which are sensitive to airborne vibrations. "Their auditory system is tuned, much like you would tune in a radio, to the call of their species. But in *Physalaemus* females, that tuning is slightly below the average male call," says Ryan, adding that it is this tuning property in the females' auditory system that makes them prefer low-frequency chucks.[68]

Only large, older males have thick enough vocal cords to produce the lower sound. So the female preference for the largest males that Ryan had earlier observed in 1980 was based on those males' ability to stimulate the female's preexisting preference for low-frequency sounds.[69] The researchers discovered that the sound frequencies with the most energy in the male's mating call "tend to match the sensitivities of the auditory papillae."[70] In other words, the male's chucks are stimulating the female's inner-ear organs.

The male's call is complex, consisting of a whine followed by from one to six chucks. The whine is necessary to attract females, but it's the chuck that clinches her preference. The chuck, however, is not adaptive. It does not enhance the female's fitness; it simply stimulates her sense of hearing.

Then the researchers set up experiments to learn whether only the male's chuck would stimulate the female's auditory system or whether other low-pitched sounds could be substituted. "We showed that there's nothing sacrosanct about that chuck," says Ryan. "You can take that chuck apart and it's still just a preference."[71] He explains that when the chuck was replaced with a blast of white noise, female frogs still found that more attractive than a call without any kind of chuck.

The next question was whether the female's specially tuned auditory system had evolved in response to the chuck or whether there had been a genetic predisposition for low-frequency sounds much like the zebra finches' genetic predisposition for a novel trait. To find out, Ryan and Rand investigated the auditory system of *Physalaemus's* next closest relative, which does not make chucks.

When they added chucks to the recorded calls of males of the closely related species, and then played them back to females, these females, which had never before heard their own males chucking, preferred them. "Now we can say that this trait did not evolve in the túngara frog. It was a trait that had been around for a while," says Ryan. "The male túngara exploited the female's preference."

So there are two aspects of the female túngara frog's choice of males that add a chuck to their whines: the female's auditory system prefers the low frequency, and the female has a genetic predisposition to respond to chucks.

When females in any animal species choose a male, they have to use their sensory system to see the male, to hear the male, and to smell the male. But those sensory systems evolved for different functions, not just for mate choice. "We think that the sensory system is shaped by natural selection for tasks that are not related to mate choice, but then this introduces biases into the sensory system," says Ryan, adding, "Males then evolved traits that match these biases that females find attractive because the sensory system has been shaped in certain ways."[72]

The idea that animals may be genetically predisposed to prefer a new characteristic—a novel arrangement of feathers, the chance appearance of a lumpy appendage, an unusual spot of color, or whatever—hints at an amazing ability to change that is apparently wired into the nervous systems of some organisms. Perhaps this genetic wiring is universal, part and parcel of life itself, holding the possibility that yesteryear's mutation may be today's common form.

It is easy to shrug and say, "Well, these are only animals. This has nothing to do with *me*." Such complacency will not get us off biology's reproductive hook, however. We humans are also animals; we, too, have evolved through the process of natural selection, and we, too, live to reproduce. The principles of parental investment, female choice, and male-male competition continue to operate—albeit with greater complexity and with some bizarre social twists—in human societies as well.

THREE

❧

FEMALE CHOICE AMONG HUMANS

O me, the word 'choose!' I may
neither choose whom I would nor refuse
whom I dislike; so is the will of a living
daughter curbed by the will of a dead father.

PORTIA IN WILLIAM SHAKESPEARE'S
The Merchant of Venice
act I; scene 2

ALTHOUGH FEMALE CHOICE applies to humans in the same sense as it does to other animals, most marriage systems allow women less personal choice of mates than that which is enjoyed by females in the rest of the animal kingdom. One could even argue that there is no individual mate choice in most human societies. More often than not, relatives—fathers, uncles, brothers, mothers, grand-mothers, sisters, and aunts—decide who will marry whom. Some marriages are arranged even before the partners are born. Western cultures may romanticize male-female relationships, but most of the world's marriages are still reproductive contracts: his wealth for her uterus. Human mate choice is one of the oldest, coldest business deals known. "For most of humanity, and possibly for all of it before modern times, marriage is less an alliance of two

59

people than of two networks of kin," says anthropologist Donald Symons.[1]

But despite all the laws, customs, religious beliefs, and taboos that restrict individual choice, humans still mate as evolutionary biology would predict. Just as many nonhuman females choose males with resources, so humans, whether families or individuals, tend to choose a groom for his wealth and status. And like many nonhuman males, the groom's family wants a fertile virgin bride for him. Her fertility promises grandchildren, especially grandsons; her virginity helps to ensure that any offspring will be sired by their son.

Virgins are treated as reproductive commodities in many societies, and the custom of paying a bride-price—wealth transferred from his family to hers—is widespread throughout the world. "Men purchase wives in the majority of human societies, and they often demand a refund if the bargain proves disappointing," write Martin Daly and Margo Wilson.[2] Among the Haya of northwestern Tanzania, for example, the husband of an infertile woman may return her to her parents and demand that her bride-price be returned.

When the reproductive market is reversed, females and their families will make considerable economic sacrifices, competing through dowry to marry into wealthy, high-status families that transfer wealth to sons. Her family's failure to pay a promised dowry can cost a young woman her life. In India in 1987, reports the United Nations, 1,786 brides were murdered for nonpayment of dowry.[3] These homicides were considered justifiable, and few, if any, were prosecuted.

Since a virgin bride is so important to the groom's family, a girl's family takes pains to preserve her chastity, sometimes by brutal and restrictive means. Her purity is essential to their family honor and is a prerequisite for a high-status son-in-law.

Both the physiological burden of reproduction and the social burden of maintaining family honor are carried by the young woman. The former is biologically obligatory; the latter is forced on girls and women through customs and laws upheld by their families and by their local governments. The equating of a young girl's chastity with family honor demonstrates the astounding power of reproduction in shaping people's lives. The entire family cooperates to protect and defend its honor. In effect, family members take collective possession of the daughter's reproductive potential; it becomes their most valuable genetic bargaining chip.

Although a woman may not have much say in the selection of her own husband, she may play a powerful role in the choice of a mate for her daughter or son. In cultures with this custom, female mate choice is simply deferred by a generation.

CULTURAL SUCCESS AND REPRODUCTIVE SUCCESS

Like female blackbirds, Mormon crickets, and bluehead wrasses, women and their families actively choose males with resources. Just as some nonhuman males compete to control food-rich territories, men compete for material riches. What ecological resources—a bountiful pasture or a protected nest—are for other animals, wealth and status are for humans. Cultural success comes to those who, by inheritance or their own work, acquire the kind of wealth and status valued by the particular society. In the United States, amassing a fortune is cultural success; among the Yânomamö Indians, being a fierce warrior and skilled hunter is cultural success. And cultural success generally contributes to reproductive success.

Among the Sharanahua Indians of Peru, for example, women prefer men who can bring home meat. In this hunting and gathering society, meat is as highly prized as money is in contemporary American society. To the Sharanahua, a successful hunt is an expression of virility. Meat is the currency of manhood and of sex. Anthropologist Janet Siskind reports a Sharanahua woman's ridicule when the men of her household returned from the hunt empty-handed: "'There is no meat, let's eat penises.'"[4]

Bringing home the meat in Sharanahua society is equivalent to bringing home the bacon in American society. Anthropological research indicates that what a society values as wealth—whether it be meat, land, cattle, pigs, or money—contributes to the status of the man who possesses it. Indeed, the reason these resources are considered wealth in the first place may be that they contribute to the owner's desirability as a mate, and thus to his reproductive success.

Studies of societies, ranging from preliterate to industrialized, show that rich and powerful men tend to have many wives and children,[5] whereas poor men may have neither. Generally women and their families do not find poor men attractive mate choices. Does this mean that the stereotype of the gold-digging female is true?

The answer is not a simple yes or no. Like all stereotypes, this one, too, contains elements of truth, but it is not exhaustive. Unraveling the larger complexity of this issue involves understanding how female choice operates in an evolutionary context.

"The data just say that females go with the money, which is parental investment on the part of males," says anthropologist John Hartung,[6] who analyzed data from some 850 societies. He found that where polygyny is possible, humans transmit wealth to male descendants. It's easy to understand why. The more wives a man has, the more offspring he sires. By transferring his wealth to his sons, a polygynist gives them means to acquire multiple wives and sire his grandchildren, thereby contributing to his own reproductive success. Of course, families in nonpolygynous societies have traditionally transferred wealth to sons as well.

In their study of 300 middle-class women in the Los Angeles area, psychologist Susan Essock-Vitale and biologist Michael McGuire found that a woman's social situation affects the way her biology expresses itself. Because U.S. society is "organized around an elaborate division of labor by sex and a strong reliance upon resource exchange, there exists a particularly large payoff for retaining a male as a provider of resources for, and care-giver to, mutually conceived offspring."[7] The high social status that accompanies wealth provides a support system that enables a woman to conceive and bear children with ease. Thus marriage in the United States is associated with a high degree of reproductive success and confidence of paternity.

Wealthy men tend to be dominant in their society, and women, like many nonhuman females, are attracted to cues of male dominance. In his cross-cultural study of traits that women find attrac-

tive, psychologist Bruce Ellis looked at three categories of dominance cues: (1) physical, such as height and body carriage; (2)
social, including family; and (3) behavioral, including aggressiveness and assertiveness. Consistently Ellis found that men
who expressed dominance cues were more sexually attractive to
women. "For women the world over, male attractiveness is bound
up with social status, or skills, strength, bravery, prowess, and
similar qualities," says Ellis.[8]

In addition to his material wealth and his status relative to
other men, a man's resources may include his network of kin, his
position in the community, his education, his reputation as a hard
worker, and his ability to father—to pass on values and skills that
will enable his offspring to succeed in their particular society.

In societies where women choose their own mates, intangibles
are also important—a man's personality attributes, such as his attitude toward women and children, his ability to be considerate,
tender, loving, kind, fair, humane, and to form intimate relationships. But while individual women will focus on the secondary resources or intangibles, material wealth and status remain power-
fully attractive.

It is possible that the achievements that a society prizes most
highly are precisely those that have enabled men to obtain wives
and sire offspring. Indeed, it has been suggested that cultural differences grew out of the reproductive strategies used to attract
mates in different environments. If this is the case, and there is increasing evidence that it is, female choice, whether individual or
familial, played a major role not only in determining how males
look and act, but also in influencing cultural value systems, social
structures, and the laws and customs for governing and maintaining those structures.

"In most human societies, cultural success consists in accom-
plishing those things which make biological success probable.
While cultural success is by definition something people are conscious of, they may often be unaware of the biological consequences of their behavior," wrote anthropologist William Irons in
1979,[9] a time when only a few anthropologists were applying evolutionary principles to human social behavior. His hypothesis was
derived from the observation that people do whatever they can,

within the limitations of their particular environments, to gain the greatest amount of *inclusive fitness*—reproductive success for themselves and their kin.

If females, or their families, consistently choose males for their resources and power, natural selection will favor behaviors that enable males to succeed in obtaining those resources. Evidence from studies worldwide shows that culturally successful males are the most desirable as mates. In the United States, for example, entrance into high-paying professions such as medicine, law, and business enhances a man's attractiveness to women. American men who marry in a given year earn nearly 50 percent more money than those of the same age who don't marry. "Part of this correlation is probably due to female preference," says Robert Trivers.[10] The other part of the correlation is probably due to male-male competition. The more money a man makes, the higher his status, and the more respect he receives among his peers and his social group in general. His dominance is thus enhanced, making him more attractive to women.

For most of human evolutionary history, status and wealth have been translated into reproductive success. According to Daly and Wilson, "Men of high status have more wives, more concubines, more children and their children survive better. These things have consistently been the case in foraging societies, in pastoral societies, in horticultural societies, in state societies."[11]

The degree to which cultural success translates into reproductive success is dramatically illustrated by a Yânomamö man known only as the father of Matakuwä, or Shinbone. Little is known about Shinbone's father other than that he was a headman who commanded great respect among his peers. Anthropologist Napoleon Chagnon learned of these men through informants in the rainforest tribe that he has spent so many years studying. Shinbone's father had 14 children, 143 grandchildren, 335 great-grandchildren, and, at the time of Chagnon's last census in 1975, 401 great-great-grandchildren. Over three-fourths of all the residents—a total of 756 individuals—of seven villages were descended in some way from Shinbone's father. In some villages 90 percent of all residents were his descendants. Through kidnap-

pings, migration, and intermarriage, Shinbone's father also had
descendants in other villages beyond those of his own tribe. As a
result, 48 percent of all Yânomamö in a particular area were descended from a single individual.[12] But Shinbone, who was a
headman because of the strength of his lineage, will have even
greater reproductive success than his father. At the time of Chagnon's last census, Shinbone had already fathered 43 children, and
two of his sons had produced 54 children. According to Chagnon,
were he to make a tally in 1992, the numbers of Shinbone's descendants would be even more impressive.[13]

Shinbone and his father's extraordinary reproductive success
is surpassed by that of Moulay Ismail the Bloodthirsty, one-time
emperor of Morocco, who reigned from 1672 to 1727, and whose
name, it is said, derives from his homicidal habit of beheading
slaves while entertaining foreign guests. Ismail is credited by *The
Guinness Book of World Records* with 888 acknowledged offspring. A devout Muslim, he was allowed only four wives, but his
religion did not limit the number of his concubines. Like many
other wealthy despotic rulers in Asia, the Middle East, sub-
Saharan Africa, and the New World, Ismail kept a harem. His is
said to have consisted of five hundred women, managed by a
senior wife. When a concubine reached the age of thirty, she was
sent packing to the harem of a provincial underling and replaced
by a younger woman.

Harems much larger than Ismail's existed in the royal courts
of China and the Middle East. Mildred Dickemann points to
harems of more than a thousand women that were managed as reproductive resources. The Arabian Caliph al-Mutawakkil, who
reigned from A.D. 847 to A.D. 851, reportedly had 4,000 concubines,
all of whom he used sexually; the Egyptian Abdur Rahman III reportedly had 6,300 concubines, and the harems of Ottoman sul-
tans ranged from 200 to 1,200 women.[14] The Chinese imperial
harem, writes Dickemann, involved the "copulation of concubines on a rotating basis at appropriate times in their menstrual
cycles, all carefully regulated by female supervisors to prevent deception and error."[15] If the reproductive bureaucracy was well
managed, considering nine-month pregnancies and two- or three-

65

year lactations, an energetic ruler might be able to have sex with a thousand women over a period of several years. However, anthropologist R. van Gulik found records of much grumbling on the part of "overburdened" polygynous males.[16]

Historically, heads of state have increased their reproductive success through exploitation of others' labors. By taking tribute and labor from their subjects, these rulers were able to support children by numerous women. And many women preferred to be one of many wives or concubines of a rich man rather than the sole mate of a poor man.

CHANGES IN AN ANCIENT REPRODUCTIVE PATTERN

Until the industrial revolution, rich people everywhere had greater reproductive success than poor people. Wealth and status translated into more children. In eighteenth-century France, however, there was an unprecedented shift in this age-old reproductive pattern. The wealthy began having fewer children than the poor, and birthrates began to decline. By the end of the nineteenth century, upper-class citizens of the United States and Great Britain were also showing declining birthrates. The decline began around 1920 in Japan, and has now spread throughout Asia. This demographic transition from a high-fertility, high-mortality regime to a low-fertility, low-mortality regime was made possible through advances in public health and sanitation. With some exceptions, most notably among African cultures and the American Mormons, the wealthy are now producing fewer children than the poor.

Just what this shift means is the subject of considerable debate and interpretation. Some critics of sociobiology say that it contradicts one of that field's basic tenets, namely that wealth and status are positively correlated with reproductive success. While admitting that the low fertility of modern humans poses a theoretical challenge, sociobiologists point out that it is too soon to tell whether this new pattern is permanent. Lower birthrates may be only an artifact of industrial civilization, a response to the novel urbanized environment in which modern humans find themselves. Or it may be the result of widespread enforced monogamy.

As biologist Richard Dawkins points out, "If a religious law limits males of a basically polygynous species to one mate each, it is hardly surprising that worldly success is no longer reflected in reproductive success."[17]

Urbanization has imposed new stresses and demands on the human animal. In agricultural societies, children were economic assets, helping their families by working in the fields. The opposite holds true in industrialized societies. Raising children has become so costly that it imposes enormous economic burdens on parents. Modern human beings may even have evolved to avoid reproduction or to limit children when the burden seems too much to bear.[18] In industrial societies, the accumulation of surplus wealth may have become a pursuit for its own sake.[19] Another fascinating suggestion is that modern humans seek wealth because they are acting in the tradition of their pretechnological ancestors, who sought resources that they could convert into mating and reproductive advantage.

For urban dwellers in industrialized societies, reproductive success is no longer a numbers game. More important is quality, the ability of offspring to compete successfully in their environment, mate, and pass on their genes. The family that has one or two children and provides high-quality parenting and educational opportunities has greater reproductive success than a poor family that produces five children it cannot support and educate to become successful members of the society.[20]

It is interesting to note, however, that despite the new pattern of declining birthrates, there has been a fertility glitch among Americans born between 1935 and 1960. When this group reached its childbearing years, wealthy couples produced *more* children. Susan Essock-Vitale's study of *Forbes* magazine's 400 richest Americans revealed that this sample had more children than the general population. As reported in the 1982 census, wealthy women had 3.1 children, compared with 2.7 in their age-matched counterparts. Not only did the wealthy have more children, but their offspring's survival rate was nearly 99 percent, high even by comparison to that of the offspring of their less affluent white American counterparts.[21]

Choosing Men for Their Resources

Women make their mate choices less directly than do nonhuman females, but choice based on resources is still a clear pattern of the human species. Because of the large parental investment made by men and their families, men with means are highly desirable mates; this gives them great bargaining power in the mating game. Men are more parental than any other male mammal, and because of their considerable investment in offspring, they have more say in mate choice than males of most other species. As a result, women often compete for men just as fiercely as men compete for women.

On Ifaluk, a tiny atoll in the Western Carolines, a salaried job makes a man more attractive. A small number of men have been able to improve their wealth and status by earning salaries as teachers or health-care workers for the U.S.-supported Trust Territory Administration. Compared with Ifaluk men who depend on fishing for income, the salaried men are rich. Anthropologists Paul Turke and Laura Betzig found that families of the employed men eat more Western food and own kerosene lanterns, stoves, playpens, transistor radios, and other consumer items. Their wives and children are better fed. Better nutrition for mothers and earlier weaning increase a woman's fertility, decrease her birth intervals, and translate into greater reproductive success.[22]

For the Yomut Turkmen of Iran, being a successful herdsman and acquiring sheep was necessary to acquire a wife. William Irons, who studied the Turkmen in the late sixties, reported that it took an average family between two and four years to acquire enough capital to give the 100 sheep required to obtain a bride for a son. The bride-price for the second or third wife was three times that of the first. As in other polygynous societies, only very rich Turkmen could afford more than one.[23]

Among the Krummhörn people who lived in Germany between 1720 and 1874, land ownership contributed to reproductive success. Anthropologists Eckart Voland and Claudia Engel studied family records from thirty-two parishes and found that wealthy men had younger brides than other men. They interpret this as an expression of a "conditional female choice strategy with decreasing standards." The mate-selection maxim might have read: "If you are young, be very choosy and marry only a high-quality mate. The older you become, the more you must reduce your standards concerning your marriage partner!"[24] Like the zebra finches described in chapter 2, the most attractive individuals had the greatest number of mating options. Attractive Krummhörn women (in this case, the youngest) had the option of being more selective and choosing the most attractive, or wealthiest, men.

Although the age at marriage of Krummhörn men rarely differed by more than one year, their brides' ages differed by as much as 4.3 years. The researchers found that the younger a woman was at marriage, the greater the likelihood that her husband owned land and enjoyed a high status. Approximately one-third of the women under twenty, but not even 10 percent of women over thirty, married a man from the highest social class. Among males, one in five farmers in the top landowning class married a woman under twenty, but only one in twenty-five landless men married a woman under twenty. From these data, Voland and Engel hypothesize that women who marry up the social ladder should marry at a younger age than women who marry beneath their social class. The older, and therefore less attractive, women had fewer marriage options.

"I consider female choice as significant as male competition in human biological and cultural evolution," says Voland. "Both aspects of sexual selection must have been balanced in the long run, since natural selection is supposed to have compromised between the different reproductive interests of both sexes."[25]

This means that the reproductive strategies of women and men have coevolved. What women want in a mate influences how men act; at the same time, what men want in a mate influences how women act. Neither sex gets its ideal mate all the time; choice becomes a compromise between what one wants and the available options. The individual women and men who are most attractive, in reproductive terms, emerge the winners.

Cultural Values and Reproductive Success

Anthropologist Monique Borgerhoff Mulder, who has studied
the Kipsigis of southwestern Kenya, found strong evidence that
wealth enhances reproductive success.[26] Until relatively recently,
the Kipsigis were a pastoral people, raising cattle, goats, and sheep
on common land. The livestock were individually owned, however, and were used both as a source of dairy products and for
bridewealth payments. In the 1930s, the British arrived and began
cultivating tea. They also introduced cash crops, which affected
the Kipsigis life-style. The Kipsigis began cultivating maize, ini-
tially for subsistence, but later selling the surplus and using the
profit to buy more livestock.

Ownership of both livestock and land was monopolized by
men and passed on from father to son. This new scarcity of land
created keen competition among men to own it, and some men became richer than others. "Land became a critical limiting resource," says Borgerhoff Mulder,[27] making the men who owned it
highly desirable as bridegrooms. Landowners in this polygynous
society can afford to support more wives, and their wives have
greater reproductive success than the wives of poorer men. In Kipsigis society, a man's ability to compete successfully with other
men for land became a prerequisite to his reproductive fitness.

Bridewealth can be a major expenditure for a Kipsigis family.
Since the sixties, a son's marriage has required the payment of approximately six cows, six goats, and eight hundred Kenyan shill-
ings to the family of the prospective bride. The livestock payment
constitutes one-third of an average man's herd, a steep price indeed. The first marriage is financed by a young man's father, but
the young man must pay for any subsequent wives himself. Since
it takes some time to accumulate the necessary wealth, Kipsigis
men usually don't take a second wife for another ten years. A
wealthy landowner may marry up to twelve wives, all of whom live
on his property and are entirely dependent on his land and livestock.[28] Just as in nonhuman polygynous societies, Kipsigis men
experience a great variance in reproductive success.

In exchange for paying bridewealth, a Kipsigis man acquires

exclusive lifetime rights to his wife's sexual and productive services. Neither divorce nor remarriage is an option for Kipsigis women, but Borgerhoff Mulder suggests that polygyny in this society "may be a consequence of the preference of females (or their kin) for wealthy males."[29] Like female blackbirds that choose to share a male with a food-rich territory, Kipsigis families may decide it is better for their daughters to be one of several wives of a rich man rather than the only wife of a poor man. The wives of a rich man have greater reproductive success; there is more food in their homes and lower incidence of illness among them and their offspring.

When a Kipsigis girl reaches menarche, she spends several months in seclusion while her parents meet with the father of each prospective suitor to negotiate the bride-price. The wealth of a potential son-in-law is particularly important. Although their wishes are not taken into formal consideration, the young can influence their parents. Kipsigis daughters are rarely forced into marriages against their wishes. The reason is that an unhappy wife will leave her husband, return to her parents' home, and continue to produce offspring with lovers. These offspring must then be fed from the produce of her parents' land. This can place economic stress on the rest of the family, particularly if the deserting bride has brothers who are already married. It is to everyone's advantage to see that a girl is happy with the choice of her husband.

Wealth not only increases a groom's mating options but also gets his family a discount on the bride-price. Sons of wealthier fathers are more likely to impregnate unmarried girls and then marry. Pregnancy before marriage demonstrates the bride's fertility. Wealthy grooms who have already impregnated a girl are charged a less exorbitant bride-price than are grooms from poorer families.

The Kipsigis study shows that in this society at least, wealth gives men a reproductive advantage and has done so for several generations. In Darwinian terms, the striving for wealth is an adaptive behavior that increases fitness. "For natural selection to operate on a trait, the trait must both confer fitness on its bearer (i.e., be adaptive) and it must be faithfully transmitted between parents and offspring, whether by cultural or genetic means," says Borgerhoff Mulder.[30]

She suggests that the strongly held view that female choice is absent or compromised in many societies because marriages are arranged by parents "may, in part, be ethnographically inaccurate." She cites the following arguments:

1. Parents may be offering guidance to their daughter rather than dictating what she must do. Thus the daughter is exercising some degree of choice.

2. Marriage prescriptions are frequently broken.

3. Information on marriage practices usually refers only to first marriages, but women often are freer to make choices in subsequent marriages.

4. In 61 percent of societies in a highly regarded ethnographic survey known as Whyte's sample (1978), the ability of women to initiate or refuse a match (not just first marriage) is "equal or greater than that of their husband; they are also equally or more able to initiate divorce than men (82% of societies), and equally able to remarry (75%)."[31]

THE INFLUENCE OF DADDY'S WEALTH

The wealth of a woman's father may be another factor in mate choice. Among the Herero, a pastoral people of the northern Kalahari Desert of northwest Botswana and northern Namibia, anthropologist Henry Harpending found a rather different slant on female choice. Women whose fathers are wealthy tend not to marry. Although they have precisely the same birthrates as married women, they choose to raise their children within their own family compound. In these cases, the children take the surname and lineage affiliation of their mother's father. The boyfriend who fathered a woman's children may visit, but if they aren't married, the couple does not live together publicly.

To understand this choice, one must realize that in Herero society, marriage requires that a young woman move away from her family and to her husband's village. Daughters of wealthy men prefer to remain in their parents' home. Sometimes the biological father of an unmarried woman's children will buy custody from her family. This doesn't mean that the children will go to live with him, but rather that they will carry his name and inherit whatever wealth he amasses. Poor Herero women with few if any prospects of inheritance for their children from their own families are more likely to marry. In general, Herero women seem to have a lot of choice and the freedom to run their own lives, Harpending reports. Although marriages are arranged, "it is not clear that young people are ever the passive pawns of politics of their elders that the elders portray them to be," he says.[32]

An unmarried woman who lives at home may have several boyfriends who visit her in a one-room house that she has constructed largely by herself. House building functions as a kind of rite de passage, a status symbol of her sexual maturity and a display of her feminine skills. In effect, the construction of a house is comparable to nest-building among other animals. The house also figures in courtship; a Herero woman's house attracts men the way a young American man's new car attracts young women. A Herero girl usually builds her first house between the ages of fifteen and twenty. First she makes a framework by tying saplings to a post. She covers this with a kind of stucco made by mixing cow dung with earth from termite mounds. Women take great pride in their houses, which Harpending describes as comfortable and cool, and they enjoy showing them off. Even if a woman marries and leaves her family home, she builds the house that she and her husband will occupy in his village. Since the materials of which the houses are constructed make them vulnerable to weather, the structures are in continual need of repair or replacement. As a consequence, says Harpending, there is a lot of house building in Herero society; and Herero men are impressed by women who build beautiful, long-lasting houses.

When Harpending asked women what they look for in a potential mate, he learned they have one set of criteria for boyfriends and another for husbands—their own double standard. Herero

73

women want boyfriends who are wealthy, good-looking, and polite; but husbands "have to be the right kind of cousin," says Harpending, adding that women talk about marriage "as if it were a business relationship."

Men pay a token bride-price, perhaps two cows or a cow and several sheep; and even that may not all be paid before the marriage. Harpending reports that families may feud for fifteen years or more over a bride-price that hasn't been fully paid. Currently, he says, bride-price throughout much of Africa is becoming inflated. Herero men, like men of other tribes, complain that they have to pay more for girls with education. Marriage among the Herero, however, is somewhat transient. A dissatisfied woman simply moves back to her family and builds another house. In this society, women are very much in control of their lives. Herero men couldn't get away with thinking of women as lesser beings, as men in some other societies do, says Harpending.

EXERCISING CHOICE IN SPITE OF THE SYSTEM

Human female choice operates in unexpected ways. In the fierce Yânomamö society, where young girls are promised in marriage by their older male kin, women find a way to exercise their own choice of subsequent mates. Napoleon Chagnon reports that a Yânomamö woman chooses her lovers and may precipitate fights between husband and lover in which the husband may be severely beaten. In Yânomamö society, the husband of an unfaithful wife is expected to challenge her lover in a club fight during which the husband may sustain serious blows to his head. If he doesn't fight to preserve his honor, he loses status. Eventually the husband becomes weary of this situation, and will "throw away," or divorce, his wife, freeing her to marry again. Of course, she risks being violently beaten by her husband for her infidelity, but she may regard this as a small price to pay to get rid of him and be with the man of her choice.[33]

Young Tongan women use elopement to circumvent arranged marriages and exercise choice. In the kingdom of Tonga, an archipelago of western Polynesia, ethnographers have long noted the frequency of elopement. In one village, more than half of the recorded marriages originated as elopements. Anthropologist George Marcus has noted that elopements are more frequent among nobility and the commoner elites, for whom the perpetuation and increase of wealth and prestige are especially important. Tongan elopement differs from the usual Western scenario in which an attractive man courts a woman and persuades her to run away with him and get married. Marcus interprets the Tongan variation as an exercise of female choice. "The real decisions about elopement are made not by the courting male but by the females in the household, who are quite aware of what the marriage system is and have actually created their own options within the system," he says, adding, "The whole idea of arranged marriages is purely in the realm of males, who control females for their own status. What has happened is that these elopement practices, which have intervened, have given females the opportunity to choose among mates."[34]

In the stratified Tongan society, an individual's status is inherited through the mother. Women have higher status than men; thus sisters have higher status than their brothers. In considering marriage, a man worries about the status his children will derive from the woman he marries. Females are also concerned about status, but not in the same way as men. For example, a girl's father may want her to marry a young man from a family in which he wishes to gain an economic or political foothold. He would have grounds for an alliance with the groom's father based on their common genetic interest in the grandchildren. Political and economic alliances have thus been formed throughout human history. But while a father wants to forge a relationship with the prospective groom's family, his daughter may want to improve her position within her own family. As Tongan women age, their position of power and authority improves within their own family. Consequently, fathers and daughters do not see eye to eye on mate choice.

Young Tongan women often make better mate choices than their fathers made for them. A father may plan for his daughter to marry a man of high status but with little or no economic means.

To a Tongan woman, status is less important than means. The landed nobility lives off its rents, but Tonga's fast-rising commoner class has entered trade and is developing wealth in overseas business. A Tongan noblewoman may choose to run off with a commoner who has better resources for supporting her and her children.

Elopement is so common that a ritual reconciliation is built into the society. As first, the young woman's father is angry and insulted and threatens to cut her and her new husband off. But after a cooling-off period, varying from a day to weeks or months, the couple, with the help of the young man's immediate family, prepare an offering of food and go to the young woman's home to ask her father to forgive them for the elopement. If the father publicly accepts the offering and apology, the reconciliation is complete.[35]

In talking with young Tongan women who had eloped, Marcus was impressed by their emphasis on the man's ability to be a good provider and to invest in their children.

REPRODUCTION AND SOCIAL CHANGE

Can a change in reproductive strategy bring about social transformation? Anthropologist Lee Cronk argues that it can and, in fact, did when Kenyan hunter-gatherers known as Mukogodo transformed themselves into herdsmen. For centuries, Mukogodo men had paid for their wives with beehives; but the stage for cultural transition was set around 1900, when British settlers entered north-central Kenya, expelling and resettling tribes that lived on land desirable to whites. The Mukogodo territory was set aside as a reserve—in effect, a tribal reservation—that was off limits to British settlement. Adjacent territories were taken over by white settlers, and this forced other tribal peoples into the reserve and thus into closer proximity with the previously isolated Mukogodo.

As the Mukogodo came into more frequent contact with their new neighbors—the herd-keeping Masai, Samburu, Ilng'wesi, and Digirri—they began to intermarry. "The British inadvertently added an incentive for the other groups to marry the Mukogodo by [threatening deportation] to other parts of Kenya," says Cronk.[36] Intermarriage with the Mukogodo would bolster the other tribes' claims to residence. But intermarriage also began to change the Mukogodo's form of bridewealth.

When a Mukogodo woman married into a herding tribe, her family received livestock as bridewealth. Many Mukogodo men obtained their first livestock by marrying their daughters to non-Mukogodo men. Mukogodo men began marrying women of the other tribes, and beehives became inadequate as bridewealth.

As more Mukogodo women married outside the group than non-Mukogodo women married into it, the tribe began to experience a shortage of women. Mukogodo men began looking for wives in the other tribes, discovering that non-Mukogodo women were more expensive than those in their own tribe. The difference was considerable—four times as many small stock and one and a half times as many cattle. Intermarriage with their neighbors thus set in motion a process of bridewealth inflation that made it necessary for Mukogodo men to acquire livestock in order to marry.[37] Cronk suggests two possible explanations for the difference between the bridewealth charged Mukogodo men by the other tribes versus that paid by men of those tribes for a Mukogodo wife: since Mukogodo men were the poorest in the area and thus the least desirable mates, they couldn't drive as hard a bargain. In addition, Mukogodo women may have been skinnier and later in maturing since their diets were poorer than those of their neighbors.[38] Another possibility is that the Mukogodo's desire to establish kinship ties with wealthy people may have made them willing to pay more for brides outside their group.

An additional consideration in the Mukogodo's transformation from hunter-gatherers to herders is that pastoral tribes expected a man to continue giving livestock to his in-laws after the formal bridewealth had been paid. The Mukogodo were also the brunt of social stigma. Pastoral tribes looked down on hunters and called them by the derogatory name *Dorobo*, which is associated with meanness, poverty, cowardice, womanishness, degeneracy, and contamination. This could also explain why the Mukogodo had to accept less for their daughters and pay more for wives outside their group.

Cronk concludes that the acquisition of livestock was a mating strategy for Mukogodo men brought about by bridewealth inflation. In asking why Mukogodo men would have preferred cattle to beehives, Cronk explains that a cow was worth several goats and sheep while a beehive was worth only one goat or sheep.

The shift to pastoralism brought other social changes as well. Most noticeably, Mukogodo men began to do less work. During the many years they had lived in caves, men had been responsible for supplying most of the food, but pastoralists leave herding, milking, and house building to women and children.

The Mukogodo's transition from hunting and gathering to herding took place in the short period between 1900 and 1936, when they left off a subsistence-level existence, began to acquire and keep cattle, sheep, and goats, moved out of caves, and began to build houses. Cronk argues that "their transformation from hunters to herders within a few decades early in this century was a response to the need to obtain livestock in order to marry."[39]

SEX DIFFERENCES IN MATE CHOICE

Choosing men for their resources and women for their fertility is not limited to tribal societies. Urban women and men share these mating preferences with women and men in pretechnological societies. Sex differences in mate choice is as universal among humans as among nonhumans.

In the largest study of sex differences in human mate preference ever done, psychologist David Buss found cross-cultural evidence supporting the predictions of evolutionary biology.[40] Using more than ten thousand responses from thirty-seven samples drawn from thirty-three countries, Buss tested five predictions about sex differences in human mate preferences. His goal was to learn whether sexual selection and parental investment are operating in humans as evolutionary theory would predict.

In setting up his first two predictions, Buss considered earning capacity the equivalent of resources in the nonhuman context. If human females were looking for men with resources, he predicted that they would value characteristics associated with increased earning capacity, such as ambition and industriousness.

His third and fourth predictions focused on male preference for fertile females. Buss suggested that in all cultures, female fertility is a factor of age. Men, he predicted, should prefer young women. Physical attractiveness, which is an indicator of age, should be more important to males than to females.

The fifth prediction concerned paternity. The old wisdom that a woman always knows who her children are but a man cannot be sure is based in biological fact. Natural selection, therefore, should have favored males who do everything they can to ensure that the children they support are their own rather than the offspring of some other male. Because of their interest in ensuring paternity, men can be expected to value a potential mate's chastity more than women do.

When the data were analyzed, Buss found the predicted sex differences in mate preference. In thirty-six of the thirty-seven samples, females valued good financial prospects in a potential mate more highly than males did. In all thirty-seven samples, women preferred mates at least 3.42 years older than themselves. Buss interprets the preference for older men as circumstantial evidence that women prefer males with a high earning capacity. Just as in the nonhuman world, a male's age can provide a cue to experience, longevity, prowess, and survival skills, which, in the human arena, can translate into success in making a living.

In each of the thirty-seven samples, males preferred mates who are younger by an average 2.66 years. As predicted, physical attractiveness in a potential mate was more important to males than to females.

Cultures differed considerably, however, about the value placed on female chastity. Samples from China, India, Indonesia, Iran, Taiwan, and Israel (Palestinian Arabs only) placed a high value on chastity. But respondents from Sweden, Norway, Finland, the

Netherlands, West Germany, and France considered a potential mate's chastity irrelevant or unimportant. Samples from Africa, Japan, Poland, and the Soviet Republic of Estonia placed a moderate value on chastity. "Chastity shows greater cross-cultural variability than any other rated variable in this study," says Buss.[41]

Although Buss's study supports the predictions of evolutionary biology and the universal pattern of sex differences in mate choice, earning capacity and physical appearance were not the highest-rated characteristics for either sex. Men and women in all samples ranked kindness/understanding and intelligence higher than earning power or attractiveness. Buss concludes that among humans, "males and females both express preferences, and it is clear that there are powerful selective advantages for doing so."[42]

Buss, like anthropologist Donald Symons, sees these results supporting the hypothesis that in our evolutionary past, males and females faced different pressures on reproductive success. Females appear to have been limited by access to resources for themselves and their offspring. Males appear to have been limited by access to fertile females. These different selection pressures in our ancestral past have presumably produced the different male and female reproductive strategies that we continue to see operating today.[43]

ECONOMIC OPPORTUNITY AND FEMALE CHOICE

In most of the world's cultures, women's social status derives from motherhood. Marriage has been an economic necessity for women, in many instances their sole means of support, a reality hidden by the emphasis on its social importance.

In her investigation of marriage as a form of labor relationship between men and women, sociologist Diana Leonard points out that in marrying, "a woman pledges for life (with limited rights to quit), her labour, sexuality, and reproductive capacity, and receives protection, upkeep, and certain rights to children."[44] Until recently, most of the world's women had few economic opportunities outside marriage, concubinage, or prostitution—all based on either their reproductive abilities and/or their sexual services.

"We continue to be second-rate citizens—no, third-rate, since our sons come before us. Even donkeys and tractors sometimes get better treatment," said a women's leader in Uganda.[45]

Second-class citizenship has been a fact of life for women in industrialized societies, too. Although career opportunities beyond motherhood and the home are available, the salaries paid women are considerably less than those paid men. In these instances, women carry not only the reproductive burden but also the economic one. Women bear 100 percent of the world's children, make up 50 percent of the world's population, grow 50 percent of the world's food, perform 66 percent of the world's work, earn 10 percent of the world's income, and own 1 percent of the world's property.[46]

81

Lack of equal economic opportunity certainly influences the quality of women's lives, but does it also influence the pronounced sex difference in mate preferences? Proponents of a theory known as the structural powerlessness hypothesis have predicted that women with power and wealth will act more like men and become less sexually selective and less interested in the economic resources of potential mates. Evolutionary psychologists, however, predict that regardless of whether women are rich or poor themselves, they will prefer attractive—high status—mates just as the zebra finches, described in chapter 2, preferred attractive individuals.

As in so many other instances, research data increasingly support evolutionary theory. Women, whether rich or poor, prefer high-status males. In fact, the more money a woman makes, the *more* she values the financial and professional status of a potential mate. As women's power and status rise, their "sexual taste become more, rather than less, discriminatory."[47] The data supporting this conclusion come from interviews of medical students and leaders in the women's movement. When asked what traits they sought in a man, the feminist leaders interviewed repeatedly used terms descriptive of high-status males: "very rich," "brilliant," or "genius."[48] Anthropologist Heather Fowler, who conducted these interviews, reported many references to lavish dinners, large tips, stunning suits, and Jaguar cars. Apparently these high-status women wanted super dominant males.

Similarly, in an investigation of second-year medical students at a northeastern university, researchers found that women medical students often became "more selective and critical in entering and maintaining sexual relationships than they had been previously. Time spent in a relationship that had no marital potential was seen as time wasted."[49] This means that as a woman's socioeconomic status improves, the playing field of acceptable men shrinks considerably.

Japan provides a case in point. Increasing education and economic independence have given Japanese women more clout in the mating game, and they have become far more choosy in selecting husbands. Young career women are making it clear that they seek husbands with a high salary, a university degree, and a very different attitude from that of the traditional man, who expected a wife to tend his every need and walk three paces behind. Today's Japanese women want mates who will treat them as equals and be supportive of their careers. Even though single men in Japan outnumber single women by 2 million, the kind of man that women want to marry is hard to find. In Tokyo, the local press has labeled this situation the Era of Too Many Men.[50] The situation is considered so desperate that two years ago a bridegroom school was opened in Tokyo to teach men how to be more supportive partners. Some companies, such as the electronics firm Meidansha, have started their own in-house matchmaking services. At one private matchmaking party in Tokyo where men outnumbered women two to one, would-be bridegrooms competed with each other introducing themselves to the assembled women. One man even sang a song he had composed. Out of the group of some eighty men, however, only eight found a match. Japanese women are not only choosier than ever, they are marrying later (the current average age is more than 27 in Tokyo) and having fewer babies. Today's birthrate of 1.57 is the lowest in Japan's history, causing politicians to offer monetary rewards to help parents pay for child care and tax breaks to encourage larger families.

New-found wealth and status are profoundly changing some aspects of women's lives, but an old mating pattern persists. Women still prefer men with resources. The data suggest that females' preference for high-status males reflects an ancient psychological mechanism that operates whether a woman's own socioeconomic status is high or low.[51] Resources may have been so scarce in the human ancestral environment or women may have been economically powerless for so long that the preference for a good provider became deeply ingrained in the female psyche. That psychological mechanism may continue to influence current behavior even though the environments in which people now live are radically different from those in which our human ancestors evolved.

FOUR

༚

SEX DIFFERENCES IN PSYCHOLOGY

*The evolutionary function of the human brain is to process
information in ways that lead to adaptive behavior. . . .
Behavior is a transaction between organism and environment.*

LEDA COSMIDES AND JOHN TOOBY
1987[1]

THANKS TO BIRTH-CONTROL TECHNOLOGY, women—at least those in
the affluent Western world—enjoy greater sexual freedom than
they have had at any other time in human history. Despite liberation from unwanted pregnancy, however, most have not changed
their criteria for mate selection. There are exceptions, of course—
women in homosexual relationships, women who choose to become single mothers—but most of the world's women keep a
man's resources uppermost in their minds when they decide to
marry. This pattern holds true whether the marriage decision is
made by the individual woman or by her family.

Modern women may emulate men in having many sexual partners, but their mate preferences are still distinctly different from
those of men. The mere sight of a young, pretty woman arouses a
man, but women remain more interested in a man's status than in
his physical appearance. In every human culture studied, whether

tribal or industrial, these differences in mate preference endure. Their universality suggests that psychological sex differences in mate preference must have evolved millennia ago.

ANCIENT WIRING IN THE MODERN BRAIN

From the beginning, the human brain has had information-processing machinery that processes input from the environment and produces corresponding behavior. Such machinery is known as a psychological mechanism. The totality of these mechanisms make up an organism's psychology. Evolutionary psychologists theorize that it is an individual's psychological mechanisms and not behavior per se that are subject to natural selection.[2] Individuals with psychological mechanisms that produced successful behaviors left more offspring to transmit their genes. Over millennia, certain highly successful psychological mechanisms became an integral part of the wiring of the human brain, making up a great deal of what we call human nature. Some of these mechanisms continue to influence our behavior today, especially with respect to mate choice.

In order to better understand why we behave as we do, some anthropologists and psychologists are now using the principles of evolutionary biology to examine human psychology. The goal of evolutionary psychology is to discover "basic psychological mechanisms—forged by natural selection operating over thousands of generations—that exist because they successfully solved adaptive problems that humans had to confront to survive and reproduce."[3]

We now live in a global village of 5.4 billion residents connected by electronic networks, but the bulk of our 4-million-year evolutionary history was spent in small, isolated groups of hunters and gatherers. Our ancestors spent their time gathering wild berries and roots and hunting wild game rather than pushing a shopping cart around a local supermarket. People got from one place to another on their own two feet, not on four steel-belted radials. Their most lethal weapon was a spear or an axe, and their property was limited to what they could carry. The overcrowded, urbanized, industrialized world that most of us inhabit today is only a flash in the evolutionary pan.

The environments in which our human ancestors solved the basic survival problems of finding food and water, obtaining mates, and defending themselves against predators and other humans no longer exist. "Our species spent over 99 percent of its evolutionary history as hunter-gatherers in Pleistocene environments," say psychologists Leda Cosmides and John Tooby. "Human psychological mechanisms should be adapted to those environments, not necessarily to the twentieth-century industrialized world."[4]

This means that many of our feelings and responses may be psychological leftovers from our hunter-gatherer past, maladapted to the crowded, polluted megalopolises where almost half of us struggle to live today. In a sense, industrialized humans invented the contemporary physical environment. The challenge now is to reinvent ourselves so that we can respond more appropriately to this environment. With the rapid growth of human population now threatening the health of the planet, our species faces an unprecedented pressure *not* to maximize reproductive success, a need that goes against millennia of genetic programming. Our conflict is not between biology and technology, as some have argued, but between our strategies for using technology and our skill at inventing new technologies. Much of the stress that modern humans feel may result from our psychological inability to keep up with our technological selves.

While our technology has taken us to the moon, our patterns of mate selection hark back to a time of untold antiquity when early ancestral men and women faced very different selection pressures. As a consequence, men and women have two quite different sexual psychologies. According to anthropologist Donald Symons and others, men are more likely than women to be aroused by the sight, or visual stimulus, of a member of the opposite sex. Symons explains this tendency by a man's ability to impregnate a woman at almost no cost to himself: "as long as the risks were low, selection favored the basic male tendency to be aroused sexually by the sight of females."[5] But a woman could incur an enormous cost of energy and time if easy visual arousal resulted in pregnancy. "Selection thus favored females who were discriminating and slow to arouse sexually, since reflex-like sexual arousal on the basis of visual stimuli would have tended to under-mine female choice," write Symons and psychologist Bruce Ellis.[6] Females are usually aroused not by the *sight* of males but by the *touch* of a favored male.

Clothes, jewelry, and makeup can enhance one's natural en-dowments and provide visual cues to status, physical vigor, youth, health, sexual receptivity, availability, and the potential for par-ental investment. Each sex does its best to display those traits that the other finds attractive, but research shows that a double stan-dard operates among men.

In a study of physical attractiveness, psychologists Elizabeth Hill, Elaine Nocks, and Lucinda Gardner[7] manipulated clothing, jewelry, and makeup with display of body. For men, differences in status were created by contrasting three-piece suits, sports jack-ets, designer jeans, and gold jewelry with nondescript jeans, tank tops or T-shirts, and no jewelry. Variations in women's status were achieved by contrasting tank tops, T-shirts, jeans, and no jewelry with formal gowns, blazers or monogrammed sweaters with button-down blouses, khaki pants or tweed skirts, and gold jewelry. Differences in male physical attractiveness were indicated by contrasting ties and buttoned shirts with unbuttoned shirts or tank tops revealing chest hair; in women, low-cut, clingy cocktail dresses, tube tops, and tank tops were contrasted with buttoned shirts, loose sweaters, or jackets.

The researchers then asked American college students to rate pictures of opposite-sex models according to four measures of at-tractiveness: physical, dating, sexual, and marital. Skin-tight clothing that accentuated the body made women more attractive as sexual partners but less attractive as a potential marital partner. The researchers explain this finding by suggesting that although a man wants a sexy lover, as a husband he experiences conflicting re-actions to sexiness in his wife. If a woman is sexy to him, she may convey sexual availability to others. One way for a man to try to ensure his confidence of paternity is to maintain an exclusive sex-ual relationship in marriage and to marry a woman who does not advertise her sexiness.

Women, on the other hand, consistently rated men wearing

high-status clothing—business suits, buttoned shirts, and ties—more favorably as a sexual or a marital partner than men wearing tight jeans or tank tops, which could denote low-status males whose only resource was their physique. Results of this study support the evolutionary prediction that females would be attracted to a high-status–low-physique-display man. The researchers admit, however, that since routine contraceptive use has diminished the risk of casual sex for females, future studies might examine the potential development of a dating-marriage double standard in women as well.

MALE JEALOUSY AND THE DOUBLE STANDARD TOWARD ADULTERY

There are other sex differences in psychology. Men, for example, are more prone to sexual jealousy than are women. The evolutionary explanation is that a male's chance for reproductive success could always be jeopardized by his mate's extramarital affair. "A husband risked having his wife's limited reproductive capacity tied up by other men and, since he could never be completely confident of paternity, investing in other men's offspring," writes Symons.[8]

Males in general try to avoid being cuckolded, a word believed to derive from the name of the cuckoo, a bird that lays its egg in another's nest, tricking the host birds into raising offspring that are not their own. Traditionally, a cuckolded man has been the object of ridicule. Among the Yânomamö Indians, there are a few cases of a man marrying a previously married woman who has a baby, and killing the infant or ordering her to do so. His reasons are clear: the baby is another man's, and it competes for the time and milk he feels the woman should put into bearing and nurturing his child. In many societies, if a man suspects that his wife has conceived a child through adultery, he has the right to kill the infant, demand that she kill it, or divorce her.

Not surprisingly, male sexual jealousy plays a major role in human violence. According to Martin Daly and Margo Wilson, it is "far and away the leading motive in spousal homicides in North America, and almost certainly throughout the world. If we include disputes between men over women, then male sexual jealousy may well be the number-one motive of homicides."[9]

Women, too, experience jealousy, but the psychological content is different. A husband's infidelity does not directly threaten a wife's reproductive success. Sexual intercourse with another woman poses a different threat—the risk that he may desert her and/or redirect his resources away from her and their children. Men and women have different anxieties about adultery. The man's biological fear is that he may have been cuckolded, his confidence of paternity cast in doubt, and the woman's fear is that she may lose access to her mate's resources.

"There are no harsher penalties in human societies than those for adultery," writes anthropologist Laura Betzig. This, plus the fact "that infidelity causes divorce more often than anything else, are most consistent with a Darwinian theory that marriage should contribute to the reproduction of husbands and wives."[10]

It is men's anxiety about paternity that has shaped the double standard in adultery laws. Universally the crime of adultery has been based on the woman's marital status, not on the man's. Although a wife's paramour may also be punished severely if discovered, *his* marital status is not a factor in the definition of the crime of adultery. It is still the woman's husband who has been wronged, and the justice meted out reflects this view. In legal systems around the world, a man who kills his wife and her lover in a jealous rage is often excused or tried on a lesser charge than murder. Jurists, citing unwritten law, have considered the discovery of a wife in flagrante delicto a justifiable provocation for murder.

Also universally, female adulterers are treated more harshly than male adulterers. For a woman, the punishment can be divorce, social stigma, beatings, and even death. The powerful men who controlled harems often took elaborate measures to ensure that no one else was permitted sexual access to their women; entire harems have reportedly been put to death when the security system was breached.[11]

"Throughout the ages and around the world, men have repeatedly invented *adultery laws* with a remarkable consistency of concept that reinforces [anthropologist] Lévi-Strauss's view of wives as property," write Daly and Wilson.[12] From a man's point of view, *he* is the victim of his wife's adultery. She has committed an offense against him, a violation of *his* property. Although some societies condemn male adultery and accept it as grounds for divorce, no society regards adultery by a married man as a violation of the *woman's* property. Few societies regard married women as victims of their husbands' extramarital affairs. Quite the contrary: married women are often expected to tolerate their husbands' sexual liaisons so long as the marriage remains legally intact.

Sex differences in jealousy and in attitudes toward adultery are exactly what evolutionary biology would predict. Like nonhuman animals, women and men act in ways that protect their genetic investments. The insights now emerging from the study of evolutionary biology show just how much of human behavior is adapted in the service of reproduction.

91

ENSURING CONFIDENCE OF PATERNITY

It is abundantly clear from anthropological research that men, like other males throughout the animal kingdom, do whatever they can to ensure paternity. Nonhuman males use genital plugs and mate guarding to protect their paternal investment. Men, too, practice forms of mate guarding, some of them quite brutal.

Anthropologist Mildred Dickemann argues that claustration, or cloistering—the seclusion of women, both married and unmarried, through such practices as veiling and restriction to prisonlike women's quarters—is a strategy for ensuring confidence of paternity.[13] Cloistered women are not allowed to talk to anyone outside the immediate family; sometimes they are not even permitted to go outdoors. In some of these women, lack of sunlight promotes rickets, which can produce difficulty and even death in childbirth. Nevertheless, this extreme isolation guarantees the virginity of daughters and the fidelity of wives, and thus the paternity of prospective bridegrooms and husbands.

In societies that practice claustration, a family's honor resides in the chastity of its unmarried women and in the modesty and fidelity of all its women. The Arabic word for honor, 'ard, also means "woman." The penalties for loss of virginity before marriage can be severe: the inability to find a husband, rejection by a suitor, or even murder of the "damaged" girl or her violator by her kinsmen. This kind of murder is considered a crime of honor.[14]

Other extreme practices for ensuring confidence of paternity are the mutilating genital surgery still inflicted on girls and women in some African countries and the now illegal Chinese tradition of foot binding. Such practices may have other rationalizations, such as promoting female purity and cleanliness, enhancing femininity, or indicating high social class, but fundamentally they function to restrict women's mobility and ensure a man's confidence of paternity.

There are also legal means of protecting paternity—laws that make women the property of their husbands, laws that forbid women to use birth control or have abortions without their husbands' consent. And there are the insidious, psychological forms of paternity insurance such as the behavioral manipulation author Betty Friedan so aptly termed *the feminine mystique*, which was designed to keep women pregnant, housebound, and out of the economic marketplace except as consumers.

Various social myths can also be viewed as part of an overall strategy to control women's sexuality and restrict their mobility: the myth of the dominant male; the myth of the weak, helpless, passive female; the myths of the intellectual inferiority of women and the intellectual superiority of men. All are human variants of male insects' genital plugs. Lacking genital glue, society ensures confidence of paternity by a kind of psychological mate guarding.

DESERTION ANXIETY

There is yet another sex difference in psychology, and this affects mental health: women experience higher levels of anxiety than men and are more often depressed. It appears that male-female differences in mental-health histories may be influenced by the different requirements of male and female reproductive strategies.

Psychologists Ada Lampert and Ariela Friedman studied 129 couples picked at random in 30 different Israeli kibbutzim.[15] They hypothesized that the unequal parental investment of males and females contributes to the feeling of greater vulnerability by women. In fact, they report, the height of female vulnerability occurs while women have three small children. During the time when demands of parenting are greatest, women are more likely than ever to feel dependent on their husbands' help in sharing parenting duties and more anxious about the possibility of desertion.

In 1990, the American Psychological Association's Task Force on Women and Depression reported that the rate of depression among American women is twice that of men. Physical and sexual abuse, poverty, sex bias in salaries, unhappy marriages, and hormonal changes during the menstrual cycle and after childbirth were included among the factors that place women at greater risk for depression than men. The report also noted that women were more likely than men to be poor and to be single parents. Depression was three times higher among professional women than among others, implying that neither income nor status protects a woman from the overload of job, motherhood, and marriage.

Some of the anxiety and depression that afflict so many American women surely results from their attempts to do it all, to be superwomen; but the differences in male and female reproductive strategies that evolved millions of years ago may also play a major part. Natural selection favored the evolution of a mother's strong devotion to her children. As women leave the home for the workplace, as more women become single heads of households because of divorce, desertion, or their husbands' need to leave home to find work, natural anxiety about their ability to nurture or provide for their offspring is compounded. Some working mothers, for example, feel enormously guilty about leaving their children with a surrogate caretaker while they go off to work. Women's greater susceptibility to anxiety and depression probably reflects an ancient female psychology that is struggling to cope with the challenges of the modern world.

Men may be less susceptible to anxiety and depression because their reproductive strategy is less focused on the care of off-

93

spring. Men, unlike women, do not have an obligate biological parental investment. One evolutionary scenario suggests that when our ancient precursors left the safety and security of the tropical forest and took up a more perilous and exposed life-style in the savanna, successful child rearing began to require the cooperation of mother and father. Female choice would have favored the more parental males. But the male tendency to mate with as many females as possible would have conflicted with the male's desire to care for his children. As a result, human males may have evolved a mixed strategy, becoming the most parental male among mammals and, at the same time, remaining easily tempted by sexual variety.

SEX DIFFERENCES IN FANTASY

The same psychological mechanisms that produce sex differences in mate preference and parenting strategies also produce sex differences in one of life's most private arenas—sexual fantasy. Men and women are aroused by different thoughts and images. Fantasies that turn on a man's sexual urges often have the opposite effect on women, and vice versa. The clearest evidence of these differences is that pornography's audience is predominantly male, while romance novels appeal almost exclusively to women.

In their investigation of sexual fantasies, Ellis and Symons administered a questionnaire to 307 college students (182 females, 125 males).[16] The researchers' starting point was that fantasies are "the most common form of human sexual experience." Since fantasies are private, they presumably express feelings that are inhibited by the demands and expectations of the real world; fantasies therefore might yield more insight into psychological mechanisms than actual sexual activities. Ellis and Symons argued that if men and women differ so in their innate sexual psychologies, dramatic differences should be revealed in their fantasies.

They made several predictions based on evolutionary biology.

1. Men would fantasize a greater variety of sexual encounters with different partners than women.

2. Men would be more likely to switch from one sexual partner to another in the same fantasy.

3. Men would have sexual fantasies more frequently than women.

4. Men would be more likely to fantasize about someone with whom they want only to have sex.

5. Men's sexual fantasies would focus primarily on visual images.

6. Women's sexual fantasies would emphasize touching, feelings, and partner response, focusing more on their own physical and emotional responses.

7. Women would be more likely than men to fantasize about someone with whom they wanted to become romantically involved.

8. Men's sexual fantasies would move more quickly to explicit sexual activity.

9. Women's fantasies would involve a slower buildup to sexual culmination.

10. Women would have a clearer image than men of their imagined partners' facial features.

11. Men would have a clearer image than women of the genital features of their imagined partners.

The findings from the anonymous questionnaires supported all the predicted sex differences except the expectation that women would have a clearer image of their partner's faces.

It seems probable that natural selection favored the evolution of sex differences in the psychological mechanisms underlying human sexual feeling and action. Female parental investment in offspring is so enormous that it would have been critical for females to choose their sexual partners carefully. "A tendency to become sexually aroused merely on the basis of cosmetic, visually-detected qualities, or a taste for sexual variety for its own sake, surely would have promoted random copulations, undermined female choice of partners and the circumstances of conception, reduced the likelihood of acquiring male parental investment, increased the likelihood of being beaten, abandoned, or killed by a jealous husband (and also by angry brothers), and drastically impaired female fitness," conclude Ellis and Symons.[17]

Sex differences in sexual fantasy are mirrored in the contrasting formulas of male and female literatures of erotic fantasy—male-oriented pornography and female-oriented romance novels. The enormous success of each of these genres indicates that they respectively fulfill the wishes in male and female sexual fantasies. "The most striking feature of male-oriented pornography is that sex is sheer lust and physical gratification, devoid of encumbering relationships, emotional elaboration, complicated plot lines, flirtation, courtship, and extended foreplay; in pornotopia, women, like men, are easily aroused and willing," write Ellis and Symons.[18]

In contrast, romance novels provide few, if any, explicit sex scenes. Rather, they offer a romantic relationship between a young woman and an older, wealthy, sexually experienced, high-status man whose passion can be domesticated by love, culminating in marriage with the heroine. Given an understanding of the role of female choice in human reproduction, this basic plot could have been predicted.

So, too, could another plot—one that happens not only in fiction but in real life—the plot to undermine female choice.

FIVE

ᘛᘚ

SUBVERTING FEMALE CHOICE

One of the most important things to realize about systems
of animal communication is that they are not
systems for the dissemination of the truth. . . .
Deceit consists of mimicking the truth.

ROBERT TRIVERS
Social Evolution
1985[1]

AS THE CHOICEMAKER in the mating game, a female is in control unless her position is subverted by deceit or usurped by force—as it often is. The phrases *battle of the sexes* and *war between the sexes* refer to this fundamental tension between female and male: while a female is doing everything she can to exert the power of choice evolution has given her, a male is doing everything he can to control or to subvert her choice. Each sex is out for his or her own genetically selfish end, and natural selection favors only the winner.

Given this built-in conflict, deception and exploitation abound. Males deceive other males, males deceive females, females deceive males, and among humans there is evidence that both sexes practice self-deception, especially in matters of love and romance. The ruses and deceits take innumerable forms, from insincere declarations of undying love to hairpieces, face-lifts, and silicon breasts. Both women and men try to appear stronger, richer, younger, and more sexually attractive than they really are.

THE GREAT DECEIVERS

We may teach our children that honesty is the best policy, but natural selection favors the skillful lie. In the context of courtship, a successful deceit carries a reproductive advantage. Nor is deception peculiar to humans. It is common among nonhuman animals and even plants. For many an animal, including the human, an ability to put one over on its fellows is a survival advantage.

One of the best-documented examples of nonhuman courtship deceit involves transvestism among scorpionflies. Courtship is risky for the male scorpionfly. Typically, he expends a considerable amount of energy catching a prey sufficiently large to attract a female. Once a male has caught a prey, he makes several short flights within his leafy habitat. After each flight, he hangs from a leaf or twig and releases a sex pheromone that attracts females. A female will investigate the prey and, if she is interested, will hang in front of the male and lower her wings. This is his signal to mate. But sometimes he falls prey to trickery. The receptive female proves to be a male transvestite that steals the prey and flies off with it to attract a female of his own![2]

The ruse works because male and female scorpionflies look alike, even to each other. When a male intent on chicanery hangs in front of a courting male and lowers his wings just as a receptive female would, the suitor invariably proffers his nuptial gift. By the time the first male becomes aware of his mistake, it is too late. Biologist Randy Thornhill, who discovered this deceit, reports that transvestite scorpionflies mate more often than those that do their own hunting. By tricking another male into handing over his prey, the transvestite scorpionfly avoids the risk of getting caught in spiderwebs as he hunts. An opportunist, he gains in reproductive success at the expense of his rival.

Male swordtail characins, South American fish related to the piranha, practice another kind of deceit. When courting, the male opens his gill cover and releases a long, almost invisible, bony appendage. Dangling on the end of this built-in fishing tackle is an imitation of a tiny crab. When the male jerks his gill cover, the fake crab appears to swim. Attracted to the lure, a female lunges for what she thinks is a meal, only to get hooked. While she struggles and chokes trying to swallow the bogus bait, the male mates with her.

Courtship deceits among humans tend to be exaggerations of qualities that are already attractive. Since women seek mates with resources, men can be expected to exaggerate their wealth by driving expensive cars, buying gifts for women, or spending more on dates than they can really afford. Since men prefer young, fertile females, women tend to do everything possible to enhance their youthfulness and personal appearance. Clothing is an important aspect of courtship for both sexes; women dress to show off their bodies to best advantage, and men dress to display status and power.

MALE COMPETITION AS SPERM COMPETITION

Whether among mice or men, all male competition for mates is sperm competition of one sort or another. Once a male copulates, he no longer controls his sperm; he cannot force a female to use them. Because of this, males use a variety of tactics to ensure that their sperm will fertilize the eggs of the female with whom they copulate. Cuckoldry is a male's greatest fear, and one over which he has little power except insofar as he can monopolize sexual access to his mate. To ensure confidence of paternity, males will do virtually anything to subvert or control female choice.

Mate guarding has a long history among humans. Wealthy Athenian men brought eunuchs into their households to watch over their wives and daughters. In *The Country Wife*, written by British playwright William Wycherley in 1675, a eunuch is presented as a gift to a courtesan who wants one "because ladies of quality alone make use of them." In his play, Wycherley pointed out how the instruments of male vigilance had become symbols of high female status.

The contemporary antiabortion movement can be seen as an extreme example of organized sperm protection with zealous groups—usually headed by men—campaigning to safeguard fertilization by *any* man's sperm. Followers of this movement are unaware that they are acting out an ancient, genetically driven program, behaving as pawns of male genes. The so-called right-to-life movement may be perceived as a highly organized effort to legislate away women's right to choose whether to reproduce.

Right now, in the closing decade of the twentieth century in the United States, political movements—supported by the highest level of government—are attempting to deny women reproductive choice and to make their bodies state property. And in Ireland, in 1992, a pregnant 14-year-old girl, an alleged rape victim, was treated like state property and held a virtual prisoner of her country while a public debate raged over her petition to leave Ireland to end her pregnancy. Finally the Irish Supreme Court granted her permission. But the fact that female reproductive biology has become subject to national debate indicates the serious degree to which sexual discrimination has been institutionalized.

The antiabortion movement seems a social aberration until placed in the context of evolutionary biology. Then it takes its place as the most recent installment in a long history of efforts, both primitive and civilized, to protect men's sperm investment and control women's reproductive biology. During the final years of the Roman Republic and continuing through most of the Roman Empire, upper-class women began practicing birth control and abortion. Like women everywhere who become educated, these wealthy Roman matrons desired freedom from pregnancy and childbirth in order to pursue other interests. But their actions outraged Roman emperors and senators. The women were publicly denounced and offered certain legal and economic concessions if they would bear at least three children. But the bribes were to no avail.[3]

At various times in history, dispensing birth-control information has been considered subversion or an act of the devil. During the later Middle Ages, midwives were often persecuted as witches for assisting women with birth control and abortion. A medieval witch-hunting manual, *Malleus Mallificarum*, accused midwives of plotting with wives to cheat husbands out of their offspring.

There is also an element of persecution in the current anti-choice movement, for it affects primarily poor women dependent on clinics. The self-righteous fervor of some of the antichoice sermons belies a class attitude that poor women who have sex and become pregnant should be forced to bear the shame and the pain of their evil ways. A 1991 U.S. Supreme Court decision that bars abortion counseling in federally funded clinics specifically targets poor women and denies medical doctors freedom of speech.

In effect, the antiabortion movement is totalitarian, the latest in a long continuum of some men's efforts to substitute political and social control of women's bodies for the biological control they can never have. Unfortunately, many women support these efforts that contribute to their own reproductive enslavement.

101

DO WOMEN WANT TO BE ENSLAVED?

The question of why so many women abet attempts to enslave themselves as individuals and as a group needs more study. Perhaps these women have traded their reproductive freedom for protection against aggression by other men. Perhaps they are cowed by men's greater physical size, strength, and political power. Perhaps millennia spent in a state of submission have affected the female psyche, the female's expectations of self, and her self-esteem. Or perhaps women only flatter men into thinking they're dominant, all the while managing life behind the scenes. All of these factors are probably filtered into women's choicemaking processes, with one or more of them assuming greater or lesser significance depending on the values of the particular society. Such questions and speculations are beyond the scope of this book, but they deserve further consideration, research, and discussion.

From a sociobiological perspective, women are in an ironic position: they share with other female animals the biological control of reproduction. Unlike nonhuman females, however, women have been handicapped in the battle of the sexes. Customs, religious doctrines, and laws function to control women's reproductive services. The human male consciously recognizes that women have ultimate physiological control of reproduction. No matter what they do, men can never give birth. All the more reason they fear women's power and try to control it through deceptions that will persuade women to participate in their own subjugation. Both sexes feel great conflict, as evidenced in the contradictory views of women.

Depending on the context of time, place and culture, woman has been considered goddess, madonna, witch, Earth Mother, temptress, nursemaid, whore, gatherer, healer, priestess, servant, slave, and sex object. She has been viewed as sexually insatiable, anarchistic and mysteriously powerful. At the same time, she has been considered the weaker sex, the domineering sex, the gold-digging sex, and the castrating sex. She has been looked on with awe, superstitution, lust, fear, ridicule, and hatred.

In the Christian religion, she has been blamed for original sin, reviled as the seat of evil and, at the same time, enshrined and worshipped as the mother of the son of God, albeit conceived by immaculate conception. In the Muslim religion, she is viewed as omnisexual, insatiable. Muslim men define woman in terms of her vagina and believe that because of her voracious sexual appetite, she should be circumcised—the clitoris surgically removed—and kept hidden in her quarters. The ideal of female beauty in Islam is obedience, silence and, immobility—the same attitudes a believer has in relation to his God.[4]

Pregnancy and childbirth put females in an extremely weak and vulnerable position. Although women seek and need additional support and assistance at this time, perhaps a bad bargain has been struck by both sexes. In many cultures marriage is a reproductive contract; women lease their uteri and men pay the rent.[5] This kind of marriage is not an intimate relationship, nor is it one in which men and women can respect and enjoy each other as friends.

Shakespeare described this view of marriage in his play *The Taming of the Shrew*, when the character Katharina, at the order of her husband, Petruchio, informs the other women where their duty lies:

> *Thy husband is thy lord, thy life, thy keeper,*
> *Thy head, thy sovereign; one that cares for thee,*
> *And for thy maintenance commits his body*

To painful labour both by sea and land,
To watch the night in storms, the day in cold,
Whilst thou liest warm at home, secure and safe;
And craves no other tribute at thy hands
But love, fair looks, and true obedience;
Too little payment for so great a debt.
Such duty as the subject owes the prince,
Even such a woman oweth to her husband;
. . . I am asham'd that women are so simple
To offer war where they should kneel for peace,
Or seek for rule, supremacy, and sway,
When they are bound to serve, love, and obey.[6]

Like Katharina, women have collaborated in maintaining marriage institutions that subjugate them. For all their ritual and lofty idealism, many marriage systems subvert female choice and make female fertility a marketable commodity. Dowries, marriage contracts, and ceremonies serve to deceive humans into thinking that something more important than reproduction is involved. The participants may focus on the trappings of wealth and power, they may be distracted by the excitement of courtship and the ecstasy of orgasm, but reproductive biology is calling the behavioral shots. Yet few people acknowledge the reproductive aspects of what they are doing, as if it were too lowly a subject for human discussion. Our illusion that we humans stand apart from the animal kingdom is the most grandiose self-deception of all.

UTERUS ENVY

One of the most bizarre deceits in Western culture was Sigmund Freud's concept of penis envy. Although this was as much an illusion as the myth of the passive female, Freud's theory created enormous anxiety for generations of women. It is difficult to imagine a more frustrated creature than a woman who felt incomplete because she lacked a penis. If she accepted this fairy tale, then she had also to accept the lack of a solution for her dilemma since she could not, like some Caribbean reef fishes, change sex. Freud would have been closer to reality had he proposed that men suffer from uterus envy.

Men's fear and envy of women's reproductive biology and seeming life-giving power are expressed in a variety of myths, from the adoration of fertility goddesses to superstitions that menstruating women can contaminate men.

Among the contemporary North American Creeks of northeastern Oklahoma, for example, menstruating women are forced to stay away from men. A breach of this separation is considered a serious crime, and the violator can be accused of causing any misfortune that might befall her people. Creek medicine men say that if menstruating women don't keep their distance from men, sickness, including diabetes, strokes, cancer, and rheumatism, can result. Menstruating women may prepare men's daily meals, but they dare not sit at the same table, eat from communal bowls, or share communal benches. While they are menstruating, Creek women must eat from a special set of dishes.[7]

Fear of contamination by a menstruating woman may also underlie the Jewish law of *Niddah*. Also known as the law of family purity, this practice holds that a menstruating woman is a source of ritual impurity. As currently interpreted, the state of impurity results from the loss of an unfertilized egg. "It is this loss of potential life, this whisper of death, that confers upon her the state of impurity," writes Normal Lamm, pointing out the Jewish religion's emphasis on life.[8] During the twelve-day *Niddah* period, which allows for five days of menstruation followed by seven days free of discharge, a woman may not marry. Thus, in Orthodox Jewish families, the wedding day is never firmly set.

Although individual practices vary among contemporary couples, the old *Niddah* laws contain some thirteen rules of conduct for husband and wife. When a woman is menstruating, she and her husband are not permitted to touch each other, eat at the same table, sleep in the same bed, or even hand anything to each other. "He may not sleep with her in the same bed, even if both are clothed and do not touch," according to Rabbi Yosef Loebenstein's translation of the *Niddah* laws. "One should therefore be careful that the beds are far enough apart to ensure husband and wife will not touch each other while they sleep. He may not sit on her bed even when she is not present. He is forbidden to take care of her when she is ill unless there is no one else, and she is in great need of it," say the *Niddah* laws.[9]

Few people today believe that touching a woman in the state of *Niddah* will bring physical or spiritual harm, but the old laws stated that a man who has sexual relations with a menstruating woman becomes ritually unclean, along with all those who come in contact with him. "Such a person brings evil sicknesses upon himself and upon the child (born from such a union)."[10] This belief comes from the Old Testament book of Leviticus: "And her impurity will be upon him."

105

Each month a woman must follow detailed rules of conduct that include self-examination during the period of *Niddah*, ending with the *mikvah*, or purifying bath. When she returns from the *mikvah*, she and her husband are required to have sexual relations. The timing of the ritual bath usually coincides with the time a woman is ovulating, so that the practice may also function to ensure conception. Jewish feminists argue that the practice of *Niddah* functions to keep a woman in her proverbial place; others believe the practice renews a marriage, enabling husband and wife to rediscover their love for each other each month as they did on their wedding night.

In some tribal societies, men's fear of women is expressed in myths about sacred instruments women are forbidden to see or touch. If we substitute the words *reproductive power* for *sacred instruments*, the sacred flutes or trumpets can be understood in a biological perspective.

In these myths, the sacred instruments originally belonged to women. Through deceit and treachery, men seized the instruments, hid them in a man's house—in many tribes, a structure to which only men have access—and forbade women to enter or to look upon them.

In reality, men have tried to seize control of women's reproductive biology through laws and customs that are biased in favor of men. Just as women have traditionally given birth apart from men, so men have constructed their separate houses—their bars, clubs, and corporate boardrooms—and declared them off-limits to women. In tribal societies, there is much uneasiness between the sexes over the possibility that women will violate these artificial male enclaves. Tribal myths reveal men's elemental fear that one day women will recapture what was rightfully theirs—control of their own reproduction. Various forms of sexual segregation in industrialized societies seem to suggest the same fear. Like the old nursery rhyme character Peter Pumpkin Eater, some types of men have tried to keep women in their place, but they continually fear that women will break out of that place, as indeed they increasingly have.

106

Much of what both sexes consider masculinity rests on a fragile house of cards, and women knowingly, although not without resentment, have set up housekeeping inside. The women of Brazil's Mundurucu tribe typify women of many cultures. According to anthropologists Yolanda and Robert Murphy, Mundurucu women are well acquainted with the men's house, which females are forbidden to enter. "They knew all about its ritual paraphernalia, though none would admit peeking, and they were neither mystified nor cowed. It is as if they had investigated the secret sources of the men's power—and had found absolutely nothing."[11]

Among the Mundurucu, relations between men and women are extremely antagonistic. Men ritualize the hostility and women verbalize it, a dynamic that is not terribly different from that found in industrialized societies.

CHASTITY BELTS AND GENITAL PLUGS

Sperm competition takes the greatest variety of forms among non-human males whose major parental investment is sperm—from insect penises that can remove a rival's previously deposited sperm to the gargantuan 900-kilogram (1,984-pound) testes of the male North Atlantic right whale. Since sperm are manufactured in the testes, males with especially large testes produce more sperm; and socially dominant males are likely to have the largest testes among their species. Dominance behavior, it seems, can effect changes in the brain that, in turn, control the size of the testes and sperm production, and ultimately determine whether a male will breed.

In remarkable new research, neurobiologist Russell Fernald has shown that brain cells in the hypothalamus of aggressive male cichlid fish are six to eight times larger than the equivalent cells of their mild-mannered peers. The hypothalamus cells produce gonadotropin, the hormone that causes the pituitary gland to release hormones that stimulate the fish's testes to produce sperm.

If a dominant male is bullied by a larger, more aggressive male, the defeated fish's hypothalamic cells shrink rapidly and so do his testes, eventually making it impossible for him to mate. The brains of other animals, including humans, may also be affected by behavior. Much more research needs to be done in this area, but it is already clear that male-male competition, at least in cichlid fish, can affect the structure of the brain itself.[12]

Species in which females routinely mate with more than one male engage in particularly fierce sperm competition. A fiction writer would be hard-pressed to conjure up more outlandish tactics than those practiced by male insects in the competition to produce high-quality sperm that will be selected to fertilize a female's eggs.

Male insects face a particularly challenging set of problems. "In insects," says Robert Trivers, "sperm competition is a major factor affecting male reproductive success."[13] Not only do female insects choose their mates, but once insects have copulated, another level of choice—known as cryptic female choice—takes place within the female's body.

Female insects mate with several males and then have the option of choosing whose sperm to select. The evolutionary pressure is for males to compete for females, and for their sperm to continue the competition within the female's sperm-storage chamber. The male insect's sperm must reach the female's sperm-storage chamber in the most favorable position to be selected to fertilize her eggs. Entomologists have noted that the general operating principle seems to be "last in, first out," meaning that the last male to copulate has the best chance of having his sperm selected. But if a male can monopolize his mate and prevent subsequent copulation with a rival, he can pretty much ensure his paternity.

One way to do this is with a copulatory plug, the insect version of the chastity belt—that twelfth-century invention that crusading knights used to lock up their ladies while they went off to fight the so-called holy wars. The copulatory plug, however, was invented tens of thousands of years before the Crusades through the process of natural selection.

The plug is usually a gluey substance secreted by the male to block the female's genital opening, preventing a rival's sperm from getting inside. But some male acanthocephalan worms seal off their rivals as well; after copulating with a female, these worms commit homosexual rape, using the same cement gland with which they sealed off the female to plug the genital orifice of their competitors.

The most extreme form of copulatory plug is found in the tiny ceratopogonid fly, *Johannseniella nitida*, the male of which gives his all in the name of paternity. Wedging himself in the female's genital opening, a male uses his body as a copulatory plug. While he's in this position, his mate eats him, using the extra protein to nourish her eggs.

Most other animals that use copulatory plugs don't engage in such reproductive kamikaze. Some male mammals, including marsupials, bats, hedgehogs, and rats, also make copulatory plugs, as do some snakes.

The snake's plug is apparently formed from kidney secretions immediately after insemination, and it probably prevents a rival from copulating with the same female. Snakes generally mate several weeks before the female ovulates. This means she could mate again after expelling the plug. But while the plug is in place, the first male's sperm may reach and occupy the sperm-storage chamber, where they would be in the most favorable position to survive until ova enter the oviducts.

Males may also monopolize females through prolonged copulation. When the South African grasshopper *Zonocerus elegans* selects his mate, he jumps on her back, wraps his legs around her thorax, and stays locked in this position for the next month or so, about a third of his lifetime. During this time, he copulates frequently, not without interference from rival males, whom he kicks off with his back legs. He remains attached to the female, providing her with several gifts of food, until she lays her eggs.

A species of walking stick, an insect whose body looks like a twig, remains *in copulo* even longer—seventy-nine days![14] This record-setting coupling keeps both female and male too occupied to mate with anybody else. The male lovebug *Plecia nearctica* copulates for a mere three days in the field, but will spend four and a half days at the job in the predator-free conditions of a laboratory. Males of these species become, in effect, living chastity belts, claiming the female's body as their territory and using their own bodies as barriers to a rival's trespass.

If extended, mate guarding can logically lead to monogamy. In termites, for example, the competition among males is so fierce that once a male finds a female, the pair stay together for life, in some cases sealing themselves inside a nest, which they never leave. This kind of situation has led Randy Thornhill and John Alcock to speculate that lifetime monogamy may have originated in mate guarding.[15] Their theory is a real twist on the commonly held assumption that monogamy is a female invention, and yet the idea is not farfetched.

Finally, there is the use of sperm itself to block the female's genital opening. Male featherwing beetles produce giant sperm that can be as large as two-thirds their body length. Just a few of these sperm can fill the female's sperm-storage organ, thereby keeping a rival's sperm from getting in.

The sperm that do go in can sometimes be removed. The penises of some male insects are multipurpose organs equipped with little horns that fit into the female's spermatheca and scrape out previously deposited sperm. The male damselfly *Calopteryx maculata* is endowed with just such an organ, which he uses not only to transfer sperm to the female but also to remove sperm deposited in her sperm-storage organ from previous matings. The penis of the male dragonfly *Sympetrum rubicundilum* has two inflatable lobes that extend into the female's sperm-storage sac and compress rival sperm to a far corner where they are unlikely to fertilize eggs.

Another means of getting rid of a rival's sperm is a kind of spermicidal douche. Some males may inject a substance directly into the female's genital tract to cause the expulsion of any previously deposited sperm. Such substances may mimic the chemical that females use to release stored sperm for fertilization. All these tactics are part of the repertoire of maneuvers that nonhuman males use to monopolize their mates and keep rivals away.

TURNING OFF THE SEX DRIVE WITH SCENT AND SONG

Males of some species protect their sperm investment by turning off females' sex drive. The ejaculates of some male insects contain substances that cause the female to lose interest in mating again. The male housefly, for example, spends an hour copulating, but only ten minutes are necessary for depositing his sperm. The rest of the time seems to be spent transferring a spermless fluid that causes the female to lose her sex drive, sometimes for the rest of her life.

Male digger bees use a different tactic—a postcopulatory song. Each spring an extraordinary sexual frenzy occurs at ground level in Arizona's Sonora Desert. Thousands of male digger bees, *Centris pallida*, dig frantically to unearth virgin females that have hatched in underground amphora-shaped brood pods, where their mothers left them nearly a year earlier. Females of this species usually mate only once in their one-month lifetime, and then become sexually unreceptive, a result of the males' ability to prevent any female choice at all.

Males generally emerge from the underground pods before females, and the competitive bouts begin. With dust flying, these noisy bees, which are about the size of bumblebees, wrestle with each other to excavate and mount an emerging female. The first male to mount is not necessarily the winner. First he must get her to a tree where they can mate. Even in midair, another male may strike the pair, causing them to fall to the ground, where a mass of males join the fray, struggling to possess the female. Usually it is a

very large male who succeeds in wresting the female from her original partner. The new pair then fly into a nearby mesquite tree,
where they copulate. When finished, the male does not release the
female. He makes what researcher John Alcock calls "a pleasant,
deep, rattling sound, a postcopulatory 'song,' while energetically
stroking the sides of the female with his legs." He also strokes her
abdomen in time with the song. After a few minutes of singing, the
male releases the female and flies off to join another frantic dig for
another virgin female.

Before releasing a female with whom he has copulated, however, the victorious male has seen to it that she will not mate with
other males. Amazingly, his postcopulatory song turns off her sex
drive. In experiments, Alcock discovered that the male's song,
which isn't sung until after he has transferred his sperm to the female's sperm-storage chamber, is necessary to make the female
sexually unreceptive to other males. Humans usually think of a
love song as part of courtship rituals, but in digger bees it has the
opposite effect, ensuring that only the victor bee's genes will be
passed on to future generations.[16]

MAKING ONE'S MATE UNATTRACTIVE TO OTHERS

The digger bee's postcopulatory love song makes the female sexually unreceptive, but males of other species use chemical substances that act as sexual repellents to keep rivals away. When
copulating, males of the bee species *Centris adani* and the but-
terfly species *Heliconius erato* deposit not only sperm but also a
substance that causes the female to smell like a male. Since most
males aren't attracted by the odor of another male, this perfume
makes the female undesirable, and the sperm investment of the
first male is protected.

The chemical also seems to be an advantage to some females
that have evolved specialized abdominal glands, called stink clubs,
for storing it. Perhaps it helps them to repel aggressive males and
possibly to avoid rape, since rape does occur among some insects.

Humans, too, take steps to reduce women's sex appeal to men
outside her family. Various religions have rules for making women

unattractive, unavailable, and unreceptive to other men. Some Christian sects forbid the wearing of makeup, jewelry, or brightly colored clothing. In some Orthodox communities, the wives of Jewish men are required to cut their hair very short and to cover their heads in public with a hat, a scarf, or a wig. In some Muslim societies, women are clothed and veiled in heavy black drapery that effectively hides their beauty, and upper-class women in these cultures may be secluded in a women's area of the living quarters, often an area without a window or any access to the outside world. Other practices that control a woman's sexuality may diminish her sex drive and impair her health; some can cost her her life.

112

Controlling Women through Surgery

The human variants on limiting a female's choice and reducing her sex drive are far more brutal than anything known in the non-human animal kingdom. In some twenty-seven African and Middle Eastern countries,[17] young girls are forced to undergo genital surgery. In these traditional African and Muslim societies, a girl is not considered marriageable unless her clitoris has been surgically altered or, in some cases, removed altogether. According to the World Health Organization, more than 80 million women have been victims of sexual surgery in Africa alone. Genital surgery is also practiced in the southern part of the Arabian peninsula, around the Persian Gulf, among Muslim groups in Malaysia, and on the island of Java. Recently it has reappeared in Europe among immigrant groups.

Although known by the misleading medical term of female circumcision, these surgeries are, in fact, forms of mutilation that would be considered criminal in most industrialized societies. Three procedures are currently being practiced in the world today. The least severe form, known as *sunna*, involves the removal of the prepuce, or foreskin of the clitoris, making it figuratively analogous to male circumcision—but only figuratively. Excision, a more radical form, involves the removal of the entire clitoris and all or part of the labia minora. The most severe and brutal form—infibulation—damages a girl even more. Not only are her clitoris and labia minora and majora removed, but the two sides of her vulva are sewn together, usually with catgut. Then her legs are bound together and she is forced to lie motionless until the wound heals. This closes the vagina except for a pinhole opening that permits urine and menstrual blood to pass drop by drop.

All of these operations, which are performed without anesthesia, cause health problems for the rest of a woman's life and sometimes result in her death. In many cases unsterile and crude homemade instruments such as razor blades and broken glass are used. Hemorrhage, tetanus, and blood poisoning commonly result. Longer-term effects include pelvic infections that can cause infertility, urinary-tract infections and painful urination, severe pain during sexual intercourse, and scars that can cause tearing of tissue and hemorrhage during childbirth.

Nawal el-Saadawi, an Arab writer, recalls her own experience:

I was six years old that night when I lay in my bed, warm and peaceful in that pleasurable state which lies halfway between wakefulness and sleep, with the rosy dreams of childhood flitting by, like gentle fairies in quick succession. I felt something move under the blankets, something like a huge hand, cold and rough, fumbling over my body, as though looking for something. Almost simultaneously another hand, as cold and as rough and as big as the first one, was clapped over my mouth, to prevent me from screaming.

They carried me to the bathroom. I do not know how many of them there were, nor do I remember their faces. . . . I . . . remember the icy touch of the bathroom tiles under my naked body, and unknown voices and humming sounds interrupted now and again by a rasping metallic sound which reminded me of the butcher when he used to sharpen his knife before slaughtering a sheep for the Eid. . . .

At that very moment I realized that my thighs had been pulled wide apart, and that each of my lower limbs was being held as far away from the other as possible, gripped by steel fingers that never relinquished their pressure. . . . Then suddenly the sharp metallic edge seemed to drop between my thighs and there cut off a piece of flesh from my body.

113

> *I screamed with pain despite the tight hand held over my mouth, for the pain was not just a pain, it was like a searing flame that went through my whole body. After a few moments, I saw a red pool of blood around my hips. . . . I did not know what they had cut off from my body. . . . I just wept, and called out to my mother for help. But the worst shock of all was when I looked around and found her standing by my side. Yes it was her, I could not be mistaken, in flesh and blood, right in the midst of these strangers, talking to them and smiling at them, as though they had not participated in slaughtering her daughter just a few moments ago.*[18]

The writer then recalls seeing her younger sister carried to the bathroom to endure the same fate. The two girls are united in terror and pain, and the pain may remain for a lifetime.

The wedding night for a woman who is infibulated also holds terror and pain, for she must be cut open to make intercourse possible. One honeymoon hotel in the Sudanese city of Port Sudan is next to a hospital. Traditionally, women are resewn after the birth of each child, which means they must repeatedly experience the vicious cycle of pain and further mutilation until they cease bearing children.

Researchers agree that these forms of genital mutilation have their origin in men's desire to control female sexuality. The medieval chastity belt and the rings that early Romans inserted through the labia majora of their female slaves to prevent pregnancy seem benign compared with the surgery being forced on young Muslim girls today.

Increasingly, African women's groups have been protesting the abuse and trying to educate women and, more importantly, male leaders in efforts to abolish all forms of genital surgery. Unfortunately, many believe that the religion of Islam requires such practices, but there is no basis for this belief in the Koran. Rather, the belief has evolved from male efforts to dominate women completely and from the myth that female genitals are unclean and must be purified by removal. In 1988, at an international conference in Somalia, some Muslim religious scholars argued that "milder forms of circumcision" should be maintained "to temper female sexuality." Yet other men opposed any strictures on genital surgery at all, arguing that eradication of the practice was a Western-motivated attack on an "important African tradition."[19]

Women around the world are challenging the legal framework that permits this type of abuse, but it will not fall overnight. Even educated women are susceptible. Those who have endured these procedures and survived subject their young daughters to the same procedure in the belief that they will not be able to attract a husband unless they are scarred for life.

In this extremely brutal example of human sperm competition, layers of deception support the underlying belief system: that the surgery is required by religion, that female genitals are unclean, that "uncircumcised" girls are undesirable mates, that female sexuality must be tempered. The one aspect of the abuse that is not discussed is the lengths to which men will go to ensure confidence of paternity and the lengths to which women will go to support them. One can only imagine the universal outrage that would erupt were men required to undergo genital surgery to temper their sexuality.

Few researchers are examining the extent to which male concern over paternity underlies these and other cultural traditions that restrict and cripple females. If they did, they would learn that no nonhuman female primate is subjected to the kind of abuse that is inflicted on women.

INFANTICIDE AND REPRODUCTIVE SUCCESS

Among nonhuman primates, rodents, and a variety of other animals, sperm competition takes another form of violence—infanticide. Infanticidal males have been widely observed among primates such as langurs, macaques, red howler monkeys, blue monkeys, gorillas, and baboons. Typically, a strange male comes into a troop, which usually consists of a dominant male and his female harem, some juveniles, and infants. The strange male usurps the old leader's position and takes over the troop. He then kills all or most of the infants in the troop. This behavior was once considered pathological, a response to crowding. But more and more field observations and research are tending to support sociobiolo-

115

gist Sarah Blaffer Hrdy's once-controversial theory that some infanticide is adaptive because it increases the killer's reproductive success.[20]

As startling and abhorent as this may be, infanticide among nonhuman animals enhances the killer's chances of fathering offspring. Infanticide has the effect of bringing the mothers of the murdered infants into estrus, the period when they are sexually receptive. The new male is then able to mate with the females and sire offspring without having to wait for them to wean infants fathered by the ousted male.

Some of the strongest evidence supporting the theory that infanticide is adaptive comes from scientists working with rodents. Laboratory experiments with collared lemmings and various strains of mice, gerbils, and hamsters show that the killing of infants by strange males reduces the period of time until the mother gives birth again.

Infanticide raises some intriguing questions. Why do females permit such exploitation of themselves and their offspring? Are there female counterstrategies? Why are only some males infanticidal and others not? Although none of these questions has been answered definitively, some extremely tantalizing data and theories have emerged.

Hrdy tackled the question of why females permit infanticide and concluded that it presents a catch-22 situation. Although females may evolve strategies to trick a male usurper, they cannot afford to boycott him because of the potential genetic gain for their future male offspring. Without an infanticidal male's genes, such offspring would lose out in the competition among males. This would mean genetic death, for they would not mate and leave offspring. "The propensity of males in a variety of primate species to kill offspring accompanying unfamiliar females is probably the most extreme cost females pay for having males around. An odd corollary of this is that in a number of species, the most important contribution a male makes is protecting offspring born in his troop from attacks by other males," writes Hrdy.[21]

Females, however, do not passively accept infanticide. Some may have evolved tactics for confusing an incoming male about the paternity of infants. One way to confuse a male is to signal sexual interest in him. Female primates usually do this by a reddening and swelling of skin on the rump. But females of some species are able to fake it by coming into a pseudoestrus or by extending estrus beyond the normal period. For example, during one male takeover of a langur troop, all the females either came into estrus or showed visual signs of estrus. One female maintained a kind of permanent estrus for four months.

For females that are already pregnant at the time of a takeover, the advantage to future offspring is obvious. If the new male can be tricked into accepting the offspring as his own, he will not harm them. Anything a female can do to affect the way males treat her offspring is important for her own fitness. This insight has caused biologists to take yet another new look at female mating behavior.

Contrary to a particularly Victorian assumption that females mate with the one best male, among wild primates as well as a variety of other mammals, including leopards, lions, and pumas, females mate with a number of males both at times when they could conceive and at times when conception is impossible. Hrdy has hypothesized that if males can remember the females with whom they mate, and if they treat the offspring of those females differently, "then there would be powerful selection pressures on females to mate with a range of male partners. Such males might be more tolerant of that female's offspring (in the sense that they would be less likely to attack the offspring), or they might be more likely to protect or care for them in situations where such behavior by males is an option."[22]

This seems to be the case among savanna baboons. Females mate with a number of different males, forming a network of friendly male associates who help her by watching the infant, allowing it to forage close by, and picking it up if it is threatened by a strange male. In harsh environments where food is scarce and motherhood takes a severe toll on females, infant survival may well depend on care by males with whom the mother has had consort relations in the past.[23]

It is not too farfetched to speculate that the threat posed by infanticidal males influenced the disappearance of visible estrus in

117

human primate ancestors. The recurring danger of infanticide may have been one of several pressures selecting for a shift among higher primates away from sexual receptivity regulated strictly by hormones toward receptivity that was determined by social situations, namely the behavior of aggressive males.

Biologists Ann Pusey, Craig Packer, and C. D. Scheel believe that the entire social structure of lions is based on the females' ability to cooperate in forming defensive maternity groups to protect themselves and their young from infanticidal intruder males.[24]

In rodents, a different type of female counterstrategy to infanticide evolved. The mere odor of a strange male induces abortion in pregnant females. Known as the *Bruce effect* (for its discoverer, biologist Hilda Bruce), this phenomenon was once considered a male strategy arising out of competition among males for mates, but more recent research suggests that it more likely evolved as a female counterstrategy to infanticidal males. The Bruce effect may be a maternal strategy to reduce, and even partially recoup, the female's investment in offspring likely to be killed by an infanticidal male.

In these species, territorial males usually prevent a strange male from approaching their mates. To a female, the scent of a strange male indicates that the dominant male has been challenged, perhaps even ousted. Female rodents even have an olfactory memory for the familiar male with whom they mated. As in some primate species, one of the first acts of a new male rodent is to kill all the infants. By resorbing her embryos when a new male takes over, a female cuts her losses. "Female rodents are primed to abort when things don't look good," says biologist Frederick vom Saal,[25] explaining that carrying a pregnancy to term in the presence of an intruder male is an enormous metabolic risk because he will kill the babies once they are born. This means that the female would lose her entire reproductive effort for that breeding period. By terminating her pregnancy through this built-in abortion mechanism, a female ends further parental investment in offspring that would be doomed, eliminates the risk of infanticide, and also makes herself sexually available to the new dominant male, insuring that her next litter will be protected.

This tactic of small rodent females is remarkably sophisticated, but female animals of many species exercise an array of more finely tuned strategies for confusing males and protecting their young than the naturalists of Darwin's day could ever have imagined. Faking estrus and mating with many males also confuse males about who has fathered a female's offspring.

One clear message that emerges from the picture of ruses and deceits to subvert female choice is that males, both human and nonhuman, will go to any lengths to protect their sperm investment; and females, whenever possible, respond with counterstrategies to confuse the issue. Unfortunately, force sometimes enters the picture. In many species, including humans, violence against females and offspring are part of this scenario. Male violence is a real threat to many females, either directly or indirectly, and it greatly affects women's choices as well as the psychology underlying those choices.

ABUSE OF POWER AND REPRODUCTIVE SUCCESS

Male violence against females and against other males is present in every human society. It is the ugly underside of the world that every woman *and* every man inhabit. On the home front, male-male competition erupts in domestic homicide; in the international arena, it erupts in war. Crime, armies, ever more destructive weapons, and threat of global annihilation are manifestations of competitive male aggression.

As this tendency becomes nationalized, the entire economy becomes dependent on the military industry with its enormously profitable arms trade. Groups of armed males are maintained to compete against other groups of armed males in the name of national security, but differential reproduction—by which some individuals, especially dominant males, produce more offspring than others—may be the real stake.

In a provocative study of the relationship between abuse of power and reproduction, anthropologist Laura Betzig examined a sample of more than one hundred societies and found that despotism in preindustrial societies "invariably coincides with the greatest degree of polygyny, and presumably, with a correspondingly high degree of differential reproduction."[26] Using the principles of evolutionary biology, Betzig argues that "men and women should have evolved to seek out positions of strength as a means to reproduction. Power, prestige, and privileged access to resources should be sought, not as ends in themselves, but as prerequisites to procreation. A lease to use power to serve one's own interests should translate into production of children and grandchildren. Despotism should be expected to coincide with differential reproduction."[27]

The data support Betzig's hypothesis. Literature on twelve despotic preindustrial societies details the methods successful men have used in order to produce children. In one ancient society after another—Dahomey, Israel, Khmer, the African Gold Coast, and the kingdoms of the Aztec and Inca, as well as others—all women were sexually available at the pleasure of the ruler. At any time, any woman could be taken from her home and added to a royal harem. Many harems contained several thousand women, far too many for even the most energetic, highly sexed ruler to impregnate; but by keeping such a large harem, the despot made these women unavailable to other men. Simply by monopolizing so many women, the ruler increased his own reproductive prowess relative to other men in the kingdom. Elaborate fortifications for defense may have served the dual purpose of hiding women and protecting their chastity.[28]

For women within harems, the only choice was between celibacy and adultery, which was punishable by death. Untold numbers of women in these societies may have spent most of their lives in seclusion to preserve their virginity. Inca women, for example, were guarded and ruled by a *mama-cuna* whose job was to make sure that if the ruler wanted a virgin, he would be sent one. If a woman was never called by the king to serve a reproductive function, she lived in the confinement of the harem until old age. Only when she was no longer fertile was she given the option of returning home.

The relationship between political power and reproduction was especially clear among the Inca in what is now called Peru. The more territory and people a leader governed, the more women he was allotted by law. The Head of a province of one hundred thousand was given twenty women; a leader of only one thousand people was permitted fifteen women; a governor of one hundred received eight; and poor Indians took whatever was left.[29]

"Political power in itself may be explained, at least in part, as providing a position from which to gain reproductively," says Betzig. "An understanding that, unless common interest overrides individual interests, individuals should have evolved to exploit positions of strength, answers the question of why power corrupts. It both predicts and explains the near universality of despotic governments in hierarchical societies prior to the development of modern industry."[30]

With industrialization, the relationship between reproductive success and despotism declined. Although Betzig admits that she has no explanation for the decline, she suggests that a key factor may have been the increasing specialization and/or scarcity of labor, as well as other events that made the interests of men in power and their subordinates overlap.

POWERFUL MALES AND FEMALE CHOICE

Male-male competition has played a major role in shaping powerful men. Dominant males wield power over other men and over women. Since natural selection favors traits that lead to the greatest reproductive success, one must also ask what part, if any, female choice may have played in the evolution of such men. Is the violent hero more attractive to women? Although some women are repelled by violent men, women in many societies are known to be attracted to powerful, militaristic, dictatorial males. In these cases, it seems as if violence has come to be equated with masculinity.

"In most social milieus, a man's reputation depends in part upon the maintenance of a credible threat of violence," say sociobiologists Martin Daly and Margo Wilson in their study of homicide.[31] They point out that in some tribal societies a young man doesn't attain his full adult status until he has killed another man. Is it possible that some women seek alliances with violent men for protection from other violent males? If so, a kind of reproductive cold war has mirrored the nuclear cold war by which the planet's two superpowers—the United States and the former Soviet Union—stockpiled tens of thousands of nuclear warheads, tit for tat, ostensibly to keep either side from detonating even one. But it's a risky strategy.

Even without violent competition, male mortality is much higher than female mortality at all ages—from fetal stage to old age—except in countries where female infanticide is still practiced or where girls have poorer nutrition and health care than boys. In addition, men generally die at an earlier age than females. Male violence multiplies that sex difference in mortality, especially during young adulthood, when men would most likely be trying to attract a woman and marry. Some researchers believe that the ultimate causes of sex differences in mortality are the different reproductive strategies of males and females. Males, human and nonhuman, simply pursue higher-risk strategies.

Men's competitive violence against other men often takes the form of murder, but male violence is sometimes directed against women as well. This violence sometimes takes the sexual form of rape—that is, forced intercourse, the usurpation of reproductive choice.

RAPISTS AS ROBBERS OF FEMALE CHOICE

Human rape is the most violent and fearsome male tactic to subvert female choice. It is aimed not only at physically controlling a woman but also at seizing control of her reproductive potential and her evolutionary right to choose her mate. Many women fear rape more than they do murder, and men have murdered because of rape, hunting down and killing the rapist of a daughter, sister, or wife. In most modern tribal societies the punishment for rape is death or castration, the same punishment meted out to rapists in a majority of ancient societies. In most modern urban societies, however, punishment is not as severe or swift in its administration. In the United States, for example, although rape is regarded as a heinous crime, rapists have a "maximum probability of about

122

0.04 of ever being punished."[32] Such ineffective deterrence probably accounts for the fact that the incidence of recorded rape in the
United States is increasing faster than that of all other violent
crimes.

For women, rape is the terrible male crime their mothers and
fathers warned them about. Anxieties about being alone in a sub-
way at night, in the parking lot of a shopping mall, on an unfamiliar street, with a stalled car on a deserted road, jogging in
a public park, or even being alone in one's own home in the middle of the night, are all rooted in the fear of rape. At some level of
consciousness, women live with this fear all their lives. Not surprisingly, many women arm themselves or take self-defense training to be prepared in the event they are ever attacked. Fear of rape
seems to be part of the female psyche that was shaped in our ancient evolutionary past, perhaps as a kind of protective awareness
that helped females avoid attack from roaming males.

Although rape rarely ends in murder, it can leave a victim
scarred for life. Against her will, the rapist—in effect, a thief of
sexual choice—has used his larger body size and his penis as
weapons to force entry to her body and burden her with his sperm.
Then he has left her at the mercy of a society that often refuses her
an abortion if she becomes pregnant. Thus do some societies protect the rapist's sperm investment. What stronger evidence is
there for the degree to which sperm competition among males influences social customs and law enforcement? Indeed, it has been
suggested that laws against rape originated not out of concern
for the woman but for the man—husband or father—whose
reproductive property had been violated, reducing her value
to each.

"It's easier to run with your skirt up than with your pants
down," an old boyfriend once said as he casually dismissed the
possibility of rape. This comment represents a fairly typical male
belief that it is difficult for a man to rape and that women who
cry rape are often lying. Another common male attitude is that
women invite rape. If a woman protests going to bed with a date,
her no may be taken for a yes. The rapist makes a woman's choice
for her. Some men believe they are justified in raping women who
dress in a "sexually provocative" manner. By this twist in logic,

women are seen as responsible for rape, and men their victims. In Lusaka, the capital city of Zambia, for example, a campaign against young single women was waged in 1972 by government authorities. The focus of the campaign was "the unaccompanied woman." The situation was summed up by a government official in a local newspaper: "It becomes dangerous for girls to loiter without an escort. In fact this is moral degradation at its worst. . . . Girls should not create situations for crimes like murder and rape, and girls can help to curb this growing rate of rape in Zambia by stopping this aimless loitering at night."[33]

There is also the belief that women exist for men's pleasure and have no sexual rights, that rape is just a normal part of the boys-will-be-boys behavioral repertoire. This attitude was all too prevalent in a midnight raid of male students on the girls' dormitory at a coed boarding school in Kenya during the summer of 1991. Some 271 teenage girls were chased into a corner of the dormitory; 19 died of suffocation in the crush, and 71 were raped. The school's deputy principal, a woman, was quoted as saying: "The boys never meant any harm against the girls. They just wanted to rape."[34]

ROMANCE AND RAPE

Some modern romance novels romanticize male violence, excusing the hero's rape of the heroine as proof of his uncontrollable passion for her—a passion that only she can transform and tame. It has been suggested that such romanticization of male violence is possible only because of readers' "willingness to be convinced that the forced taking of a woman by a man who 'really' loves her is testimony to her desirability and worth rather than to his power."[35] Perhaps such novels express women's *wish* that male violence could be transformed into tender, loving behavior. Perhaps these novels help their readers deal psychologically with an abusive husband or boyfriend by providing a few hours of escape. But they do not solve the problem, nor do they suggest solutions. They function only as a kind of drug, temporarily taking the reader away from the real world but doing nothing to help her change it.

The enormous financial success of these novels, however, cannot be overlooked. At some level, they are speaking to women's psychological needs, a phenomenon that surely deserves more study.

"By suggesting that rape is either a mistake or an expression of uncontrollable desire, it may also give her [the reader] a false sense of security by showing her how to rationalize violent behavior and thus reconcile her to a set of events and relations that she would be better off changing," writes Janice Radway in her study of the romance novel.[36]

In the real world, rape has nothing to do with romance; it does have something to do with power, with aggression, with contempt for women; and however repugnant the idea may be, it may also have something to do with reproduction. Traditional psychology has considered rape a pathological act, the behavior of a diseased mind. But studies indicate that rapists tend to be normal; in prisons, rapists are considered the most normal of inmates. Apparently something more than a diseased mind is involved in rape. Pathology is not a sufficient explanation.

In an attempt to learn how rape may have evolved, two recent, complementary studies by husband-wife research teams (biologist Randy Thornhill and anthropologist Nancy Wilmsen Thornhill; biologist William M. Shields and social-science researcher Lea M. Shields) looked at rape in the context of evolutionary biology.[37] This meant asking an altogether distasteful question: does rape in any way enhance the rapist's fitness—his ability to reproduce offspring that will, in turn, survive and reproduce?

If rape has any reproductive component, evolutionary biology would predict that the victims would be in age groups of highest fertility. This prediction is supported by rape statistics from the U.S. Department of Justice and from police departments in a variety of American cities. Women from ages sixteen through twenty-four report rape more than women in any other age category.[38] These are the ages of highest fertility, when pregnancy is most likely to be carried to term successfully. The most underrepresented females among reported rape victims are those in age categories of zero fertility—under ten and over fifty.

What kind of men rape? The Thornhills' and the Shieldses'

studies offer different hypotheses. The Thornhills propose that rape is a last-ditch, desperation strategy by losers to achieve reproductive success. Only a small percentage of rapes result in pregnancy, but those few may give the rapist his only chance to reproduce. Even minimal reproductive success is enough for natural selection to have favored the potential of some males to rape. The Shieldses propose that all men possess the potential for rape and will do so whenever the benefit far outweighs the cost, as in times of war or under other conditions of female vulnerability and powerlessness.

If rape does indeed have a reproductive component, however slight, evolutionary biology would predict that men would be most likely to rape at the ages when the competition for females is most intense. This corresponds to ages prior to the age at which men usually marry for the first time. During this period of life males take the greatest risks in sexual competition; it is for them a time of high mortality.

Once again, statistics support the prediction from evolutionary biology. As shown by the major studies of rape offenders, young men between the ages of fifteen and twenty-five predominate.[39] Depending on the study, the median ages for rapists ranged from twenty to twenty-three.

A third prediction is that males who lose out in sexual and social competition will be more likely to rape than those who can gain access to resources. Surveys of the socioeconomic status of rapists in the United States indicate that the vast majority of offenders come from lower socioeconomic classes and are unemployed or unskilled laborers with only an elementary-school education or less. Cross-cultural studies from Denmark and Australia also confirm that unskilled, unemployed, and poorly educated males—those who lose out in sexual competition—are more often rapists than other men.

The data suggest that rich men rarely rape, and that rapist and victim most often live in the same neighborhood (82 percent).[40] According to one study, a female living in the inner city stands a one-in-seventy-seven chance of being raped in her lifetime. In more affluent areas the risk becomes one in two thousand,

and in a rich neighborhood she stands a one-in-ten-thousand chance of being raped.[41]

There are exceptions. Some married men as well as men of power and wealth commit rape. Rather than fitting the profile of losers in sexual competition, such men are winners. Although they make up a small percentage of rapists, they demonstrate that rape is not committed solely by subordinate males.

All males are capable of rape given certain conditions, suggest the Shieldes. According to their hypothesis, all men have three basic reproductive behavior patterns: honest courtship, seduction-deception, and rape. Using a cost-benefit analysis, they argue that any man will rape in situations such as war, where there is no cost connected with the crime.

War presents conditions of intense male hostility and female vulnerability. From tribal wars to world wars, rape in war is commonplace. War allows the full expression of male aggression, legitimizing murder, torture, and rape. Susan Brownmiller devotes an entire chapter of her book on rape to this subject, pointing out that during the Japanese invasion of Nanking in 1938, there were approximately twenty thousand cases of rape during the first month of occupation. During the nine-month West Pakastani occupation of Bangladesh in 1971, between two hundred thousand and three hundred thousand rapes occurred, and thousands of raped women became pregnant.[42]

Rape in war is so prevalent that it implies an underlying cultural attitude that rape is a right of the conquerors. This attitude goes back at least to biblical times, and is probably much older. In an Old Testament story, the Hebrews conquered the tribe of the Midianites by slaying all of their men. Moses then ordered his officers: "Now therefore kill every male among the little ones, and kill every woman that hath known man by lying with him. But all the women children, that have not known a man by lying with him, keep alive for yourselves."[43] Thus have conquering men, like nonhuman male primates, committed infanticide after ousting the old male leadership. In the biblical story, the conquerors also murder the pregnant women but keep the virgins alive for their own reproductive advantage.

The evolution of rape appears to follow one of sociobiology's basic principles: if there is any benefit and no cost to any behavior, then it is likely to evolve. Genes are essentially selfish, as pointed out by British biologist Richard Dawkins.[44] For genes, there is no morality, no good and bad, no fair play, no sense of justice; any means justifies the end, which is reproduction. The Shieldses speculate that "during human evolutionary history, males that possessed a mating strategy that included rape were favored by natural selection over those that did not."[45]

Although finding that rape does potentially enhance the rapist's fitness, the Shieldses agree with feminists that rape "is a violent act rather than a sexual act."[46] They argue that the motivation for rape is quite different from the motivation for sex by a male seeking a bond with a female to produce offspring. The ultimate gain may be offspring, but the immediate act, say the Shieldses, is triggered by hostility.

RAPE AND POLYGYNY

Human rape most likely evolved in ancestral polygyny. Polygyny is an important factor in the evolution of rape because competition for resources is more intense among polygynous males than among monogamous males. In polygynous societies, a few men have more than one mate. This means that a number of other men are denied access to mates and are forced into bachelorhood. These men may try however they can to sneak or seize copulations, for the reproductive stakes are high. In polygynous societies, the difference between male and female reproductive success is much greater than in monogamous societies, where male and female reproductive success may be equal.

Even in monogamous societies, however, male reproductive success may be greater than females' for three reasons: (1) infidelity that results in offspring; (2) divorce followed by a second marriage in which the man sires additional offspring; and (3) differential access to females by married men. "Thus," argue the Thornhills, "all or most human societies exhibit some degree of polygyny, even those in which monogamy is socially imposed." They point out that in the United States, and probably in other

128
ℬ

countries as well, more males than females are unmarried for all reproductive adult age categories, and more males than females never marry.[47]

The sociobiological analysis of rape is not popular. Critics mistakenly assume that such an analysis justifies or excuses rape, but this criticism misses the point. Investigating rape from an evolutionary perspective doesn't justify it any more than research on AIDS viruses justifies the disease. The reason for examining the sociobiology of rape is to gain a clearer understanding of its dynamics and, through this understanding, to design more effective punishment. To deny rape's sexual and reproductive aspects is to fail to understand it fully. Rape *is* a violent act. But it is a violent *sexual* attack on females that sometimes results in offspring. The sociobiological perspective illuminates the full horror of the rapist's crime, which is aimed at seizing control of a female's reproductive potential and undermining her fitness.

Most writers on rape, whatever their persuasions, agree that current penalties are not preventing rape, especially in industrialized countries. The sociobiological perspective "implies that a society can most effectively control rape by ensuring that a rapist can expect to pay a sufficient genetic cost to outweigh any potential genetic benefit," say the Shieldses.[48] They point to societies in which rape was controlled by punishments of death or castration, which effectively eliminate any genetic benefit.

Urban societies seem to have reduced the cost of rape to such an extent that the threat of retribution no longer acts as an effective deterrent. "We predict," write the Shieldses, "that when a society regards the rape of *any* [emphasis theirs] woman the way individuals perceive the rape of their daughters, sisters, or mates, and then resists, pursues, and punishes the rapist accordingly, rape will cease to be a major problem."[49]

NONHUMAN MALES THAT RAPE

Rape can be seen in an evolutionary context most clearly in nonhuman animals. Among primates, only humans and orangutans are known to commit rape; but males of various species of colonially nesting birds, such as swallows, gulls, herons, and alba-

129

trosses, are known to try to rape their neighbors' unattended mates. North American puddle ducks, including mallards, shovelers, and pintails, are notorious rapists. Males of several species of fishes and insects also rape. Most nonhuman rapists have been excluded from the usual avenues of courtship. According to Randy Thornhill, who has done the most detailed research on nonhuman rape, "Rape is the only option for reproduction for a male without resources because he cannot deceive a female about his quality as a mate."[50]

Thornhill has observed rape in eighteen species of scorpionflies in the genus *Panorpa*. As noted in chapter 2, a male must come courting with a nuptial gift of a dead insect to offer a female. The competition for insects is so intense that some males risk their lives by stealing one from the web of a spider, their chief predator. Males that are unable to obtain a dead insect may manufacture a nuptial gift by using specialized salivary glands to make a spittle ball, which a female may mistake for a dead insect. But if a male has been unable to eat for several days because of competition from other males, his salivary glands become shriveled and useless; and he is without resources.

Thornhill has found that whenever a male can neither obtain nor manufacture a nuptial gift, he is likely to rape. Those males whose salivary glands have become useless are particularly aggressive rapists. Although only 11 percent of rape attempts result in insemination of females, and raped females lay fewer eggs than females receiving nuptial gifts, males still pursue this option when they cannot produce a nuptial gift.

Female scorpionflies, on the other hand, are strongly selected to avoid rape. Females flee from males without a nuptial gift. Whenever a female copulates, she becomes sexually nonreceptive for a day or two. During this time, she will not invite copulation even with a male bearing a gift. If she is raped, her entire fitness may be imperiled because she may not lay as many eggs as she would have had she mated with a male of her choice. In addition, the rapist may pass on bad genes that the female's choice would have rejected. Thus rape both subverts her choice of mate and reduces her reproductive success.[51]

Fortunately, rape is not that common in the animal kingdom, suggesting that natural selection has favored female tactics to resist rape more strongly than it has favored rape itself. But the fact that rape occurs at all means that females of some species, including humans, must ever be wary of aggressive, rogue males.

For females, especially mammals that invest so heavily in reproduction, pair-bonding with a male may offer the greatest security, with respect both to undivided resources and to protection from other males. But monogamy goes against the male's strategy of trying to mate with as many females as possible. Nevertheless, some animals have indeed become monogamous, although sometimes the alliance is uneasy.

131

S I X

ന്റ

MONOGAMY, PAIR-BONDING, AND FEMALE CHOICE

Monogamy . . . is maintained by the way females deploy
themselves both socially and geographically, and by female
reproductive strategies which make male assistance
(either in maintaining the territory or in actually rearing young)
imperative. Neither sentiment nor sexuality enters the picture—
until later.

SARAH BLAFFER HRDY
The Woman That Never Evolved
1981[1]

MONOGAMY SUPPORTS the female reproductive role better than any
other social system, yet few animals mate for life. When animals
bond at all, it is usually because the young require the care of both
parents; the duration of a pair-bond is related to the time needed
to raise offspring to maturity. There is no biological necessity for
any animal to mate for life. Therefore, among the birds and the
bees—and most other animals as well—monogamy is the exception, not the rule. Less than one in ten thousand invertebrate species is monogamous, and only a small fraction of vertebrates are

monogamous. Even among those animals that supposedly developed monogamy, such as many species of birds, infidelity is rampant; both females and males cheat.

Biologists who once believed that as many as 94 percent of bird species were monogamous are now revising their views. Using new techniques to determine paternity, they are finding that almost a third of the chicks in any nest are not sired by the resident male. Males pursue a predictably promiscuous strategy, and females philander as well.[2]

The difference between the two sexes is that female dalliance is not random. Among the black-capped chickadee of North America, for example, female infidelity follows a strategy that would be predictable under the principles of female choice. She goes for a higher-ranking male than the mate she left on the nest. Similarly, the female barn swallow seeks males with longer tails than that of her mate. The longer tail is evidence of a male's resistance to parasites, a trait that would benefit her young.

Male birds, like males of other species, have a roving eye. After establishing a nest, attracting a female, and reproducing, some older male purple martins—the world's largest species of swallow—begin singing songs that lure younger males. When a younger male moves in and sings a courtship song that attracts his own mate, the elder martin rapes her. Similarly, older male mallards and other ducks that are already paired with females often try to seduce or rape a neighbor's mate.

For many species, pair-bonding may be more than anything else a marriage of convenience. The bond keeps male and female together long enough to raise their young, but it also leaves an opening for a bit of cheating. As more complex creatures, we human beings pursue a mixed strategy, practicing monogamy under some conditions and polygyny under others. In most societies, we extol the virtues of monogamy while sneaking extramarital sex on the side. As anthropologists Lionel Tiger and Robin Fox have noted, "All cultures may not be monogamous, but they are all certainly adulterous."[3]

Many biologists and anthropologists consider humans basically a polygynous species although monogamy is practiced—at least in principle—by most humans today. Evidence for polygynous ancestry lies in the size difference between men and women.

In monogamous nonhuman species, the sexes tend to be equal in size and sometimes look exactly alike—even to each other. Among pigeons, for example, male and female are indistinguishable. The same is true for gibbons, the most monogamous of primates. In polygynous species, however, males are larger than females and, in the case of nonhuman primates, males have large and prominent canine teeth. These differences in form and structure between male and female are known as sexual dimorphism. Darwin noted the size difference in his two-volume work, *The Descent of Man, and Selection in Relation to Sex.* The more polygynous the species, the greater the size differential.

In general, male gorillas and chimpanzees tend to be 25 percent (or more) larger than females. The theoretical explanation for this kind of sexual dimorphism is that polygynous males need additional size and strength to compete with other males and to safeguard their group of females and infants. Although females may copulate promiscuously, as in the case of chimpanzees, they tend to choose larger, more dominant males to father their offspring. This ensures that their sons will inherit genes for larger size and strength, enabling them to compete successfully with other males for mates and status. Both natural selection and sexual selection work to maintain sexual dimorphism in polygynous species.

Contemporary men are only 5 to 12 percent larger than women, but fossils of our 4-million-year-old hominid ancestors indicate a much greater size difference, suggesting that we were once much more polygynous than we are today. For this reason, biologists classify modern humans as a mildly polygynous species. Our social evolution has been in the direction of monogamy. Approximately 80 percent of contemporary human societies are polygynous and 20 percent are monogamous, but even where polygyny is sanctioned, most men have only one wife. According to anthropologist Joseph Shepher, "An overwhelming majority of all males of the species live in pair-bonding—not only because the cultures comprising the largest populations are monogamous

(American, Russian. Chinese, Japanese, etc.), but . . . even in explicitly polygynous cultures only a low percentage of males are married polygynously."[4]

In general, observed Shepher, human polygyny can be extensive only if something happens to upset the sex ratio, such as systematic male infanticide, sterilization, or war, which would reduce the number of available males. Other factors might be practices that prevent a large percentage of males from marrying, such as celibacy or long military service, or circumstances that effectively postpone male marriage until a late age. A further limitation on the number of males practicing polygyny is that in polygynous societies, only wealthy men can afford more than one wife. Many more men have one wife, and some men have no wife. Most men and women, then, are living in monogamous arrangements.

What is unclear is whether human monogamy arose out of some ecological necessity or whether it has been imposed by law and religion. Depending on the specific culture, a combination of factors may have been operating. In any case, monogamy among humans, as among barn swallows and black-capped chickadees, is often breached by extramarital affairs.

Monogamy runs counter to the male's reproductive strategy of spreading his sperm around and inseminating as many females as possible. But monogamy supports the female's general strategy of choosing her mate and enlisting as much male parenting assistance as she can. Monogamy in humans also supports the male's desire to be certain that he is the father of his children, as we'll see a little later in this chapter. The duration of a strong pair-bond in any species usually depends on the length of time the young need the care of both parents.

Biologists and anthropologists differ over how much importance should be attributed to female choice in the evolution of monogamy. Some believe that monogamy evolved as a direct result of female choice. Others believe that a number of female reproductive strategies were involved. Whatever the case, without female direction at some level, it is inconceivable that monogamy would have evolved in any species.

Although humans—some humans, anyway—tend to think of monogamy as a lifetime contract, animal behaviorists use a loose definition when speaking of nonhuman monogamy. Monogamy generally means any relationship in which male and female mate and stay together to raise their offspring. This relationship may endure only through the breeding season. But with a few animals, such as gibbons and the California mouse, it can, indeed, last for life.

CONDITIONS FOR THE EVOLUTION OF MONOGAMY

In the few species in which monogamy has developed, some factor or combination of factors required the involvement of males in parenting. Biologists James Wittenberger and Ronald Tilson have presented five hypotheses to explain its evolution. Monogamy should evolve, they say: (1) when male parental care is nonshareable and indispensable to female reproductive success; (2) when a female in a territorial species benefits more from mating with an unmated male than with a male who is already mated; (3) when the majority of males in nonterritorial species can reproduce most successfully by defending exclusive access to a single female; (4) when female aggression prevents a male from acquiring two mates; and (5) when males are less successful with two mates than with one.[5]

In all cases of monogamy, the care required by offspring emerges as a critical factor. "In the animal world, fidelity is a special condition that evolves when the Darwinian advantage of co-operation in rearing offspring outweighs the advantage to either partner of seeking extra mates," says sociobiologist Edward O. Wilson.[6]

PRIMATE MONOGAMISTS

Of all mammals, primates—the order to which humans belong—are the most monogamous. This isn't surprising because primate young need parental care much longer than do the young of other animals. "Monogamous breeding systems are four times more common among primates than in mammals generally," writes sociobiologist Sarah Blaffer Hrdy.[7] She points out that of some two hundred species of primates, thirty-seven, or roughly 18 percent, are monogamous, although most of these animals are "rare and endangered, little known even to scientists."[8]

Significantly, monogamy turns up in all four major evolutionary groups of primates: prosimians, the most primitive group, which includes tree shrews and lemurs; New World monkeys, such as marmosets and tamarins; Old World monkeys, such as the Mentawei Island langur; and apes, including gibbons and humans. But among all monogamous primates, humans are the only ones that do not live in trees. All other ground-dwelling primates are polygynous.

Some biologists speculate that monogamy evolved among primates whenever environmental conditions pushed animals to speed up reproduction—to produce more young in the same period of time or the same number in less time. The tiny marmosets of Central and South American rain forests may have developed monogamy under such circumstances. A tip-off is that these tiny females usually bear twins, which each weigh at least one-fifth, and sometimes up to one-quarter, of their mother's weight. Without a male to help carry and feed such large young, a female marmoset might not be able to raise any offspring at all. Male parenting is indispensable for the survival of young marmosets and, therefore, for both male and female reproductive success.

The marmoset reproductive system may have evolved in response to ecological changes. Marmosets feed primarily on insects; they also eat lizards, tree frogs, and small birds when these prey can be found. Fruits and tree sap are part of their diet, too. Pointing out that insect-eating primates are small because they must survive on such tiny morsels of living protein, Hrdy theorizes that "ecological necessity" may have selected for smaller and smaller females. This would have created the dilemma of females trying to deliver babies through pelvises that were too small. "Twinning evolved as a practical solution to this difficulty. Instead of bearing one enormous baby, mothers produced two or three infants that were merely large."[9]

The marmoset's life-style as a colonizer of disturbed, short-lived, and unpredictable areas—such as forest openings created by a fallen tree—probably favored increasing the number of offspring per pregnancy rather than producing fewer offspring with longer spaces between births. Animals that live in fluctuating habitats need to move in and reproduce quickly. The marmoset does this well by producing two babies at a time; but the female's remarkable reproductive capacity wouldn't be possible without a breeding system that supports her. A marmoset mother is very assertive; both her mate and the nonbreeding members of the group defer to her. Her mate's behavior is especially important to her as he assumes primary responsibility for his offspring except when they are being suckled. Hard times, such as periods of food scarcity, can change marmoset reproductive behavior. During such times, only the healthier of a pair of twins may survive. Females may also lengthen the space between births. According to Hrdy, "Marmosets, like many small mammals, must be ecological double-agents, shuttling back and forth along a continuum" of reproductive strategies.[10]

139

The choices are between producing more young more rapidly to take advantage of fluctuating and unpredictable environments—known as R-selection—or producing fewer, more slowly maturing young—known as K-selection. R-selection is an opportunistic strategy. The most extreme example is the oyster, which may produce as many as 500 million eggs a year. K-selection is the strategy of more stable species that inhabit long-lived, self-perpetuating environments such as mature old-growth forests or coral reefs. The most extreme example of K-selection is the great apes—gorillas, chimpanzees, and orangutans—which produce only one infant every five or six years. K-selection such as this places animals in danger of extinction if their habitat is disturbed. Because of habitat destruction, gorillas, chimpanzees, and orangutans are endangered species today.

Whichever strategy animals follow, it is really the female's pattern of maternal investment that determines how much care the father must provide. For example, if the female marmoset produced fewer young with longer birth spaces and was able, therefore, to provide the kind of maternal investment chimpanzee mothers do, her mate would be free to breed with other females. "Female choice may be a factor in monogamy, but ultimately monogamy derives from constraints imposed by females at a more basic level," says Hrdy. "One way or another, females in these species are deploying themselves so that there is only one breeding female in each territory or group. Any prospect of polygyny would be precluded by fierce antagonism among females of breeding age. In most monogamous species, rival females are physically excluded from the territory by the aggressiveness of its mistress. In cases where the presence of other females is tolerated (as in wild tamarins), the integrity of the breeding unit is maintained by suppression of ovulation in subordinate females.[11]

In the gelada baboon, for example, dominant females take fewer cycles to conceive than subordinate females, even when they are cycling simultaneously. Biologist R. I. M. Dunbar suggests that delayed conception among the lower-ranking individuals is caused by stress, the result of dominant females harassing subordinates. Or higher-ranking females may have earlier access to the dominant male and receive higher-quality sperm.[12] Among vervet monkeys, subordinate females may show a delayed conception time because males mate less frequently with lower-ranking females.

There is another explanation for the increased involvement of male primates in parenting; they may have been preadapted to fathering. This would be a new slant on the prevailing assumption that monogamy and certainty of paternity paved the way for the evolution of male caregiving. Hrdy asks that one consider an alternative possibility: "whether the extraordinary capacity of male primates to look out for the fates of infants did not in some way pre-adapt members of this order for the sort of close, long-term relationships between males and females that, under some ecological circumstances, leads to monogamy!"[13] Although no one will ever know exactly how monogamy evolved, it is clear that in species where it has, the behavior enhances the reproductive success of both partners.

MONOGAMY AMONG HUMANS

Human beings present an extremely complex and often contradictory picture of a species with both polygynous and monogamous tendencies. Repeatedly, in various cultures, humans have promoted monogamous marriage as the ideal. Monogamy with a wink, however. The same civilizations that have legislated monogamy are also forced to recognize that adultery is common. Are we humans monogamous? Or is monogamy an ideal that we strive for but, with some exceptions, never quite achieve? Do we enter into formal monogamous contracts because we can express promiscuous tendencies on the side? And how much of our massive denial of our animal nature is really denial of our sexuality? These questions will be the subject of research for years to come. For the moment, we must acknowledge that the kind of monogamy biologists and anthropologists find in humans is not necessarily the "till death us do part" ideal.

141

Four factors appear to have been involved in the development of human monogamy, not necessarily in this order: (1) an evolutionary pressure for greater male parental investment; (2) upright walking; (3) the disappearance of visible estrus in human females; and (4) the evolution of the distinctively human pair-bond. There are numerous theories as to how each of these may have evolved, and it is beyond the scope of this chapter to present all of them. What follows are those theories that seem most pertinent to female choice.

UPRIGHT WALKING—A REVOLUTIONARY POSTURE

According to anatomist Owen Lovejoy, upright walking was the most revolutionary change in primate behavior, and female choice played a major part in this phase of human evolution.

Although walking on two feet seems perfectly normal to us, it is, says Lovejoy, one of the most inefficient forms of locomotion in the animal kingdom: "It makes you slower, more awkward, more prone to injury, and it deprives you of the basic primate niche, which is the arboreal canopy." In one of the most controversial articles ever published in *Science* magazine,[14] Lovejoy presented his theory that upright walking must have enhanced reproductive success or it wouldn't have evolved.

"Think about the disadvantages of taking away your climbing ability," he says. "It eliminates most of your food supply and your places of safety. It's just a totally unexpected adaptation for any primate; therefore, the adaptation itself must have been intensively crucial in terms of directly increasing reproductive success in some way."

Lovejoy theorizes that the earliest human ancestors must have stood upright to carry something valuable. From his study of fossil bones dating back 4 million years, Lovejoy concluded that ancient hominids were walking upright long before any evidence of tool use and long before the savanna, or tall grasslands, evolved in Africa. With this, the old theories that apes stood upright to carry tools or to see over tall grass were laid to rest. But why *did* these creatures stand upright? What could they have been carrying? What could have been so valuable that a primate would risk losing its food supply, its shelter, and even its life to stand on two legs?

Lovejoy's controversial answer was that the earliest human ancestors must have stood upright to carry food back to a home base where it could be shared with females and their offspring.

Human babies are the most helpless in the animal kingdom; they require many years of care before they can survive on their own. Like gorillas, human beings pursue a K-selected reproductive strategy of producing fewer children and taking better care of them over their long period of maturation. At some time millions of years ago, human ancestors may have experienced some evolutionary pressure to speed up reproduction and produce more young. The only way it would have been possible to do this would have been to bring more male energy into reproduction. "Basically, the only way you can do it is to use a monogamous mating strategy. Female selection is the *sine qua non* of monogamy," Lovejoy says, adding, "In selecting a male who'll reliably provision her and her offspring, she increases her reproductive success."[15]

But what could a female do to ensure that her mate would continue bringing home the bacon rather than taking it to some other female? One possibility would be to keep him guessing as to when she was ovulating—the period when conception is most likely to occur and, therefore, the time when a male would be most attracted. The old sex-for-food ploy also could have contributed. Among humans, sex in exchange for food and protection may be the most ancient motive for monogamy. For such a trade-off to succeed, however, females needed to be able to have sex at any time, not just during a period of estrus. Just how this adaptation may have occurred is unknown, but the result is that women do not show visible signs of estrus. In humans, then, the pursuit of sex became a continuing preoccupation.

CONCEALING OVULATION

The fact that ovulation in women is hidden—even from women themselves—has generated numerous theories as to how estrus was lost. But perhaps it wasn't lost at all. Perhaps natural selection favored concealed ovulation in a number of ancient primates, including the line that was to become distinctively human.

The theory that visible display of ovulation was somehow lost by women is based on the observation that most other primate females advertise ovulation through conspicuous behaviors, genital swellings, and odors. These changes are controlled by ovarian hormones, especially estrogens. They occur in cycles, and females tend to be interested in copulating only during the time when they are in heat. For some animals, this period can be quite brief. In the galago, a small primate in the loris family, estrus lasts only a few hours. Among chimpanzees and savanna baboons, copulations are generally limited to about two weeks in the middle of each thirty-five-day cycle.

When a female primate is in estrus, rising estrogen levels cause the skin around her genitals to swell and redden. These large, conspicuous sexual swellings and accompanying odors signal ovulation. The female becomes a walking sexual beacon, flashing her readiness to copulate. Sexually receptive females attract males, sometimes inciting them to fight. In addition, female primates are no shrinking violets. They don't wait passively for interested males to saunter over and mount. Extensive field research shows that female primates in estrus approach males aggressively, present their swollen rumps, and invite copulation. Sometimes estrus females rub males' genitals.

Whether the primate ancestors of human females ever had

such conspicuous sexual swellings will never be known, but many of the highly speculative theories attempting to explain the loss of estrus in humans assume that our early hominid ancestors had sexual swellings like chimpanzees. Loss of visible estrus is interpreted as a strategy by which females became sexier, entered into a kind of sex contract[16] with males, and motivated males to form pair-bonds and share the bounty of their hunting with females and offspring. No one can truly reconstruct how prehuman primates lived some 3 million to 10 million years ago, however. The least speculative option, says Hrdy, is to investigate reproductive behavior in living primates. In doing so, one discovers enormous diversity in primate breeding systems. One also discovers that we humans are not as unique in our sexuality as we may like to believe.[17]

144

CONCEALED OVULATION IN OTHER FEMALE PRIMATES

Women are not the only female primates that conceal ovulation, and they are not the only female primates that can have sex at any time during the menstrual cycle or even during pregnancy. Female tamarins, marmosets, and other monogamous New World monkeys may copulate on any cycle day, and they show no conspicuous sign of ovulation.[18] Nor do these primates menstruate. Among most monkeys and apes, however, female interest in copulation seems to peak at the fertile midcycle. Females may also be most attractive to males at that time. Significantly, some species that visually display estrus may also be sexually active at other times, some of them even more sexually active than women.

Concealed ovulation does not necessarily lead to continuous receptivity. The continuously receptive human female turns out to be as much a myth as the passive female. "No human female is continuously receptive . . . and any male who entertains this illusion must be a very old man with a short memory or a very young man due for bitter disappointment," biologist Frank Beach is reported to have remarked.[19] Numerous studies have shown that human female sexual receptivity depends as much on mood, ambiance, and, most especially, the right partner as it does on hormones. Research on different groups of women from different cultures has shown that human females, like other primate females, also show a peak in sexual activity at midcycle. What then is the major difference between women's sexual patterns and those of primates? Apparently it is the *ability* of women to have sex at any time, which is quite different from the *desire* to have sex at any time. Cultural attitudes, values, religion, and education also play important roles in regulating human sexuality and sexual receptivity.

The biologist's old query of why human females lost estrus may need to be rethought. Perhaps human females never had a visible estrus. According to Hrdy, the questions that should be asked are: "Under what circumstances do primates generally shift from cyclical to more situation-dependent receptivity? Under what circumstances do we find conspicuous signaling of receptivity? When is it absent?"[20] These questions place concealed ovulation in the broader context of evolutionary biology. In short, when would natural selection favor sexual swellings and when would it favor hidden ovulation?

Apparently, sexual swellings evolved in species that live in social units containing more than one male, such as the common chimpanzee, savanna baboons, and twenty-two other primate species. Females in such multimale groups probably benefit by conspicuously advertising ovulation. Sexual swellings entice and excite males, drawing them to a female when she's ready to copulate. The whole process is much more energy efficient for females because they don't have to take time away from their food-finding activities to solicit each male. Instead, a female advertises to the whole male community. This strategy has the effect of shifting to the male the energy burden of finding an opportunity to mate.[21]

How could a female benefit by mating with many males? What happens to female choice in this context? Is there a strategy underlying the promiscuity of some female primates? Hrdy offers the intriguing hypothesis that females may use multiple matings to forge alliances with many males. In this way, a female may confuse the issue of paternity and trick each of her sexual partners into suspecting he is the father of her offspring. As a result, they may help to protect her, share food with her, and assist in caring for her young. Among savanna baboons, for example, several males often assist a female by babysitting, carrying, or protecting her infant. Recent research indicates that male care may be critical to the survival not only of young baboons but of more young primates than was previously believed. "Being carried by males—typically males with whom the female had past consort relations—is essential for infant survival," says Hrdy.[22]

Another possible explanation for multiple matings, proposed by primatologist Meredith Small, is that female primates may be improving the possibility of conceiving by keeping a steady supply of semen in their reproductive tracts during the days close to ovulation. "Under some circumstances sperm may be a limited resource," says Small, adding that "excessive sexual activity is an adaptive strategy for females that maximizes their chances of conception."[23] Each ejaculation reduces the sperm supply. When females mate repeatedly during nonfertile periods, they are temporarily reducing the supplies of sperm available to competing females. After repeated ejaculations, males become exhausted and sperm are less available.

Multiple matings may enhance a female's reproductive success in several ways: (1) by confusing the issue of paternity, thereby securing the help and protection of several males; (2) by functioning as a counterstrategy to infanticidal males; (3) by improving the probability of conception; and (4) by reducing the quantity of sperm available to competing females.

Wherever females are mating with many males, as in multimale social groups, sperm competition is intense. The male counterstrategy, apparently, was to evolve large testes. If a male is one of many copulating with a female, his chances of fathering her offspring will depend on more than seduction. To win in the competition for reproductive success, he will need to produce more sperm as well as sperm of higher structural and chemical quality than his rivals. The battle to father offspring will be won or lost inside the female's reproductive tract.

A comparison of testes size in comparison with body weight shows that males in multimale societies are more amply endowed relative to males in monogamous or one-male/several-female breeding units. A male chimp's testes, for example, account for 0.27 percent of his body weight, and female chimps are among the most sexually active of all primates. The testes of the male macaque, which also lives in a multimale group, account for 0.80 percent of his body weight. Similarly the testes of the savanna baboon and the squirrel monkey make up 0.21 and 0.41 percent respectively, of their body weight.

Males in more monogamous societies have a significantly lower ratio between testes and body weight. A man's testes, for example, constitute only 0.06 percent of his body weight, a gorilla's 0.02 percent, and an orangutan's 0.05 percent. In gorilla groups, only one silverback male at a time breeds. Orangutan males pursue a solitary existence, mating when a female solicits them or when they happen to encounter a female while foraging through the forest.

Small points out that one of the striking differences between *Homo sapiens* and other primates is the poor quality of human sperm. Human sperm are known for their abnormalities, great variances in structure, and such variation in chemical properties that many quickly lose their ability to fertilize eggs.[24] According to studies of infertility in the United States, males are "the sole identified problem" in one out of every five infertile couples.[25] Research demonstrates that toxic substances can reduce the overall number of sperm, increase the number of abnormal sperm, and decrease the sperm's ability to move. Radiation and smoking especially are known to impair sperm quality.[26] Given the Earth's current population, such impairment of sperm poses no immediate threat to the species, but over the long term of thousands of years, reproductive capacity could suffer.

Small theorizes that if males or sperm are scarce, females should be selected to (1) choose males with the highest quality and greatest quantity of semen and seek exclusive access to them; (2) mate with many partners at every opportunity; and (3) try to improve their reproductive success relative to other females by depleting sperm supplies that would otherwise be available for their rivals.

For females in multimale groups, sexual advertising is an energy-efficient way of getting the job of mating done. But what about females in monogamous pairs or in groups in which one male travels with a number of females and their offspring? Such females don't need sexual swellings. Living in a harem serviced by one male, females don't need a way to call in all the males; instead, they have more to gain with flexibility, by being able to shift strategy and become receptive depending on conditions. For example, if a female hides her ovulation, she is free to copulate when a strange male suddenly comes into her troop. This enables her to trick a possibly infanticidal male. If she is already pregnant, she can still copulate with the stranger, thereby confusing the issue of paternity and possibly saving her offspring's lives. (Intruder males rarely kill offspring of females with whom they've copulated, but they are known to kill the young of other females.)

Humans, then, have no monopoly on continuous sexual receptivity, a state with a number of benefits for females that are not at all related to pair-bonding. In fact, there is no necessary connection between continuous sexual receptivity and pair-bonding. The most monogamous primates—gibbons—mate for life but engage in very little sexual activity. Female gibbons come into estrus only every two or three years. During that time, they breed for only a few months.

Evidence from other primates does not support the widely circulated theory that human females became continuously receptive because it forced males into pair-bonds and motivated them to bring food back to females and their offspring. Nor does the pair-bonding theory explain other characteristics of human sexuality: face-to-face copulation, female orgasm, and women's prominent breasts. The missionary position is not unique to humans. Both pygmy chimpanzees and orangutans, neither of which are monogamous, copulate in this position. Nor is female orgasm reserved solely for humans. Field researchers report a similar response in other primates. The one feature that *is* uniquely human is permanently enlarged breasts. In other female primates, the breasts enlarge during lactation and then shrink considerably after weaning. Women's breasts also enlarge during lactation, but they never shrivel after weaning. The pair-bonding theory assumes that women's breasts were sexually selected to enhance a female's attractiveness to her mate. An alternate hypothesis is that a woman's permanently enlarged breasts are a signal to men that she has stored enough fat to support pregnancy and lactation. Breasts may have become attractive to men because they indicate the trait that most interests males in choosing mates—fertility.

Looking at humans in the context of other living primates, we see how much of our behavior reflects our animal heritage. We are not as unique as we thought we were. The size difference between males and females, even though slight, is evidence that early humans probably did not live in monogamous pair-bonds but rather in polygynous groups. But since contemporary men do not show as much sexual dimorphism in size as the 4-million-year-old fossils, it seems as if polygyny has steadily decreased in humans, although it has not disappeared altogether. "Male strategy is still polygynously colored and even in the most modern societies strong, influential males have *de facto* access to more females than the average male," writes Shepher.[27]

The relative size of human testicles also makes it unlikely that human ancestors lived in multimale groups. "Humans resemble the small-testicled orangutans, gorillas, and gibbons, suggesting that one-male breeding systems may have been the most ancient adaptation among hominoids," writes Hrdy.[28]

When all of this evidence is considered and compared with evidence from other primates, the likeliest breeding system for human ancestors would seem to have been a one-male polygynous group in which a male lived with several females, or a group in which individuals pursued a mixed mating strategy of polygyny and monogamy. Concealed ovulation and continuous sexual receptivity would have been compatible with either situation.

IS CONCEALED OVULATION AN EVOLUTIONARY DECEIT?

In an extremely original theory, biologist Nancy Burley suggests that concealed ovulation could be an evolutionary deceit to trick women into getting pregnant. In this scenario, concealed ovulation evolved through natural selection "as a response to human and perhaps protohuman attempts to practice contraception."[29]

Other theories try to explain continuous sexual receptivity and concealment of ovulation as a way of deceiving a female's associates, especially the males, but Burley focuses on the fact that ovulation is also hidden from females themselves.

"The self-centered human may often be at odds with natural selection," writes Burley. "Culture does not always oppose natural selection, but it has considerable power to do so.[30] With the development of intelligence, early humans may well have understood the relationship between ovulation, sexual intercourse, and conception. Childbirth is painful and, in preindustrial societies, frequently fatal to women. Even today, somewhere in the world a woman dies as a result of pregnancy or childbirth every minute—more than 500,000 maternal deaths a year.[31]

It is not unreasonable to assume that our ancient female ancestors may have tried to avoid pain and risk of death by abstaining from intercourse near the time of ovulation. "As a result of female desire to avoid conception, physiological changes which lessened female awareness of ovulation were selected for, and eventually ovulation that was not detected resulted," hypothesizes Burley. "Ovulation concealed to females evolved because women less aware of ovulation left, on average, more descendants."[32]

If women were in the dark about the timing of ovulation, they would not know when to abstain and they would be unable to practice this basic method of birth control. Concealed ovulation, then, might well be a grand deception perpetuated through natural selection to ensure reproductive success in spite of females' wishes.

Concealed ovulation also greatly complicated the human male's efforts to ensure certainty of paternity, says Burley. Among nonhuman animals, when signs of estrus are visible, a male knows when his mate is ovulating and can copulate with her frequently and guard her from other males. Not so when her ovulation is concealed. Among humans, a man has to extend courtship and remain with a woman until conception occurs to ensure that only his sperm fertilize her egg. He has no other choice if he wants to be as certain as he can that he will be the father of her offspring.

As with other animals, courtship gives a man and a woman the time to form a bond, test its endurance, and ensure that neither partner has outside interests. The woman would want assurance that the man does not have alliances with any other women; the man would want to know that she has not been impregnated by a rival. Courtship, then, requires a certain amount of time. Overnight courtships would not serve either partner's reproductive success.

As we have seen, families and societies take additional steps to provide a prospective bridegroom and his family with certainty of paternity. The desire for certainty is elaborated into cultural systems that aim to control female sexuality and preserve female chastity for the benefit of both the bride's and the groom's families. Biologist Richard Alexander has argued that legal systems in technological societies can be explained altogether in terms of reproductive competition: *"The function of laws is to regulate and render finite the reproductive strivings of individuals and subgroups within societies, in the interest of preserving unity in the larger group."* (The italics are his.)[33] The unity of society pertains to that segment of society that controls, changes, and enforces the laws.

Certainty of paternity is important to all males, but its importance is intensified in wealthy families because the family holdings—money, land, livestock—will be inherited by children and grandchildren. There is a vested interest on the part of both the bride's and the groom's families in making sure that these children are fathered by the high-investing male.

Adherence to cultural strictures on female chastity and modesty becomes critical, for unless traditions are observed, a woman's family would not be able to marry her to a high-status man who would provide for her and her offspring. It seems that cultural selection has worked hand in glove with natural selection to ensure that women produce offspring in a prescribed manner, whether they want to or not. This has been the pattern not only in tribal societies but also in industrialized countries. To take one extreme example, in 1966, Romanian President Nicolae Ceausescu banned all abortions and contraceptives. By 1986, married women who had not borne at least one child by age twenty-four faced substantial tax penalties. Ceausescu's twenty-five-year campaign to increase Romania's population by 8 million before the year 2000 resulted in great human misery. Today thousands of abandoned children fill crowded orphanages.[34]

Two themes run through human reproductive history: on the one hand, both men and women, like males and females of other species, strive for reproductive success; on the other, women have tried to control their own reproduction by avoiding or terminating pregnancy.

In tribal societies, women practice contraception through the use of herbs, postcoital cleansing, natural spermicides, expulsion of semen, magical concoctions, and rituals. If these methods fail, women attempt abortion through use of very tight belts, the introduction of various objects into the vagina, starvation, and abrupt jolts or leaps. If abortion also fails, people practice infanticide, which anthropologist Marvin Harris has called "the most widely used method of population control during much of human history."

Even today, women in parts of the Third World practice some of these primitive forms of birth control and abortion, especially where they lack access to contraception or where abortion is illegal. Recent surveys by family-planning workers around the world indicated that except in sub-Saharan Africa,[35] women say they would have had fewer children if they had had more choice in family size and access to contraception. In most Third World countries, the husband decides how many children the family will have, and women—even educated, professional women—believe that he has this prerogative, that it is their duty to obey. It has been observed throughout Asia, Latin America, and in a growing number of African countries that as women receive more than a primary education, the birthrate drops. Improvements in women's status and economic opportunities cause the birthrate to drop even more.

But some husbands violently oppose their wives' use of birth control, and not just in the Third World. During the fall of 1991 in Salt Lake City, Utah, a 39-year-old Mormon father of eight stormed a hospital maternity ward with a handgun, a shotgun, and a bomb consisting of forty-two sticks of dynamite. His mission was to kill the doctor who had performed a tubal ligation on his wife two years previously. He explained his rampage, which left a nurse dead, by saying that he had one more baby in heaven waiting to be born.[36] This kind of violent outburst against a doctor is rare, but anthropologists and family-planning professionals have found that in much of Latin America, Africa, and the Middle East, husbands oppose their wives' use of contraception, partly out of a machismo that is associated with having many children and partly out of the fear that if they do not keep their wives pregnant, the women will take lovers. Some of these men reason that wives who use contraception can have affairs without becoming pregnant. A man who lives and works far away from his home most of the year, as many men in developing countries do, would not be able to tell that his wife had an illicit affair in his absence if she did not become pregnant.

153

In many Third World countries, male attitude is a major impediment to reducing birthrates. "Machismo is one of the cultural obstacles, and it has been a major factor in keeping families large," says Julia Henderson, former secretary-general of International Planned Parenthood Federation and one of the founders of the United Nations Fund for Population Activities, which is now known as the United Nations Population Fund. "Since a man has traditionally been head of the household, he had to be listened to with respect to family size," she says. "In many countries a man is more distressed by losing a son than by losing his wife; so you have to convince him that his children will be healthier, and his sons will grow up stronger and be better able to help him, if he and his wife have fewer children."[37]

Biologically, men have little motivation to practice birth control. Some men view pregnancy as altogether a woman's problem. It is, after all, easy for a man to reproduce; he can launch his sperm and run. When men provide little or no parental investment beyond this biological minimum, there is not even an economic motivation for them to practice birth control. In sub-Saharan Africa, for example, husbands provide very little financial support for their offspring; women are responsible for themselves and their children. Yet it is in these areas that men are most adamantly opposed to contraceptives. The same is true in some of America's inner cities, where households headed by females are on the rise.

Everywhere, it seems, certain groups of men stack the cultural dice to encourage women to make babies. And most women, expecially those in the developing world, have few choices aside from marriage and children. In many societies, tradition places a very high value on childbearing and almost none on anything else a woman does. In most societies, a married woman who doesn't have children is held in low esteem. She may even become a kind of household slave. Furthermore, women may be punished for practicing contraception, abortion, and infanticide. Childless women are considered to have a failure of character. In some societies a husband may divorce a wife who has no children, and some cultures permit a man to take an additional wife if his first wife is barren. Such options are not open to the wives of infertile men.

Although concealed ovulation, in some respects, gave women greater reproductive choice, culture has often negated that choice. Indeed, at every turn culture seems to have worked in the interests of natural selection to ensure, even to *compel* pregnancy.

THE HUMAN PAIR-BOND

In their attempts to trace how monogamy, such as it is, evolved among humans, many anthropologists and psychologists theorize that men and women first formed some kind of pair-bond. According to Joseph Shepher, the human pair-bond probably evolved during the first 2 million years of hominid existence, "but *Homo sapiens sapiens* (modern human beings) is a facultative monogamist [practicing monogamy under some conditions and not under others] and therefore pair-bonding is highly sensitive to ecological, demographic and cultural factors."[38]

Depending on whether hominids lived on the edge of a forest, in the savanna, or in semidesert conditions, they probably experimented with different types of sexual strategies and social organization—one male, multimale, and semi-promiscuous. But, speculated Shepher, these groupings probably shared the following traits:

1. There was no division of labor by sex; both males and females were gatherers and/or scavengers.

2. Females had an estrus cycle and a comparatively long lactation period without estrus.

3. There was no significant selection by females, but males showed preference for mature females in peak estrus to adolescents, leaving the latter to subdominant males or apprentices.

4. Male dominance was the norm in all three types of social organization.

In some hominid groups, males began hunting wild game to supplement the food provided by gathering; these groups, which anthropologists believe led to modern humans, presumably developed quite differently. Brain volume began to grow and the brain began to evolve through the processes of tool using, tool making, and hunting. Larger brain volume could have created a major physiological problem for females, however—the difficulty of delivering babies with huge heads. Shepher speculated that this problem could be solved only by compromise. "Those females that could earlier bear a baby whose head was still not so big that it would kill the mother were selected. But since the baby was born earlier, it needed a long extrauterine gestation. Wider hips and long lactation created a relative disadvantage for the females in hunting as compared with the males. This created gradually the well-known sexual division of labor between the sexes."[39]
Hunting would also have had other social consequences, including the forging of cooperative bonds among males and the reinforcing of the existing male dominance. But hunting was often

unsuccessful, and the gathering of fruits, roots, seeds, and other vegetable food continued to be indispensable for survival. Nevertheless, as hunting earned males more and more dominance and prestige, they may have stopped gathering altogether, leaving that role to women and children. When men returned to the group's camp, females probably exchanged gathered food for pieces of meat. "It is possible," theorized Shepher, "that males were paradoxically attached to females not because hunting was successful, but because . . . it was often not. The quantity or even quality of gathered foods enhanced the economic importance of the females' activity."[40]

156   Such an exchange of food could have pushed sexual size difference even further. Since females were not on the run hunting with men, they stored more calories for pregnancy and lactation; fatty rather than muscular tissues evolved in the female body. The traits associated with childbearing—rounded buttocks, wide hips, and enlarged breasts—may have become especially attractive to males. Sex probably also entered the picture. "At the same time, food exchange and sharing between the sexes probably involved exchange of sex against food. Females that were both more attractive and more frequently ready for intercourse became better fed and had better chances of their own as well as their offsprings' survival."[41]

If the male was attracted to a female both economically and sexually, he may have been motivated to invest in her and in her offspring, preferring her to others as the bearer of his own offspring. But he wanted to know that the offspring in which he invested were his. No conscious association between sex and procreation would have been necessary. Other animals living in mating systems with high paternal investment don't have conscious knowledge of the correlation between the two, but they act as if they do. The only way a male could achieve certainty of paternity with a female that showed no visible sign of estrus would be to make exclusive the sexual contact with his female.

In the hunting-gathering society, females would be interested in bearing the offspring of powerful hunters who could provide them with more meat and protection. Since females could be sexually receptive whenever they chose, they could take their time selecting mates. Of course, not all the females could choose the best hunter as the father of their children; nor were all females equally attractive. It is in the context of hunter-gatherers that Shepher saw the human pair-bond evolving. "Male and female selection and sexual strategy matched each other, creating the pair-bond as a specific human innovation," he said.[42]

As with other monogamous primates, the essence of the human pair-bond is both male and female parental investment in their offspring. But the dependence on the pair-bond is different for the two sexes. The birth of children has a different impact on men and women; the presence of children may strengthen or weaken the pair-bond. "In 'normal' conditions when males have the wherewithal to support the mother and baby, it strengthens the pair bond for both sexes," says Shepher. "But if not, it weakens it, as the alarming number all over the world of matrifocal [female-headed] families indicate. For the female, the birth of children *always* strengthens *the dependence* on the pair bond."[43] For a woman with an infant, being able to count on the reliable assistance of a man would be critically important both to her survival and to that of the offspring.

If the psychological state of love also evolved between man and woman, the bond was reinforced by emotions, becoming more than a sex-for-food-and-protection contract and extending beyond the breeding period. If female choice operated as it should have to select the most parental men as mates, this would have had a profound impact on behavior, influencing human males to become more and more involved in child rearing, eventually making men the most parental of male mammals. As men were motivated to invest more of their time as well as their resources in their mate and children, a more monogamous arrangement could evolve.

Again, reproductive success—viability of offspring—is the master control of the male-female bond. According to psychologists Ada Lampert and Ariela Friedman, parenting is the most ancient and significant connection of the two sexes and the most ancient difference between the sexes. These researchers speculate that when human ancestors left the security of the forest and started life in the dangerous savanna, successful child rearing became so difficult that cooperation of both mother and father was essential. The male probably had a combined reproductive strategy of great investment in care for his children along with a temptation for promiscuous affairs, which would risk only his minimal biological investment. But the mother, strongly committed to her children and bound irrevocably to her parental investment, learned to expect her partner's help and to fear his desertion. "Thus, the unequal parental investments create unequal parental strategies, which put the parent that invests more, in a state of *'relative vulnerability,'* by which we mean the *apprehension of being deserted and the feeling of dependency on the partner* [emphasis mine]."[44]

For the human female, monogamy may have guaranteed protection, food, and even love . . . for a while. But the price may have been a gradual loss of economic independence and a dependence on males from which she is still trying to recover.

SEVEN

ιℚ

LOVE: THE ROMANCE OF REPRODUCTION

Love is a means of reproducing, and human beings, no less than other animals and plants, tend to be very good at it.

DAVID BARASH
The Hare and the Tortoise
1986[1]

LOVE MAY BE the ultimate ruse in the reproductive game, the grandest trick of all for ensuring that humans produce babies. We say that love makes the world go round, that we can't live without it, that it is the essential ingredient in male-female relationships, that life would be colorless and deficient without it. But all of this is poetry. In the context of evolutionary biology, the key question about love is whether it evolved as an adaptive psychological state.

Biologically, the end point of passionate love seems to be pregnancy, as many an unprepared couple have discovered. Of course, love isn't a prerequisite for copulation or pregnancy. Most of the world's children are born within arranged marriages, not within love matches. The notion that love and marriage "go together like a horse and carriage" is not universal. Throughout history, love has gone together with adultery, not marriage.

Love and Mate Choice

Marrying for love is a relatively new phenomenon, and one that is also predominantly Western. Most of the world's marriages have been and continue to be arranged by parents for social and economic reasons. Even today, a woman who marries for love is considered by many cultures to lack good judgment. "To marry for love without land or chattels could assure nothing but a life of penury," notes Barbara Hanawalt in her study of marriage among English peasant families during the Middle Ages.[2]

160

The same could be said for women of any period who, for lack of education and economic opportunity, were forced to depend on men for their livelihood. This is still the situation of many Third World women and, until the twentieth century, was true for most women in the Western world as well. As Betty Friedan observed in her classic book, *The Feminine Mystique*, "Only economic independence can free a woman to marry for love, not for status or financial support, or to leave a loveless, intolerable, humiliating marriage, or to eat, dress, rest, and move if she plans not to marry."[3]

In societies that permit individuals to marry for love, both women and men can be more selective. "Freedom of choice is . . . associated with greater romantic love as a basis of marriage, with impractical grounds of choice, and with greater male-female antagonism in courtship," write anthropologists Paul Rosenblatt and Paul Cozby, who conducted a cross-cultural study of courtship patterns. Of seventy-five societies in their study, forty-three permitted freedom of choice of spouse. In these societies, there was greater contact between men and women and a greater frequency of dances, which provided socially approved opportunities for women and men to meet. There was also more frequent marriage to someone within the local community. Wherever there is freedom of mate choice, people tend to marry individuals whom they see often. In the United States, for example, people tend to choose mates who live close by.

The researchers found that for an individual to experience love, it seemed sufficient to be psychologically drawn to a member of the opposite sex and to label this arousal as love.[4] Feelings of affection and courtly love were more important among individuals with greater freedom of choice, but there was also greater exaggeration of qualities (versus objectivity), and sex was more important as a source of attraction.

THE ROOTS OF LOVE

Romantic love grows out of sexual attraction, which is the impetus for mating in all species. The feeling we identify as human love may have evolved among our hominid ancestors in the context of friendships. Such friendships have been observed among some nonhuman primates. "Attraction to members of the opposite sex at times when sex itself is unlikely, strong individual partner preferences, and long-term special relationships between males and females indicate that in some nonhuman primates, as in humans, mate choice is intimately related to social bonds," says biologist Barbara Smuts.[5]

Among some macaques and savanna baboons, for example, certain males form a sustained consortship with a particular female. "In some cases, males continue to prefer a favorite female even when she is not near peak estrus and other females are," says Smuts,[6] adding that male savanna baboons that have lived in a group for several years form friendships with middle-aged and old females—a striking contrast to the preference of older men for young women.

Adolescent male and female savanna baboons also form friendships. "These friendships increase the reproductive success of both females and males by facilitating reciprocal exchanges of benefits," says Smuts. Females and their infants are protected by their male friends from other males and possibly from predators as well. The male friend, in turn, is favored by his female friend as a mate.

It is possible that a psychological state beyond conscious control evolved in our human primate ancestors as part of the attraction process. The psychological condition that we call love could have made the attraction overpowering, leading not only to erotic pleasure but to culmination in a breeding bond between male and female.

161

THE NAKED APE DISCOVERS LOVE

In *The Naked Ape,* written in 1967, British zoologist Desmond Morris speculated that the evolution of the pair-bond was critical to human development. He defined the pair-bond in terms of an emotional attachment: "Male and female hunting apes had to fall in love and remain faithful to one another."[7] Such a pair-bond, suggested Morris, solved three problems: (1) females remained bonded to their individual males and faithful to them while they were away on the hunt; (2) serious sexual rivalries between males were reduced, and this helped them to develop cooperation; (3) the development of a one-male-one-female breeding unit benefited the weak, dependent human offspring.

More recent research on human and nonhuman primate behavior suggests that Morris, like other biologists before him, may have projected onto evolutionary history more of the Western attitude toward monogamous marriage and sexual fidelity than the facts would support.

Since behavior leaves no fossils, it is impossible to know with certainty how our human primate ancestors behaved more than 3 million years ago. But we may not have changed as much as our technological advances would indicate. The most widely spread "relic" we have of early man is modern man, says behavioral scientist and physician David Hamburg.[8] "It's useful to think of ourselves as an ancient species in a modern world. Our biology hasn't had much time to change since the Industrial Revolution. Our bodies, including our brains, are very largely shaped by millions of years of evolution prior to these few generations since modern technology burst upon the scene and transformed the world."[9]

For this reason, anthropologists find the few remaining pre-industrial cultures of special interest. By studying the Yânomamö, the Sharanahua, the Kipsigis, the Herero, and other tribal societies, we learn more about our species, *Homo sapiens,* as we were prior to urbanization and industrialization. With advances in communications technology, we can look each other in the eye across vast distances, fax letters to remote islands, and beam images of different life-styles into tribal villages and Western living rooms. Never before in the history of human evolution has it been possible for so many people to see for themselves that despite our many cultural differences, we have no biological differences. Men and women everywhere court, mate, and reproduce. Everywhere women are attracted to high-status men with resources. Everywhere men are attracted to voluptuous young women. Culture aids and abets reproduction . . . everywhere.

The feeling of love bridges cultural differences, but on its most fundamental level, love bridges sexual differences. Medical psychologist Dr. John Money defines falling in love as "the experience of establishing a pair-bond."[10] He speculates that this bond "maintains itself at its level of highest passion typically for a maximum of two or three years. It may be construed as nature's guarantee that a pregnancy will ensue."[11] If this indeed is the case, if love evolved as a psychological state contributing to an individual's reproductive success, it is surely one of the most complex mechanisms of mate choice.

The growing number of researchers who are looking at the biological aspects of love include psychologists Phillip Shaver, Cindy Hazan, and Donna Bradshaw. They write, "Our idea, which needs further development, is that romantic love is a biological process designed by evolution to facilitate attachment between adult sexual partners, who, at the time love evolved, were likely to become parents of an infant who would need their reliable care. Romantic love and infant care-giver attachment thus both contribute to reproduction and survival."[12]

The biological goals of love, says psychologist David Buss, are (1) to attract a mate, (2) to retain that mate, (3) to reproduce with that mate, and (4) to invest parentally in the resulting offspring.[13] Just as evolutionary biology would predict, the ways in which men and women in love go about attracting each other reflect the differences in male and female reproductive strategies. Buss points out that "the first goal of acts of love is resource display." Whatever the culture, courting males tend to display their resources—

their wealth. In Western countries this display among middle- and upper-class men takes the form of gifts, dinner dates at elegant restaurants, large tips, expensive clothes, cars, or anything else that conveys the message "I can provide." Women, on the other hand, tend to display their physical appearance, emphasizing their youth and health, which, in biological terms, convey the message "I can have a baby."

In addition to displaying their resources or fertility, the love-smitten couple tend to do all they can to demonstrate their faithfulness to each other. For a man, a woman's display of fidelity ensures that he will father any offspring resulting from the union. For a woman, a man's display of fidelity ensures that his resources will be directed toward her and their children.

Although the biological link between love and babies seems clear enough, most of the literary rhapsodizing about love omits any association with reproduction. It's easy to understand why. The heat of passion seems to have little connection with diaper rash. Being on call twenty-four hours a day until a child leaves for college is hardly the stuff of love songs. Romance enables lovers to deceive themselves about the likely consequences of their overwhelming passion. And, like it or not, self-deception figures prominently in love.

What Is This Thing Called Love?

As the popular song title suggests, love is almost impossible to define. Psychologist Dorothy Tennov even felt that the word *love* was inadequate to describe the intense emotional preoccupation that afflicts some individuals to such an extent that they are hardly able to focus on anything else. She applied the word limerence to this state, emphasizing that it can happen to any person of any age, that it is "entirely involuntary once it takes hold," and that "for many individuals, recovery is never complete." Tennov speculates that limerence is related to reproductive choice and points out that in most cultures in which marriages are arranged, "there are powerful anti-limerence forces operating." According to Tennov, those who experience the limerent state feel that it is necessary to life, although they also may feel that "it is odious in retrospect after full recovery. . . . What conditions foster the state, the biology of the state, these are as yet total unknowns."[14]

Whether we call the condition love or limerence, it has traditionally been attributed more to women than to men. "Love is the whole history of a woman's life, it is but an episode in a man's," wrote the eighteenth-century French author Madame de Staël.[15] Over the centuries, poets, novelists, and philosophers of many cultures, from ancient Greece to contemporary America, generally have agreed that women are more strongly affected by love. But this view may be the result of cultural conditioning. Western societies in particular have promoted an image of women as weak, love-smitten creatures, inadequate for politics and economics. A woman who is preoccupied with romance has no time to challenge the male bastions of power.

In the literature of fiction, poetry, and psychology, love has been called a sickness, a form of insanity, a state of ecstasy, an exquisite passion, and the ultimate psychological bond—all conditions that Tennov found among the subjects who admitted to having experienced limerence. But love or limerence may also function as a form of deceit, making the love-smitten or limerent person highly susceptible to his or her own fantasies. "What is true love itself if it is not chimera, lie, and illusion?" wrote the eighteenth-century French philosopher Jean-Jacques Rousseau. "We love the image we make for ourselves far more than we love the object to which we apply it. If we saw what we love exactly as it is, there would be no more love on earth."[16]

No phrase in English or, perhaps, any language gets a more knee-jerk response than "I love you." Women in particular seem to have an intense need to hear it, to read it, and to fantasize about it, as the booming market in romance novels demonstrates. Although men, too, can become obsessed by love, they seldom make it the central focus of their lives. No social rewards and customs have taught men that their lives depend on love. Men learn that love is one of life's highlights, but not the essential experience on which to judge their success or failure as human beings. Not surprisingly, men seem to learn early on how to manipulate love for sexual gratification, and many women allow themselves to be manipulated.

"It's easy to get American women to go to bed with you," a wealthy young man from India told me years ago. "All you have to do is say you love them and call them darling." A male artist friend of Russian descent observed, "If a man can talk, he can get any woman to go to bed with him; it doesn't matter what he looks like." An urban American man told of courting a woman who was distressed because he never said, "I love you." He explained that that was because he didn't love her. He was astounded when she replied, "Even if you don't mean it, just say the words. I need to hear them."

Three little words. We are a verbal species with language— spoken and written—and words are loaded with meaning, emotions, memories, and promise. Entire scenarios can be embodied in a word. A conversation is an experience—of a different order than walking or swimming, but an experience nonetheless. Words, and their associated feelings, linger in the mind long after physical actions have been forgotten. And we learn to expect certain words in certain situations. Love words, in particular, are imbued with power.

THE POWER OF LOVE

Although the condition we call love may have entered the human psychological inventory millions of years ago, the word *love* first entered the English language around A.D. 825. Its Latin root, *lubet*, means "it is pleasing." The variation, *lubido*, means "desire," and the Sanskrit root, *lubh*, means "to desire." The ancient Greeks recognized two kinds of love—agape and eros. Agape was brotherly or spiritual love, such as a god might have for humankind, and had no sexual implications. Eros, personified as the god of love, referred to sensuous desire. In the context of attachment between the sexes, love means intense attraction between a man and a woman. For some anthropologists and psychologists, love means pair-bondedness. In the context of families, love refers to the bond of attachment between parents and children, most particularly between mother and infant. Some experts say that this first love bond is the basis for all others.

Probably more has been written about love in all languages than about any other subject, yet it remains a nebulous, undefinable feeling of varying intensities. Each individual professes to know when he or she is in love, but that knowledge is not objective. Love is an interior, subjective condition that, in its intense limerent state described by Tennov, can be akin to a disease; the victim is feverish, dizzy, and vascillates from ecstasy to despair. People in love often describe feeling out of control, their lives dominated by the force of the attraction for the beloved.

167

One may even be temporarily blinded by love; the love-smitten person tends to project his or her own idealized image onto the loved one, often overlooking certain unpleasant realities of that person's character and behavior. In no other state of mind are people more caught up in fantasy, in seeing only what they wish to see. A sophisticated riddle goes like this: what do lovers have in common with the Rorschach inkblot test? The answer is, they project their own image onto each other. A long-lasting love match, John Money speculates, is one "in which there is reciprocally a very close love-blot match."[17] How a man thinks his lover feels about him may be much more important than how his lover actually feels, and the same applies to women.

Psychologist Robert Sternberg describes his "triangular" theory of love as containing three components: (1) an emotional component—feelings of closeness, intimacy, and bondedness that one experiences in loving relationships; (2) a motivational component, which encompasses the drives that lead to romance, physical attraction, and sexual consummation; and (3) a cognitive component, which encompasses, in the short term, the decision that one loves another, and in the long term, the commitment to maintain that love. "The amount of love one experiences depends on the absolute strength of these three components, and the kind of love one experiences depends upon their strengths relative to each other," writes Sternberg.[18]

Sternberg's research shows that the single most important

element for success in a romantic love relationship, for both men and women, is the sharing of ideas and interests with one's lover. Also high on the list is the sense of growing personally through the relationship and taking pleasure in doing things for the other person. Any of these factors is more likely to lead to a long-lasting relationship than the initial attraction of sex. Sternberg and others agree that emotional involvement appears to be at the core of all loving relationships, whether between children and parents, siblings, lovers, or close friends.

Sternberg divides the cognitive component of love into two aspects: (1) the short-term—the decision that one loves a certain other; (2) the long-term—the commitment to maintain that love. These two aspects don't necessarily go together. As almost everyone knows from personal experience, the decision to love doesn't necessarily imply a commitment to stay in love. In effect, the institution of marriage as we know it in the West represents a legal contract to love another throughout life. Sternberg suggests that the cognitive component may help people get through the ups and downs of a loving relationship.

But why do we feel love? What accounts for that love-at-first-sight attraction? Love as an intense psychological state could have served an adaptive purpose in our ancestral past, ensuring that male and female mated, conceived, and stayed together in a harsh environment long enough to care for weak and dependent offspring. The environmental context in which love may have evolved has long since disappeared, but the feelings and longings have been programmed in our genes. The contemporary emphasis on romantic love may represent a degeneration of what was once adaptive behavior into a futile craving for flowery words and empty phrases. The feeling that we call love may be a kind of emotional appendix, a vestige of a former time.

THE QUEST FOR LOVE

In spite of the deceptive aspects of love and the discomfort of its emotional highs and lows, the quest for love in Western culture has become almost an addiction, running through every literary form known—poetry, essays, short stories, novels, films, soap operas, and songs. It is difficult to read a book or see a movie—in any language—that does not have a love story as either the main plot or subplot. In fact, the quest for romantic love has been a dominant theme in Western civilization for more than eight centuries. Its roots are found in the Middle Ages.

Love as both a literary and a social theme was initiated by medieval troubadours. Young French noblemen—usually the younger, landless sons of wealthy families—became traveling poets during the twelfth and thirteenth centuries. Since land was inherited by the eldest son, a younger son lacked resources to attract an upper-class woman as a wife. It was the custom of a noble house to marry off only the oldest son unless an heiress could be procured for a younger son. Most of these young men were simply forced into bachelorhood. With no opportunity for reproductive success through the usual channels of courtship, they could have become fodder for war, like so many other young men without resources. Instead, they invented an ingenious ploy to take care of their sexual and social needs: they redirected the values of knighthood from service in defense of a feudal lord's holdings to service in defense of love for a lady.

169

What set the troubadours apart from any previous literary or social tradition was their veneration of women and their belief that romantic love was life's supreme experience. This view marked a radical departure from the prevailing Christian teaching that passionate love, even between husband and wife, was a sin. "The medieval Church was obsessed with sex to a painful degree," writes historian G. Rattray Taylor. "The sexual act was to be avoided like the plague, except for the bare minimum necessary to keep the race in existence. Even then it remained a regrettable necessity. It was not the act itself, but the pleasure derived from it, that was damnable."[19] According to Taylor, some medieval European men and women tried to diminish sensuous pleasure by wearing a heavy nightshirt known as a *chemise cagoule*, which had a strategically placed hole through which a husband could impregnate his wife without touching her in any other way.

According to the earliest Christian teachings, every woman

was Eve, the temptress responsible for man's fall from innocence. Saint Jerome considered women the gate of the devil, the patron of wickedness, the sting of the serpent. Throughout the Middle Ages, pious Christian writers noted how women sought to woo men from God, displaying their sex appeal even at Communion. And during the time of the plague, men were advised not to sleep with a woman or even to go near a woman's bed lest they increase the risk of infection.

Attitudes handed down from the early Greeks and Romans were not as neurotic, but even they limited love to sex, the only bond recognized between men and women. The Roman poet Ovid viewed love merely as sensual gratification, a kind of cheerfully immoral sport with few sporting rules. Ovid's well-known book of advice on seduction, *The Art of Love*, concerned the pursuit of another man's wife; love and marriage were considered completely different states. Love, in fact, was considered inappropriate to marriage.

Classical literature also held that love was a punishment—a "chastisement inflicted on men by the gods."[20] All of the classical views of love reflected only a male perspective. The poetry of the troubadours departed from the past in taking a kinder, more respectful attitude toward women, at least toward those of the upper class. The main components of troubadour poetry were: (1) homage to a lady; (2) true love as endless suffering; and (3) chastity as the highest expression of true love. This tradition of courtly love appeared during a period when some aristocratic women were gaining economic power. The absence of husbands off to fight in the Crusades gave medieval Frenchwomen the opportunity to control land just as the absence of men in World War II gave American women the opportunity to join the work force. By the beginning of the tenth century, women were in charge of a number of fiefs in the region of southern France known as Provence. With women holding the authority associated with land ownership, the militaristic values of feudal society were open to challenge. Opportunistic young noblemen looking for work as knights in the service of a wealthy lord suddenly had to plead their cases to powerful women. Their strategy was artful—the invention of troubadour poetry, which might be considered the medieval version of the modern romance novel.

Turning the tradition of military knighthood to the service of women, the troubadours became knights of love, pledging their loyalty, obedience, and service to the wife of a feudal lord. In this feudalism of love, the troubadour became a vassal to the aristocratic lady, even addressing her in the masculine form, *midons*, meaning "my lord" in Provençal French. He wrote highly romantic poetry extolling her virtues and committing himself to her in heart and spirit, and whenever possible in body. Accompanied by hired musicians called jongleurs or gleemen, troubadours traveled from castle to castle entertaining the aristocracy. But there was a social message hidden in their love songs.

171

Troubadour lyrics contained the seeds of social change. The poetry gave women the same status as men, but this wasn't its most subversive message. Love ennobled, sang the troubadours, making lover and beloved equals regardless of social class and wealth. The impact of this democratic idea on a rigidly stratified medieval society was equivalent to the tearing down of an emotional Berlin Wall. A great division between social classes was being attacked, not because of any democratic ideal, but from the desire of the troubadours for access to power through powerful women.

Andreas Capellanus, the twelfth-century codifier of courtly love, wrote model arguments that young men might use in a variety of different situations. For example, Capellanus suggested the kind of plea a middle-class young man might make to a noblewoman: "Love is a thing that copies Nature herself, and so lovers ought to make no more distinction between classes of men than Love himself does. Just as love inflames men of all classes, so lovers should draw no distinctions of rank, but consider only whether the man who asks for love has been wounded by Love. Supported by this unanswerable argument, I may select for my beloved any woman I choose so long as I have no depravity of character to debase me."[21]

In feudal society, the idea that love could overcome barriers of social class and wealth was revolutionary. The argument served the troubadours well, however. It may have been in their own self-ish interests to tout love as a democratizing force, but the larger social implications did not remain locked in poetry. In 1209 Pope Innocent III waged a campaign known as the Albigensian Crusade against various forms of expression that the church considered subversive and heretical. Targets included troubadour poetry and courtly love. Many troubadours became exiles in Italy or Spain. Those who stayed behind and continued writing camouflaged their passion for woman in religious symbolism, making her immortal, the Virgin Mary. It was a grand poetic deceit.

The thirteenth-century troubadour Uc de St. Circ wrote: "To be in love is to stretch toward heaven through a woman." The Italian poet Dante adopted the concept in the form of his beloved Beatrice. In the *Divine Comedy*, Dante proclaimed love the supreme experience of life, setting forth a major theme in Western literature—the quest for love through woman. The catch was that the woman was put on an ideological pedestal where she was expected to stay, restricted from full participation in life. This limitation, however, was not immediately apparent. For wealthy medieval women, the concept of courtly love represented new freedom.

In their pursuit of romantic love, troubadours let the genie of democracy out of the bottle. Author C. S. Lewis remarked that the troubadours "effected a change which has left no corner of our ethics, our imagination, or our daily life untouched, and they erected impassable barriers between us and the classical past or the Oriental present. Compared with this revolution the Renaissance is a mere ripple on the surface of literature."[22]

Today it's hard to imagine how medieval love songs could have had such a profound influence, but keep in mind that few people were literate at the time. What television and VCRs are to us, troubadour poetry was to the medieval upper classes. Troubadour ballads were the Middle Ages' pop music, the first literature written in common, everyday speech. Many princes hired small armies of copyists and illuminators to write down the music and lyrics, which bespoke youthful passion. By the beginning of the thirteenth century, imitations of the Provençal *chanson*, or love song, were being written in Italian, German, and Spanish.

Love, you make me tremble so violently that because of the joy I have I do not see or hear or know what I am saying or what I am doing. A hundred times do I discover, when I think about this, that I ought to have good sense and a sense of proportion (and I do have this, but it lasts but a little time for me), for when I contemplate it, my joy turns to pain. But I know well that it is the custom in love that the man who loves well has scarcely any good sense.

So wrote the celebrated troubadour Bernart de Ventadorn. Then as now, some men made fools of themselves over women, and the knights of love had their own living caricatures. One of these, Ulrich of Lichtenstein, a German knight and minnesinger, or troubadour, reportedly had his upper lip amputated because it displeased his mistress. It is also alleged that he cut off one of his fingers and used it, set in gold, as a clasp for a volume of poems that he sent to his lady.[23]

The love celebrated by the troubadours was centered on adulterous passion. "The game of love was . . . the expression of profound hostility to marriage," remarked anthropologist Georges Duby in his book about marriage in twelfth-century France.[24] "Love can have no place between husband and wife," wrote Capellanus in his book, *The Art of Courtly Love.* Scholar Meg Bogin suggests that the poetry penned by troubadours may have been a medieval con game. The troubadour's cunning ruse was to work his way into his lordship's service by working his way into his ladyship's bed. "Courtly love was essentially a system men created with the dreams of men in mind," Bogin reminds us.[25] Both the noblewoman and her husband felt honored by the troubadour's verses. In many cases, the husband invited the troubadour to live in his court . . . at least so long as the poet's admiration for his wife maintained the pretense of literary idealism. Just how often poet and lady were swept away by the power of the lines is impossible to say.

Troubadour poetry can be seen as a form of male-male competition, younger men using their songs to sneak a copulation with the wives of older, dominant men. "Romantic love was at first

173

adulterous and seen as totally incompatible with marriage," writes anthropologist Robin Fox. "In its troubadour form, it exquisitely embodies the agonies of the underprivileged males from whom the 'ladies' had been taken by the hard old warrior knights."[26]

The troubadours' view of life persists to this day. The romantic love they defined, as French writer Denis de Rougemont points out, was "perpetually unsatisfied." The endless longing embodied in courtly love profoundly influenced European romanticism, which "may be compared to a man for whom sufferings, and especially the sufferings of love, are a privileged mode of understanding," writes de Rougemont.[27]

174

Throughout the long popularity of troubadour poetry, the pedestal on which woman was placed grew higher and higher, until, in Dante's *Divine Comedy*, it reached Heaven itself. But there is evidence that the wealthy ladies to whom this poetry was addressed preferred a more down-to-earth relationship. Women's feelings about love were expressed in the poetry of female troubadours, or *trobairitz*, who were largely unacknowledged by literary historians. Bogin's scholarship uncovered twenty known women troubadours. Some were the objects of the male troubadours' adoration, and all were aristocrats—the only level of society in which people had sufficient education, wealth, and leisure to pursue the arts. Some of the *trobairitz* exchanged verses with the male troubadours, but their writing differed. "The most striking aspect of the women's verse is its revelation of experience and emotion," says Bogin. "Unlike the men, who created a complex poetic vision, the women wrote about their own intimate feelings. In all their poems, the women argue for a *real*, as opposed to a symbolic acknowledgement of their importance."[28]

The Countess of Dia, for example, penned these sentiments:

"Handsome friend, charming and kind,
When shall I have you in my power?
If only I could lie beside you for an hour
and embrace you lovingly—
Know this, that I'd give almost anything

to have you in my husband's place,
but only under the condition
that you swear to do my bidding."

In a tenson, or poem taking the form of a dialogue between two people, the two troubadours Maria de Ventadorn and Gui d'Ussel argued about the rank of lovers. Maria posed the question:

"When a lady freely loves a man, should she do
as much for him as he for her,
according to the rules of courtly love?"

Gui replied:

"The lady
ought to do exactly for her lover
as he does for her, without regard to rank;
for between two friends neither one should rule."

But Maria disagreed:

"Gui, the lover humbly ought to ask
for everything his heart desires,
and the lady should comply with his request
within the bounds of common sense;
and the lover ought to do her bidding
as toward a friend and lady equally,
and she should honor him the way
she should a friend, but never as a lord."

Gui argued that the lady owed her lover equal honor since they were equally in love, but Maria disagreed again, pointing out that a new suitor got down on his knees and asked permission to serve the lady. Thus, argued Maria, "to me it's nothing short of treason if a man says he's her equal *and* her servant."[29]

Clearly, these medieval women enjoyed manipulating the young men who were so ready to do their bidding in the name of love. For both sexes, courtly love was a sporting game.

A *trobairitz* poem with three female characters, Alais, Iselda and Carenza, addressed the question of whether to get married. One character states she doesn't want to marry, "for making babies doesn't seem so good, and it's too anguishing to be a wife." Another agrees: "Lady Carenza, I'd like to have a husband but making babies I think is a huge penitence; your breasts hang way down, and it's too anguishing to be a wife." Any of these sentiments could have been written today.

A social by-product of the troubadour movement was an obligatory deference to women as the weaker, purer, more virtuous sex. This attitude, while an improvement on the older view of women as property, provided yet another male argument to isolate women from politics and power. Although the manners of aristocratic men softened, their attitude toward poor women remained unchanged. In a chapter called "The Love of Peasants," Capellanus advised male aristocrats that it's all right to rape lower-class women: "If you should, by some chance, fall in love with a peasant woman, be careful to puff her up with lots of praise and then, when you find a convenient place, do not hesitate to take what you seek and to embrace her by force."[30] The lord of a fief had the absolute right to rape his serf's bride on her wedding night. This practice, known as *ius primae noctis*, was widespread and continued into the fifteenth century.

Despite the new emphasis on romantic love and the poetic elevation of women, marriage in medieval France continued to be "a creation of the aristocracy, an economic and political contract designed to solidify alliances and guarantee the holdings of the great land-owning families," writes Bogin.[31] A medieval woman's value—like that of many women in the world today—was based on her ability to bear sons. If she failed repeatedly, she was sent home to her parents or to a convent. Nevertheless, troubadour poetry was a harbinger of sexual and social liberation; it set the stage for Western courtship as a period during which men and women could see each other often and reciprocate tender feelings, allow romantic love to influence mate choice, and, perhaps, forge a lasting bond between them.

Modern Romances and Female Choice

The contemporary version of troubadour poetry is the romance novel. Written by and for women, romance novels apparently fulfill the romantic fantasies of millions. Sales figures indicate that the market is insatiable.

Romance novels are structured according to this general formula: a worthy young woman, usually innocent and childlike, falls in love with an older, sexually experienced, extremely masculine, wealthy, high-status man—exactly the kind of male predicted by the principles of female choice. Throughout a long courtship beset with obstacles, the heroine's sensuality is awakened. The leading man finally initiates her into sex and adulthood. Through the heroine's love the hero's promiscuity, his rough edges, and sometimes his violence are tamed. The ending is always a happy confirmation that love, courtship, and marriage are the supreme experiences of a woman's life. As literary analyst Kay Mussell has noted: "Romances suggest that the greatest adventure for a woman occurs when she finds the one man with whom she will share the rest of her life."[32] And, indeed, that *is* the great adventure in the lives of most women.

The romance novel is a curious genre. Women derive enormous pleasure from reading these fantasies even though they reinforce the sexual double standard: the hero should be sexually experienced, the heroine virginal. He may have other women in his life, but she waits to choose him, acting out the one-best-man fantasy. She also acts out the female fantasy of beauty and the beast—finding a prince behind a beastly countenance. Through love, the heroine domesticates the man, overcoming his wildness with her innocence, her tenderness, her childlike honesty. "Women in romances appear to be self-deceived. They often do not know what they want until they are told by the hero, who offers both love and adult identity in the same package," writes Mussell.[33]

The one-track formula of contemporary romance fiction seems sinister, but there is no evidence that publishers are engaged in deliberate behavioral manipulation to keep women subordinate.

The primary behavior that interests publishers is the book-buying habits of their readers. Publishers are out to make money, and they have discovered that the romance novel is an enormously successful formula that appeals to women. Publishers give romance readers exactly what they want. Feminists may not like the messages, but there is no denying their popularity.

Critics like Mussell, however, have pointed out that in the process of providing a few hours of fantasy escape, the romance novel reinforces the patriarchal status quo and functions to keep women in their proverbial place. The romance, like a drug, yields temporary, illusory relief and wish fulfillment but provides neither ideas nor encouragement to help women deal with the real problems from which they might wish to escape—a domineering or abusive husband or boyfriend, an enslaving marriage and/or job, a sense of low self-esteem. "In summary, romances can be termed compensatory fiction because the act of reading them fulfills certain basic psychological needs for women that have been induced by the culture and its social structures but that often remain unmet in day-to-day existence as the result of concomitant restrictions on female activity," comments literary scholar Janice Radway.[34] She sees romances functioning as "a kind of cultural release valve, enabling women to experience the anger and outrage at men that society does not encourage them to feel."[35]

When a reader closes the final pages of a romance novel, her faith in the power of love and marriage has been reinforced. During the time she has spent reading, she has felt empowered in fantasy; she has been able to exercise more choice than she can in her real life. But that empowerment, like the high from intoxication, ends when the romance ends. The only cure is to get high again—to read more of the fantasy. Unable or unwilling to change the real conditions from which she wishes to escape, the romance reader has accepted the illusory freedom of a romantic deception. "Romance is a form of insanity in which one projects onto another a response to needs unmet and ignores the reality of the other person," writes anthropologist Janet Siskind.[36]

The success of romance novels implies that women are so susceptible to the verbalization of love that they willingly choose to be deceived, even to the point of staying with a mate who repeatedly abuses them. When asked why they remain with an abusive man, many a battered woman has replied: "He said he loved me; he said he'd change." When it comes to love, words are sometimes permitted to speak louder than actions. Indeed, love may be one of the most dangerous conditions of the human psyche, for it seems that people will tolerate, excuse, and commit almost any act in its name.

EIGHT

⟨∾⟩

FEMALE-HEADED FAMILIES BY CHOICE AND BY DEFAULT

Women's unique role in childbearing and rearing, and the risks and benefits therein entailed, is possibly the most fundamental distinction between their experience and that of men.

DAISY DWYER AND JUDITH BRUCE
A Home Divided: Women and Income in the Third World
1988[1]

With or without the resources of men, women are genetically programmed for maternity. Once a woman commits her biology to reproduction, she reaches a point of no return. And when social conditions subvert female choice and block male parental investment, women—and society—are left at the mercy of the selfish genes.

A combination of overpopulation, growing poverty, and lack of jobs is now thwarting these basic evolutionary processes. As a result, family structures, both monogamous and polygynous, are breaking down. The number of female-headed families is increasing all over the world, with dire consequences for most of the women and children involved. Households headed by women are the poorest, their children the most undernourished and undereducated, the standard of living the lowest. Entire groups of people have been forced into the ecological niche of scavengers.

WOMEN AND MEN WITHOUT CHOICES

What happens when female choice for males with resources is denied women? When men must leave their families in order to find work? When the only economic opportunity open to young men is crime? When young women's only route to status is through motherhood? The result is the female-headed, or matrifocal, family, which, for the most part, has become a widespread social disaster. In the countries where female-headed families are prevalent, there are few economic opportunities for women. The household is still the major center of work for most women, and that work is largely unpaid. According to the United Nations, women in many developing countries, especially poor women, are now working sixty to ninety hours a week just to maintain their meager living standards of a decade ago.[2] Although urban growth is providing new economic opportunities for women in Africa, Latin America, and the Caribbean, salaries and status are not commensurate with those of men. Nearly 80 percent of working women in sub-Saharan Africa and at least half in Asia, except western Asia, are in agriculture. Although they work the land, women in Colombia, Nepal, Kenya, Panama, Chile, Iraq, and Egypt are not permitted to own it. In Zambia, Tanzania, Ethiopia, and Nepal, the new so-called land reform laws exclude divorced women from owning land.[3] In effect, societies restrict women's economic mobility and access to wealth, reinforce the female reproductive role to the exclusion of any other, and then punish women for accepting the role.

There appear to be certain predisposing conditions for the emergence of matrifocal families: (1) early marriage age for women; (2) delayed marriage age for men; and (3) a surplus of male migration or abnormally high male mortality.[4] Some minimum of supporting institutions—whether benign or malign—is necessary to perpetuate the female-headed family. The institution of slavery, for example, ruptured many black families in Africa and later in the United States. Similarly, the spread of the Western money economy throughout the world has disrupted traditional cultures and their small cottage industries. The money economy is also associated with even greater division of labor between the sexes and the separation of men from their families as they migrate in search of jobs.

During the late fifties, reports of female-headed families began to appear in the ethnographic literature. These family constellations were found mainly in the Caribbean and the Guianas, and anthropologists considered them an exotic phenomenon. In the Caribbean societies, a girl usually became pregnant at an early age, bore her child in her mother's house, and reared it there. Male children left the household as soon as they were able to work, sometimes traveling great distances to find jobs. When they returned to visit their mother, they usually had a short affair with a young girl of a neighboring household, impregnated her, and then returned to their wandering life.

Since then, more and more evidence of female-headed families has appeared in the literature, and not just from the Third World. The United Nations reports that the percentage of births to unmarried women is rising rapidly in many countries and regions. Some thirteen developed countries, including Australia, Austria, Germany, France, and the United States, show increases in the percentage of births to unmarried women. In Denmark, for example, 11 percent of births were to unmarried women in 1970; in 1985, the figure was 43 percent. In Sweden, births to unmarried women increased from 18 percent in 1970 to 46 percent in 1985, while the U.S. figure jumped from 10 to 21 percent.[5]

Although high divorce rates have influenced the rise in individual cases of female-headed families, larger economic and social shifts have prevented many men from ever acquiring the means to invest in their children.

In their study of the matrifocal family, Pierre van den Berghe and Joseph Shepher[6] describe four types of contemporary female-headed families. The first is the American-Caribbean type, with a historical background of chattel slavery imposed by a ruling class who lived in a monogamous mating system. Female slaves became pregnant by male slaves, who were then prevented by sale or separation from investing in their children. In other cases, slave women were impregnated by ruling-class males who indulged

183

themselves sexually but had no intention of investing in the off-spring. Even if these men had wanted to provide for their mistresses and children, social taboos prevented such investment. But since owners usually wanted more slaves, they did enable the female slaves to provide the minimum care necessary for the offspring's survival. Not even the abolition of slavery changed the economic conditions that perpetuated this type of female-headed family.

A second kind of female-headed family has emerged in India, where there is institutionalized, quasi-hereditary prostitution. In this situation, women are the only providers; males either are pimps or leave the community. Generations of females share the child-care responsibilities.

A third type of matrifocal family occurs among lower classes in Third World cities, especially in western Africa. In these areas women control trade in foodstuffs and textiles in open markets. The price for their economic freedom, however, has been male neglect of offspring and the rise of female-headed households. "The rate of growth of women's labor-force participation since 1950 has outstripped the rise in male workers by two to one," report anthropologists Daisy Dwyer and Judith Bruce. "Apart from this, it has been established that women's compensated labor combined with household production renders them substantial and sometimes predominant economic contributors in all the developing regions of the world. . . . Almost universally, women in Africa are viewed as ultimately responsible for fulfilling children's food needs."[7]

Third World women may be trying to gain a foothold in two areas where they traditionally have had almost no freedom of choice—improving their access to income, and gaining control of their own fertility.

In some societies, however, as women earn more income, men seem to decrease their parental investment. Researcher Joan Mencher found that women in south India "contribute proportionately more of their income to the houshold and withhold less for personal use than men. Even in the months when both earn little, men continue to give a lower proportion of what they earn."

184
ೞ

And when a woman's income was at its lowest point, instead of increasing their contributions, men reduced theirs and kept enough to socialize with their friends at the local tea or toddy shop.[8] In general, no matter how low the family income drops, men in these societies reserve some money for personal status-raising activities. Women, on the other hand, spend less of their income on themselves and more on their families.

The message that emerges from these societies is that when women find a way out of traditional roles that have kept them dependent on men, the men reduce their parental investment. According to anthropologist Ilsa Glazer Schuster, "A common response [of Zambian men] to an increase in income is not to improve the standard of living of one's wife and children—as the wife would expect—but to become promiscuously involved with other women, fathering children as a non-essential by-product."[9] By their actions, these men are telling women that if they want economic independence, they can shoulder the entire family burden. In a sense, men are punishing women who want reproductive and economic freedom. If a woman won't be subservient, a man will withdraw his support, feel no guilt, and pursue his polygynous tendencies. Women then find themselves liberated only to take on additional responsibilities.

A fourth type of matrifocal family occurs in modern, urban industrial welfare states where racial or ethnic discrimination has prevented some groups from acquiring the work skills necessary to earn a decent living. Suffering from unemployment and high job instability, men have been forced to migrate to find jobs. Women, too, are part of the waves of urban migration, but in the main, women with children are left to eke out a bare survival by accepting low-paying, exploitative menial jobs.

In the United States today, there are virtually no jobs for many young men and women. As a result, approximately 50 percent of black American children are now reared in families headed by single females. Many of these children will never know their fathers. Their outlook for the future is grim. Lacking any chance to choose mates who will help to provide for them and their offspring, their mothers have settled for the minimal male parental investment—

sperm. This represents less paternal investment than almost any other female primate finds acceptable. In these cases, it seems that female choice is not functioning at all.

If they have no means of providing paternal investment beyond their sperm, men lack choices, too. Cultural success and reproductive success generally go hand in hand; but if the avenues to the former are closed, the genetic predisposition to breed will assert itself no matter what. The result is an entire underclass of people cut off from full participation in the larger society.

BABIES AS STATUS

Throughout most of recorded history, women have been enslaved by reproduction. All the while, men have tried to control women's fertility. The myth has been that women want babies above all else, that they want babies more than men do, that they trick men into becoming fathers. Observations and field studies, however, support a very different conclusion. Men desire offspring more than women do, and they generally want more children than women want. Although this concept defies conventional wisdom, when viewed through the perspective of evolutionary biology, men's desire for more children isn't surprising. It fits the male reproductive strategy of trying to inseminate as many females as possible to achieve the greatest reproductive success. Of course, men are not *consciously* trying to enhance their reproductive success. They perceive themselves as trying to achieve status, to compete with other males, to prove their masculinity. In much of the world, however, these goals are tied to fathering children, especially sons.

In an unforgettable scene from a Bill Moyers television documentary on the breakdown of black families in America's inner cities, a young man named Timothy McSeed reacts to the birth of his newest illegitimate son by exclaiming, "Yay, a little boy. Little boy. I'm the king! I'm the king."[10]

But illegitimate children are all he has to establish his claim to nobility. McSeed, a high-school dropout, has fathered six children by four women. He does not support any of them, and he has no steady job. Asked by Moyers how it feels to have those children, McSeed replies they are "like artwork. . . . You look at your art, you say, 'This is something that I've done.' It's like carpentry, it's something that you've done. You can see what you've done."

The mothers of McSeed's children raise them with the help of welfare checks. From the jobless McSeed's perspective, what he can't provide the government does. After all, he's contributed his sperm. "I'm highly sexed," he says. "Like most women say, 'You're a baby maker.' I've just got strong sperm, that's all."

For McSeed, the mothers of his children, and others like them living in inner-city poverty, the only success possible in American society may be found in producing babies. "It seem like that's all they be doing around here, is making babies and stuff," Darren, a jobless eighteen-year-old high-school dropout, who has fathered a baby, tells Moyers.

Many jobless young men in America's inner cities put together what is, in effect, a harem of welfare mothers. But unlike the wealthy polygynous man who has resources to support his several wives and their offspring, these unemployed, unskilled young American males have become sexual scavengers who deposit their sperm where they can and accept handouts from their welfare women. "There's a lot of guys that . . . just goes around looking for welfare mothers. And they may have six of them like that, and get a little piece of money out of each of them. That's their job, you know, that's their hustle," says Detective Shahid Jackson, whose beat is McSeed's neighborhood in Newark, New Jersey.

WHEN MALES CAN'T PROVIDE

The young men in Moyers's documentary belong to a growing population of poor minority men in the United States who have no economic opportunities, and thus lack the resources for paternal investment. Deprived of earning a living in legitimate ways, some of them turn to crime.

In 1990, at its national convention in Los Angeles, the National Association for the Advancement of Colored People (NAACP) held a workshop entitled "The Endangered Black Male," during which some alarming statistics were released:

• One of four black men in their twenties is either in jail, in prison, on probation, or on parole.

• Violence is the number-one cause of death for black males between the ages of fifteen and twenty-four. In California, black males are three times more likely to be murdered than to be admitted to the University of California.

• Black males are the only U.S. demographic group whose life expectancy was shorter in 1990 than it was in 1980.

These statistics were given further support by a subsequent report from a nine-year study by the national Centers for Disease Control. "From 1978 through 1987, annual homicide rates for young black males were four to five times higher than for young black females, five to eight times higher than for young white males, and 16–22 times higher than for young white females," says the report. Since 1984, the disparity between homicide rates for young black males and other groups has increased substantially.

The report noted that from 1984 to 1987, the homicide rate for black males between the ages of fifteen and twenty-four leapt more than 76 percent in Michigan, 71 percent in California, and 40 percent for the nation as a whole. This meant a national average increase from 60.5 homicides per 100,000 in 1984 to 84.7 per 100,000 in 1987. In Michigan, the figures were 231.6 murders per 100,000 black men in 1987, and in California, 153 homicides for every 100,000. By comparison, the 1987 national homicide rate for white men in the same age group was 11 per 100,000. Of every 100,000 young females, 17.7 blacks and 3.9 whites die of homicides.

The factors identified as important contributors to homicide in young black men include "immediate access to firearms, alcohol and substance abuse, drug trafficking, poverty, racial discrimination, and cultural acceptance of violent behavior."[11] Homicide has been the leading cause of death for young black men for some years. The Centers for Disease Control pointed out that if a disease had increased by the same percentage as the rate of black male homicides, a massive public-health effort would have been mounted.

The lack of national programs to counter this trend leads to the uncomfortable conclusion that the majority society is unconcerned. The implication is that the dominant white males in American society do not want lower socioeconomic or minority groups—most particularly black males—to achieve either reproductive or social success. In effect, the black male population is being systematically destroyed. By reducing the ability of black males to compete in the marketplace and gain the economic means to invest in their children, society has undercut both female and male mate choice, making itself the provider and, by default, the mate that the female could not choose.

189

But government doesn't really want to provide paternal investment for the poor, either. In the United States, the first casualties of budget cuts usually include maternal and infant health care, early childhood education, day care, and school lunches and breakfasts for poor children. In spite of politicians' avowals that children are the nation's future, official policies do much to ensure that a sizable proportion of children have no viable future at all—and that neither do their parents. The woman is left with the obligatory biological burden of being the sole parent to her children. She usually drops out of school and goes on welfare, thereby reducing her chances for getting an education and the kind of job that would help her to achieve economic independence. The man is deprived of legitimate economic options. Their children join the ranks of the impoverished, malnourished, and uneducated. Society is burdened. Nobody wins.

Some knowledge of evolutionary biology could help people understand that when men are deprived of livelihoods or when they are forced to leave their families to make a living, the result is the female-headed family.

THE DOUBLE BURDEN OF FEMALE-HEADED FAMILIES

Racism and poverty thwart mate choice throughout the world. According to a United Nations Population Fund report, a study of seventy-four developing countries revealed that 22 percent of the households in Africa, 20 percent in the Caribbean, 18 percent in Asia, 16 percent in the Near East, and 15 percent in Latin America were headed by women. It is estimated that worldwide as many as one in three households are headed by women. The majority of these are without men because of migration to find work. In Kenya, for example, where over two-fifths of rural households are headed by women, about sixty thousand men leave drought-ridden Burkina Faso each year to look for jobs in the neighboring Ivory Coast. Two-thirds of these men never return. The story is the same in other countries of the developing world. In Lesotho in 1980, 45.2 percent of rural households were headed by women; fewer than half of those received any money from the absent men. In India, households headed by women comprise 35 percent of the landless rural people.[12]

With men cut off from full participation in marriage and parenting, the basic sex differences in reproduction come into play. It is not that either partner necessarily prefers it that way; it has simply become a circumstance of their lives. Like other female mammals, women have no choice with respect to their biological investment. Although a male can always deposit his sperm and walk away, once a female mammal is pregnant, her parental investment is obligatory and will continue after birth for a period of time that varies with the species. In a very real sense, female mammals subsidize males' reproductive success with their time, energy, and sometimes their lives.

According to the World Health Organization, 1 million or more women die each year from pregnancy-related causes. Ninety-nine percent of these deaths occur in the Third World, where complications arising from pregnancy and illegal abortions are the leading killer of women in their twenties and thirties.[13] As shocking as it seems, maternal mortality accounts for some 25 percent of deaths of women aged fifteen to forty-nine in the Third World.[14] No wonder, then, that women worldwide prefer having fewer children than men do.

According to the World Fertility Survey, from 1974 to 1984, 40 to 50 percent of women of reproductive age in eighteen developing countries desired no more children but had no access to family planning.[15] In traditional Third World societies where both fertility and mortality are high, women may desire fewer children for at least four reasons: (1) health risks, including maternal death, associated with pregnancy, birth, and lactation; (2) social and economic costs of child rearing; (3) the lower likelihood that women will gain the benefits of children because of inheritance patterns and sex bias that favor males; and (4) high fertility, which reinforces men's dominance of women by keeping them so preoccupied with children that they have no time for anything else.[16]

Of course, women also gain status from motherhood. And women, too, desire sons because in many social systems women's only access to economic resources is through their male offspring. But sometimes even a son is no security for his mother. In Uganda, for example, a woman may not have any rights to the land she has spent years cultivating. Traditionally, the son inherits on his father's death, and a widow may not stay in the same house as her son. Her brother may find her a new husband, or someplace else to live.

Daughters, on the other hand, are valuable helpers with a woman's many domestic chores. In parts of Latin America, Africa, and other less developed countries, little girls are kept home from school to carry out tasks that include child care, farming, gathering firewood, hauling water, preparing food, cleaning, washing, and building houses. Little girls in Tanzanian villages, for example, spend two hours every day searching for firewood that is now scarce because of deforestation. Most men are free from the primary role in subsistence. "Fairly consistently, women in all parts of the world put in more work hours (paid and unpaid) than do men of the same age," say Dwyer and Bruce, adding that this pattern occurs from early childhood through old age.[17] At the same time, men often keep the money earned by their wives.

"Women have to kneel to their husbands every morning, begging even for money for matches, paraffin, sugar, or soap," says Joyce Mpanga, Uganda's minister of education. She points out that women produce 90 percent of Uganda's food crops and

191
ౘౘ

60 percent of the cash crops, but men do the marketing and keep the money.[18]

Why do women put up with this kind of domination? There are no hard and fast answers, but the burden of caring for children, and the lack of educational and economic opportunity, can cause a woman to feel that she has no other options. She may also fear that her husband will kill her if she tries to leave. Domestic violence by men against women occurs everywhere, in all regions, classes, and cultures. The full extent of this violence is unknown because only a few small studies have been conducted, but many criminologists believe it to be the most underreported crime. The United Nations has compiled available information on domestic violence in thirty-six countries in the mid-1980s. India, for example, had 999 registered cases of dowry deaths—murder of wives for lack of payment of dowry—in 1985. The numbers were 1,319 in 1986 and 1,786 in 1987. In a study of married women from Bangkok's largest slum and construction sites, more than 50 percent were beaten regularly by their husbands. In 1985, violence against the wife was cited as a contributing factor to the breakdown of the marriage in 59 percent of Austria's fifteen hundred divorce cases. And, in the United States in 1984, nearly a third of the female victims of domestic homicide died at the hands of a husband or partner.[19] Such statistics reinforce the fact that women are consistently treated far worse than females of any other primate species.

THE FEMALE AS SOLE PROVIDER

Most societies consider the desertion of children by their mother a heinous crime, a mental derangement, a violation of the natural order. Desertion by a father, while not praiseworthy, is not treated as an aberration. In some sectors of industrialized society and in many countries of the developing world male desertion, if not accepted overtly, is actually encouraged by withholding job opportunities. In South Africa, men who must migrate far from home to find jobs are permitted to return to their families only once a year—usually around Christmas. Under these conditions, relationships between women and men fracture, and some men never return. The woman is left to raise her children alone or with the help of her family.

Across cultures, in families with a single parent, that parent is overwhelmingly female. Why are there so few male-headed families? The explanation goes back to the fundamental difference between male and female parental investment. Women, like other female mammals, tend to nurture and care for their babies even under the most adverse circumstances. As almost any woman who has given birth can testify, the biochemical bonding between mother and infant is intense. In the early days and weeks following birth, the baby's cries for nourishment and the mother's milk production are perfectly synchronized. It is not unusual for a lactating woman to awaken with milk dripping from her nipples just seconds before her baby cries to be fed. She may feel an inexplicable identification with the tiny being she so recently carried in her womb, and she may be overcome with waves of the most all-consuming love she has ever felt. Nonhuman female mammals also experience an intense biochemical bond with their young and are known to be fierce defenders of their offspring. Natural selection has selected for females that aggressively protect their young.

193

SOCIAL COMPLICITY IN THE FEMALE-HEADED FAMILY

Although ostensibly established to help women and dependent children, the welfare system in the United States has only encouraged further male desertion by supporting female-headed families through welfare payments. In some states, evidence of a male in the household has been grounds for cutting off further payments. Had social planners deliberately set about breaking up families and damaging men, women, and children, they could not have designed a more successful system than welfare, or what is also called aid to dependent children. This system set in motion a vicious cycle, beginning with discouraging men's role as fathers and rewarding women for having babies. As women took new lovers, certainty of paternity was further reduced, damping any man's desire to invest in children whom he could not be sure he had fathered.

WHAT FEMALE-HEADED FAMILIES SAY ABOUT MEN

In some of the instances discussed above, female-headed families evolve by default when economic opportunities are lacking for men of lower socioeconomic status. But one must also ask whether cultures have encouraged men to extend love, to be playful with their children, to listen to them, to help them grow. Some men have developed these facets of their personality, facets that are present in all men but which are not always nurtured. In some societies a display of feelings is considered weak and unmanly. All too often, men have learned to suppress their tender feelings and to cultivate their competitive, aggressive ones. The highly materialistic Western society rewards a man who can pay the bills. But parenting involves far more than bill paying. Money can't buy tenderness, kindness, gentleness, understanding, compassion, respect, fun, creativity. These are character traits—the inner resources of human beings. Unfortunately, in much of Western culture, the father's parental investment as well as his concept of self-worth has been reduced to money.

Researchers Elizabeth and Anne Hill have suggested that "if society could increase men's feelings of responsibility for direct care of children, it could interrupt the feminization of poverty and redress the gender inequality in earnings."[20] In some Scandinavian countries and among some forward-looking Western businesses, paternal-leave policies are encouraging more male participation in child rearing, a great benefit to both the fathers and their children.

CHOOSING TO BE A SINGLE MOTHER

In contrast to the women who become single mothers by default, there is in Western countries a rising group of older, professional women who deliberately choose to become mothers without hus-

bands. They, too, have decided to accept the minimal male parental investment—sperm. But they don't accept just any man's
sperm. These women shop for the best sperm they can find. They
go to sperm banks, study profiles of sperm donors, and choose
what they consider the most desirable paternal genes to pass on to
their child. Or they seek out a man with desirable qualities, sometimes a friend, to impregnate them.

Most of these women choose motherhood at the outer limit of
their childbearing years. For a variety of reasons, they have not
found a man whom they wish to marry and they see little hope that
one will come along. Desiring offspring and aware of the relentless
ticking of their biological clock, they choose to bear a baby alone
rather than remain childless. These economically independent career women, however, are not in the same social or financial straits
as teenage mothers. They can afford to invest both their biology
and their resources in raising a child. Some of these women have
decided that they simply do not want to be bothered with having a
husband as well as a child to care for.

The choice of single motherhood by this stratum of women is
no doubt influenced by feminism, higher education, and economic and social independence. And it is their independence that
many of these women are intent on protecting. They have decided
that they do not need to take on a husband in addition to their
other responsibilities simply to reproduce.

WHEN WOMEN COMPETE FOR MEN

Unlike most of the nonhuman animal kingdom and many human
societies as well, an unusual situation has arisen in the Western industrialized world. Some researchers estimate that females nine-
teen years of age and older have outnumbered like-aged males in
Western societies for perhaps one thousand years.[21] This im-
balance does not contradict the pattern of male-male competition
and female choice that has been discussed throughout this book.
Mating strategies are governed by parental investment, and mate
choice is the prerogative of the sex that makes the greater invest-

ment. Among most animals, this is the female; but there are species, especially *Homo sapiens*, in which males make a considerable parental investment. In these species, males also have varying degrees of mate choice, and in some instances females are the ones who compete for mates. This is the case in the Western world. In some age groups, the enormous variation in men's abilities to provide resources makes marriageable men scarce. As a result, there are fewer males than females, and women are competing for mates more intensely than men.

This reversal of the common mating strategy can be seen quite clearly among some nonhuman species. Some katydid females fight over males that produce a particularly large spermatophore that nourishes the female's eggs and ovaries. The more spermatophore a female eats, the greater the number and size of the eggs she produces. Some male katydids produce such a large spermatophore that they may lose up to 40 percent of their body weight in a single copulation. This would be equivalent to a medium-sized man losing sixty pounds from one act of sexual intercourse! The size of a male katydid's spermatophore, like the size of a man's bank account, is his ticket to reproductive success.

Male tettigoniid katydids of the species *Anabrus simplex*, commonly called the Mormon cricket, are highly desirable mates. These males produce a spermatophore that is almost 25 percent of their body weight. The male expends so much energy producing it that he may copulate only once before he dies.

Like other male katydids, when the male Mormon cricket is ready to mate, he climbs on a plant and begins to sing. Attracted by his courtship song, several females hop quickly across open ground to reach his perch. If two or more females arrive at the male's perch simultaneously, they grapple and bite each other like territorial males of other species. Sometimes the fights last so long that the male leaves and neither female gets him.[22] If the skirmish ends within a reasonable time, the winner climbs on the male's back and jerks up and down as she gets in position to lower her ovipositor—the tube through which the eggs are laid—to receive the spermatophore. If the male accepts her, copulation occurs.

Near the end of copulation, the male contracts his abdominal muscles and inserts a packet of sperm into the female's genital opening. Then he squeezes out a large white mass, known as a spermatophylax, which remains attached to the sperm packet. The spermatophylax and the sperm packet make up the spermatophore. After male and female uncouple, the female reaches around and eats the spermatophore, sometimes feasting on it for several hours.

For some females it's feast or famine, since male Mormon crickets are quite choosy and reject certain females. The male wants the most fecund female—the one with the greatest number of eggs. He may be able to assess the female's fecundity by her body weight. On average, the females accepted by males are heavier than those rejected. Heavier females have larger ovaries and more eggs. They may also be genetically better adapted to survive in an environment where food is scarce.

In other species of katydids, food availability plays a part in determining which sex is more selective. In areas with a rich food supply, such as a clover patch, where females are not as dependent on the spermatophore for food, they become more selective and the males less choosy.[23] By manipulating food availability in the laboratory, researchers have induced a reversal of courtship roles.[24] Biologists D. T. Gwynne and L. W. Simmons took their cue from the behavior of an undescribed genus and species of zaprochiline katydid that feeds only on pollen of certain plants that flower in spring. When these plants are in flower, large numbers of feeding individuals and males calling for mates can be found on a single plant. In nature the role reversal—choosy males—occurs early in the season when flowers are not producing very much pollen and there is a food scarcity. Later in the season, when pollen is more abundant and females can find their own food, they become the choosier sex. Thus even in the nonhuman world economic independence is a factor in female choice.

In their experiments Gwynne and Simmons manipulated the amount of pollen available to the insects and discovered they could switch the role reversal on and off. The switch followed Robert Trivers's theory of parental investment. When provided with supplemental pollen, the females were choosy. In the control field group, however, where pollen was scarce and available only in a male's territory, females competed for additional courtship meals and males were choosy. The scarcity of a needed food resource and the ability of one sex to control that resource are major factors in mate choice in this species.

In the human scenario, high-investing men have become so valuable as mates that women actively compete to win them. Researcher Margaret Hamilton has called this a biologically bizarre situation: women are still making their enormous obligatory biological investment in reproduction, yet they also expend energy to compete. Competing men, it must be remembered, are not, at least at the time, making a huge biological investment in offspring. Their physiological contribution is sperm. But women, whether rich or poor, are stuck with the major biological investment in reproduction. "The fact that females compete despite this huge investment suggests that the male contribution to rearing young is critical to female reproductive success," Hamilton says.[25]

Unlike male sea horses, which have a brooding pouch and actually gestate and give birth to their young, human males have no built-in, anatomical parenting structures. Boys and men have to learn parenting behavior, but, suggests Hamilton, "in unstable eras such as our own, the social process for such learning tends to break down. Thus, females are 'locked in' to their reproductive costs while males are not, a difference that has produced a great deal of tension in modern sexual relationships. The 'sexual revolution' has liberated women from the stigma of freedom in sexual relationships, but it has not liberated them from the biological costs of reproduction."[26] The impulse to reproduce is strong, even when an overwhelming reproductive investment falls to women. It seems as if the stage has been set for an increasing incidence of female-headed families.

If men are not encouraged to be responsible parents, if men do not have economic opportunities that enable them to provide for their offspring, they are in the position of lekking animals without defensible resources. Such men are, in effect, freed from any parental investment at all. Unwittingly or unwillingly, they have been emancipated from the nest. As these men move on to inseminate

198

the next receptive female, women are left to bear and raise the kids as well as to provide their economic support. Or social agencies step in and provide support. This no-win situation is surely not immutable. The fact that humanity remains locked in this maladaptive social dilemma implies irresponsibility on the part of government policymakers and perhaps even a malign unwillingness on their part to empower people to make other choices.

199

NINE

॰ॐ॰

BEYOND THE REPRODUCTIVE IMPERATIVE: THE NEXT STEP IN HUMAN EVOLUTION

*Through most of history the survival of the species has been
dependent upon the willingness of women to bear
(on the average) six to eight children so that two or three might
survive to adulthood. Until the decline of mortality rates in the
nineteenth century, the rebellion of even a minority of women
from this taxing maternity regimen could threaten a group
with slow or rapid extinction.*

SHEILA RYAN JOHANSSON
1976[1]

*The most far-reaching social development of modern times is the
revolt of woman against sex servitude. The most important force
in the remaking of the world is a free motherhood.*

MARGARET SANGER
1920[2]

As ANIMALS, we are relative latecomers on the evolutionary stage;
but we share in a universal heritage of sexual strategies and mating behavior that go far back in time. In a period of less than a

201

century, however, conditions that gave rise to an ancient pattern of human reproductive behavior were irrevocably altered. Technology intervened in natural selection to eliminate some of the harsh controls on population and make resources more widely available to more people—all worthy objectives. But the ancient genetically programmed behavior patterns of male-male competition and female choice, and the drive for reproductive success, did not change accordingly. Within the new context of improved living conditions, the ancient patterns were no longer necessarily adaptive, but people continued to pursue them and to manipulate them for various social or political ends. Acting out of total ignorance of evolutionary biology, humans began misusing sexual differences in reproductive behavior, resulting in the major problems confronting our species today: (1) sex discrimination—the use of biological sex differences to support social systems of sexual inequality that have led to abuses of women; (2) war—the legitimization of state-subsidized male-male violent competition for resources; (3) overpopulation—the natural consequence of the drive for reproductive success in an environment where fewer infants die and more people reach old age.

Not surprisingly, many of our critical quality-of-life problems today center on reproduction. No longer are we threatened by extinction should we produce too few children. Now we are endangered by our reproductive success, our numbers boosted to astronomical heights by advances in sanitation and preventive health care, and cures for diseases that formerly killed young and old alike. Couples need no longer produce six to eight children so that two or three may survive to adulthood. With good prenatal and infant health care, a child born today can look forward to a long life. Lifesaving interventions by medicine and public health, coupled with the ancient drive to have many children, confront us with an unprecedented dilemma: some 5.4 million of us now make up a human swarm that is depleting the planet's resources and lowering the quality of life for all.

As a species, we must now consciously strive to have fewer children so that those we do produce may enjoy an existence on a level higher than the scavenging to which more than a billion impoverished humans—one out of every five people on Earth—have already been reduced. Obviously, we will not stop mating. No matter what the conditions of human life—poverty or wealth; wartime or peace; flood, famine, or pestilence—mating and reproduction will never stop. But there are ways to limit reproduction without devastating consequences for ourselves, our offspring, and our planetary home. A first major task is education. Although our technology has soared into the space age, our self-awareness seems stuck in the age of superstition. Evolutionary biology is as necessary in the curriculum as language. Without a knowledge of evolutionary biology, we cannot hope to understand the human animal or the problems we face.

SEX DISCRIMINATION

In the attempt to control women as reproductive commodities, humans subvert female choice in ways more brutal than those of any other species. These subversions are the source of much social injustice. Among animals, humans present a curious and unique case. We appear to have used sexual differences and inequality in reproductive investment to develop grossly unequal social systems, but with an ironic twist. The female, who makes the greater reproductive investment, has been forced into the subordinate social position. In most societies, men have favored themselves at women's expense; and because enough women have accepted their subordination, the system is perpetuated.

Most Third World societies continue to provide better educational and economic opportunities for boys and men than for girls and women. In some countries male infants receive better nutrition and medical care than girls, resulting in an abnormally higher female mortality. According to the 1991 *Human Development Report*, in Asia and North Africa 100 million women are "missing."[3] Societies in which girls are treated much the same as boys have about 106 females for every 100 males because women, on average, live longer. In Asia and North Africa, however, there are, on the average, only 94 females for every 100 males, a shortfall of about 12 percent from the norm. Throughout the world, by both law and custom, women and girls have traditionally been treated with contempt and derision. Practice of female infanticide, most notably in India, poignantly dramatizes the end point of female inequality and the lengths to which a society will go to achieve reproductive success.

In her studies of the Rajputs, Sikhs, and other eighteenth- and nineteenth-century high-status dowry societies in North India, anthropologist Mildred Dickemann[4] found that the upper class of the highest-ranking castes routinely practiced female infanticide. In some groups there were four boys for every girl; some high-status families had not allowed a girl to survive for many generations. The name of one of the Sikh clans—*Kuri Mar*—means "daughter destroyers."

Today some wealthy Indians are using a new method of skewing the sex ratio in favor of males. Through the prenatal diagnosis techniques of amniocentesis and ultrasound, couples are determining the sex of their offspring. And it has been reported that so many abortions of female fetuses are being performed in Haryana state, the second richest in all of India, that only 874 females are being born for every 1,000 males.[5] As this generation reaches sexual maturity, social strife will be virtually guaranteed as an oversupply of men begin competing for a scarcity of women.

However repugnant practices that discriminate against females may be, it cannot be overlooked that women, having collaborated with and participated in these sytems, are complicit in their own domination.

WAR, WOMEN, AND MALE SUPREMACY

War, the violent form of male-male competition, may have figured in efforts to control both population and female choice. In their analysis of 561 local band and village populations from 112 pretechnological societies, anthropologists William Divale and Marvin Harris concluded that warfare "was formerly part of a distinctively human system of population control. The principal component in this system was the limitation of the number of females reared to reproductive age through female infanticide, the benign and malign neglect of female infants, and the preferential treatment of male children."[6]

Warfare, the researchers argue, was the most important support of male supremacy with its sexual division of labor, which assigns drudge work, such as fetching water and firewood, to women. Hunting with weapons, they note, is a virtually universal male specialty. "Almost everywhere men monopolize the weapons of war as well as weapons of the hunt. Nowhere in the world do women constitute the principal participants in organized police-military combat."[7]

In the pretechnological societies Divale and Harris studied, men were trained for fierce and aggressive behavior, and they showed a preference for male children. Women became the reward for military bravery, and they were reared to be passive and to submit to men's decisions concerning their sexual, economic, and reproductive services. Societies that produced the largest number of fierce warriors were likely to gain a survival advantage, so women who produced warriors gained status. The sex ratio was then skewed toward an excess supply of males through the practice of female infanticide. Female infants were killed by strangling, blows to the head, exposure, and other direct acts. Excess males died in battle—a so-called noble death, although one was no less dead. Divale and Harris suggest that male combat deaths could always be blamed on the enemy—an acceptable means of population control. They also suggest that female infanticide was probably a more socially acceptable means of controlling population than the deaths of mothers through abortion. The deaths of adult women would have been both an economic and an emotional loss to the society. In that context, female infanticide could be seen as less costly.[8]

Such research illuminates the full horror of pretechnological birth-control practices: the rearing of excess males to die in war; the limiting of female numbers through infanticide, thus curbing female fertility.

Today warfare is not pursued to control population, but the kind of large military-industrial complex that contributed to the economic collapse of the former Soviet Union and which continues to dominate the U.S. economy represents a dangerous social investment in violent forms of male-male competition. Modern warfare no less than ancient warfare expresses the male drive to expand men's power and resources to achieve reproductive success. Today that drive is rhetorically called national security, but the ancient dynamics of male-male competition for resources underlie all militarism; the recent war over Middle East oil is a case in point. As the population gap between the rich industrial nations and the poor developing nations continues to widen, resource wars among nations of competing males may become more frequent unless greater intelligence intervenes to radically alter policies and transform economies. The destructive power of modern weapons makes such forms of male-male competition obsolete. And modern humans do not have to resort either to battle or to infanticide to control births. Besides the inhumanity of these methods, we are now so numerous that neither war nor infanticide could possibly solve our population problem. Some 93 million of us are added to the global population each year—more people than have been killed in all wars during the past century. It is clear that we cannot rely on war, natural catastrophes, or dreadful diseases such as AIDS to control population. We must choose to do so ourselves, both as individuals and as groups. And this means redefining reproductive success in terms of quality instead of quantity.

UNDERSTANDING THE HUMAN ANIMAL

Evolutionary biology and studies of female choice shed light on how we got into our dilemma and how we may get out of it. Humans, no less than other animals, strive for reproductive success. When men try to control women by opposing their use of contraceptives, it is because they associate masculinity with siring many children. When they try to restrict women's social mobility, it is because they want to ensure certainty of paternity. When women acquiese in their own domination, it is because they want the resources of high-status men. When men pick fights and resort to violence, it is, in part, because they feel the ancient push of male-male competition. But men could just as easily meet their reproductive needs by creating a new definition of competitive masculinity for themselves—one that encourages strength of character rather than strength of arms.

Women need to recognize why so many deliberately seek out well-heeled men. The risk in this behavior is that they may be computing a man's resources in dollars and cents to the exclusion of the inner qualities that are so important to male-female relationships and so essential to fathering.

Obviously, women's reproductive services are indispensable, but instead of valuing those who provide the service, both church and state—or their equivalents—have made the control of women's reproductive biology a major objective. Even as we have rocketed men to the moon, we have formulated laws to prevent women from exercising the most basic and intimate of choices—whether to reproduce. And again women have not mounted a successful revolt. Evolutionary biology teaches us that males will do virtually anything to ensure confidence of paternity. And it is in this context that we need to analyze the many laws and customs that restrict, punish, and discriminate against women. Evolutionary biology can help us to understand the powerful influence that reproduction has on our lives. With this knowledge we can develop constructive, nonabusive means of meeting the same human animal need.

There is nothing in evolutionary biology that justifies unequal treatment of the sexes, nothing that condones the elevation of one sex over the other. Evolutionary biology makes no value judgments; it only widens the window through which we see our world.

THE CONTRACEPTIVE REVOLUTION

Birth-control technology truly sets humans apart from the rest of the animal kingdom. A combination of education and birth control may also be our best hope of solving not only the problem of overpopulation but also the problems of sex discrimination and war. Contraception can free both sexes from enslavement to their reproductive biology. The biggest hurdle is convincing people to control family size by exercising choice before conception rather

207
ᘮᘮᘮ

than after birth. Convincing the world's people to accept that new freedom, to choose to reduce births to replacement level, is the major ecological challenge of our time, for it goes against millennia of genetic programming to do just the opposite. The greatest hope for meeting this challenge lies in educating women. All over the world, even the slightest improvement in women's education lowers the birthrate. Once men are educated to understand that the entire family benefits from fewer children, they, too, prefer smaller families: there is more money to go around, everyone has more to eat, and mother and children are in better health. Men, too, are enslaved by reproduction when they must provide for too many children.

208

Although birth control seems like old news, its revolutionary promise has still not been fully realized. There is even a current backlash to contraception, indicating that the primitive attempt to control women's reproductive services continues to this day. "No woman should be a mother against her will," wrote Margaret Sanger, the pioneering American advocate for woman's reproductive health services.[9] Although these words were penned in 1920, birth control is still not widely accessible to the world's women. Even in the United States, where modern contraception was created, support for research and development has been severely curtailed. "The United States is the only country other than Iran in which the birth-control clock has been set backward during the past decade," wrote chemist Carl Djerassi, who was one of the creators of the birth-control pill.[10] Three decades after the introduction of the pill, sterilization is the most popular way of preventing pregnancy among American couples, as it is in many developing countries.

As monumental as the task of lowering birthrates seems, there are signs of hope everywhere. According to the United Nations Population Fund, birthrates are now dropping significantly all over the world. In developing countries, average family size has decreased from 6.1 children per woman in the early 1960s to 3.9 today.[11] In some European countries where women have more birth-control choices than are available in the United States, birthrates are already below replacement level.

Given a quality of life beyond the necessities of mere survival,

people have other options—choices for a more educated, cooperative, and creative society; choices for peace, environmental quality, and individual health; choices to share resources and live in
harmony with one's neighbors; choices to be fully human rather
than slaves of the gonads.

Critics may charge that the human animal we know doesn't
want to choose—even that people don't want to be fully human.
The struggle now is between those who want to be free of the re-.
productive imperative and those who wish to remain enslaved.
This struggle represents a crucial battle in the ongoing process of
human evolution. Just as the agricultural revolution freed people
from dependence on hunting and gathering and set the stage for
the technological revolution, so the contraceptive revolution could
liberate people from their reproductive biology.

In pointing out the myths that underlie traditional views of
women, men, and concepts of gender, I hope to have revealed how
narrowly humans have viewed the sexes. We are far more multifaceted than our definitions of gender suggest. Art, science, and
civilization demonstrate humanity's enormous potential for creativity, but we regularly destroy that potential with our male warfare systems, which a growing number of women seek to enter.
Developing solutions to the problems of sex discrimination, war,
and overpopulation requires that we address our ancient sexual
strategies and drive for reproductive success with a fresh attitude.

Both women and men need to be aware of the traps evolution
has set to ensure that we reproduce. With awareness, each sex has
at least a chance to avoid falling into a stereotypical role. In the
modern world, reproduction is easy; it is assuring quality of existence that proves difficult.

Birth-control technology and biological literacy provide the
means of moving to a more rational level of social development
where abilities other than reproduction are valued and nurtured.
In this sense effective, reliable, inexpensive contraception is the
most revolutionary advance in human evolutionary history. But
the challenge to exercise new choices beyond reproduction calls
for significant changes in attitudes, customs, and political structures. Some individuals have already made these changes, but societies as a whole have not.

209

• The definition of womanhood must go beyond child-bearing and mothering. The definition of manhood must go beyond an erect penis, an unsheathed sword, and a drawn gun. By centering concepts of gender on reproductive functions and their related psychologies and mythologies, we have, in effect, denied our intelligence and constrained our potential for personal growth.

• Men and women must be equal under the law. The sexes have different anatomical features, but these differences do not make either one superior. It is essential for our children to learn that the facts of biological difference do not support theories of sexual superiority. With this one bit of knowledge alone, humankind could take a giant step toward its own intellectual liberation.

The meaning of the contraceptive revolution is that births can be limited, and that sex can be enjoyed without fear of pregnancy. This is not to say that children will be less important, that the miracle of procreation will lose its impact, that marriage and families will be denigrated. Rather, these aspects of life would become more precious because they happened by choice and not by chance. With fewer children, women and men have more time to devote to themselves, to each other, to enjoying the wondrous adventure of helping their offspring grow into successful adults. Most of all, real liberation is not just freedom from sexual taboos and discrimination; it is the freedom—for both women and men—to discover and develop *all* the multifaceted aspects of human nature, not just the reproductive aspect.

Through birth control, women finally have the option of being freer than females of any other species. "The liberation of woman has become possible only with fertility control," writes Lynn Baker. "Contrary to what many believe, what she is being liberated from is not the tyranny of men but the rule of her physiology. Members of both sexes need to recognize this. It was scientists, predominantly male, who freed woman from her reproductive biology."[12]

210

The threat of overpopulation demands that we go beyond the reproductive imperative encoded in our genes. The precedents already exist. Studies of female choice and evolutionary biology reveal that females of many species limit births through a variety of strategies. In fact, if humans had not limited births in one way or another from time immemorial, there would be far more of us than there are today.

Freedom from the reproductive imperative can affect profoundly the way men and women relate to each other. The question is whether people—women as well as men—want this option. Evolutionary biology teaches us that the struggle for reproductive success dominates the lives of individuals of all species. Very likely, it will continue to dominate ours, too, unless people choose otherwise. If we do not change our current ways, individuals will reproduce beyond the planet's limits, and we will continue maintaining the most abusive system of male dominance in all of nature, destroy ourselves by fighting resource wars, and push the species toward extinction. Humanity's tenure on Earth would be all too brief. We are a young species, barely 4 million years old. Surely, with our enormous brains, we can have as long a run as the small-brained dinosaurs, whose reptilian reign lasted some 260 million years.

Nothing in biology makes the human situation inevitable or irrevocable. If there is one thing our evolutionary history shows, it is humanity's enormous flexibility and inventiveness. The next step demands that we give up values tied to quantity, focus on quality of life, develop the arts of living, and accept ourselves as members of one species, one part of the great panoply of life.

ɡᴏ

NOTES

CHAPTER 1

[1]Cox and Le Boeuf 1977, p. 317.
[2]Symons 1979, p. 27.
[3]Chagnon 1979a, p. 375.
[4]Chagnon 1988, p. 986.
[5]Chagnon 1983, p. 7.
[6]Chagnon 1988, p. 986.
[7]Ibid., p. 985.
[8]Daly and Wilson 1988, p. 149.
[9]I am indebted to anthropologist Mildred Dickemann for pointing out this substitution, which modern biology teachers now use to clarify what Darwin really meant.
[10]Darwin [1871] 1981, Vol. II, p. 38.
[11]Ibid., Vol. I, p. 296.
[12]Ibid., p. 259.
[13]Ibid.
[14]Ibid.
[15]Schopenhauer 1942, pp. 72–73.
[16]Darwin [1871] 1981, Vol. I, p. 273.
[17]Hrdy 1981, p. 128.
[18]Frederick vom Saal. Personal communication, 1990.
[19]vom Saal 1983.
[20]Frederick vom Saal. Personal communication, 1992.
[21]Frederick vom Saal. Personal communication, 1991.
[22]Henry Harpending. Personal communication, 1991.
[23]Hrdy 1986, p. 140.
[24]Bateman 1948, pp. 349–68.
[25]Hamilton 1964, pp. 1–51.

[26]Alexander 1981, p. 511.
[27]Wilson 1975, p. 3.
[28]Dickemann 1979b, p. 367.
[29]Trivers 1972, p. 141.
[30]Ibid., p. 139.
[31]Lancaster 1984, p. 7.
[32]Edward O. Wilson. Personal communication, 1983.
[33]Hrdy 1981, p. 18.

CHAPTER 2

[1]Trivers 1985, p. 331.
[2]See Ellis 1992.
[3]John Hartung. Personal communication, 1982. See Hartung 1981a, p. 392.
[4]Thornhill and Alcock 1983, p. 426.
[5]Lloyd 1979, p. 22.
[6]Eberhard 1985, pp. 12–13.
[7]Ibid., p. 110.
[8]Ibid., p. 70.
[9]Ibid., p. 17.
[10]Ibid., p. 79.
[11]Smuts 1983a, 1983b.
[12]Smuts 1986, p. 398.
[13]Davis 1991, p. 53.
[14]Verner 1964, pp. 252–61. Also Verner and Willson 1966, pp. 143–47.
[15]Yosef 1991, p. 37.
[16]Sarah Lennington. Personal communication, 1981. Also see Lennington 1980, pp. 347–61.
[17]Wolf 1975, pp. 140–44.
[18]Alcock 1984, p. 417.
[19]Thornhill 1980b, pp. 162–71.
[20]Randy Thornhill. Personal communication, 1983.
[21]Thornhill and Alcock 1983, p. 385.
[22]Wilson 1975, p. 157.
[23]Cockburn and Lee, 1988, pp. 41–46.
[24]Thornhill and Alcock 1983, p. 396.
[25]Robert Trivers. Personal communication, 1989.
[26]Trivers 1985, p. 353.
[27]Sarah Lennington. Personal communication, 1981.
[28]Hamilton and Zuk, 1982, pp. 384–87.
[29]Ibid., p. 385.
[30]Zuk et al. 1990, pp. 477–85.
[31]Randy Thornhill. Personal communication, 1990.
[32]Ibid.
[33]Ibid.

[34]Milinski and Bakker 1990, pp. 330–33.

[35]Papers from this symposium are published in *American Zoologist* 30, no. 2(1990).

[36]Low 1990, p. 325.

[37]Ibid.

[38]Ibid., p. 335.

[39]Chung I. Wu. Personal communication, 1990.

[40]Wu 1983.

[41]Chung I. Wu. Personal communication, 1990.

[42]Shepher 1971.

[43]James Lloyd. Personal communication, 1983.

[44]Kirkpatrick and Ryan 1991, pp. 33–38.

[45]Bert Hölldobler. Personal communication, 1983.

[46]Clutton-Brock 1991, p. 38.

[47]Jack Bradbury. Personal communication, 1991.

[48]Robert Gibson. Personal communication, 1990. See Gibson and Bradbury 1985.

[49]Robert Gibson. Personal communication, 1990.

[50]Pruett-Jones and Pruett-Jones 1990, p. 499.

[51]Bruce Beehler. Personal communication, 1990. See Beehler and Foster 1988.

[52]Jack Bradbury. Personal communication, 1982.

[53]Zahavi 1975, pp. 205–14. Also Zahavi 1977a, pp. 603–5.

[54]Kodric-Brown and Brown 1984, p. 310.

[55]Thornhill and Alcock 1983, p. 132.

[56]Scott Kraus. Personal communication, 1990.

[57]Smuts 1986, p. 392.

[58]Rosenthal 1991, pp. 22–27.

[59]Thornhill and Alcock 1983, pp. 398–99.

[60]Parker 1970, pp. 525–67. Also Thornhill and Alcock 1983, p. 321.

[61]"Chemical May Draw Sperm to Egg." *New York Times*, Medical Science, Apr. 2, 1991, p. B6. The article refers to the study of Dr. Dina Ralt and Dr. Michael Eisenbach of the Weizmann Institute in Rehovot, Israel. The finding was reported in the *Proceedings of the National Academy of Science*, April 1, 1991.

[62]Burley 1985, p. 43.

[63]Burley 1988, p. 627.

[64]Burley 1986, p. 1200.

[65]Ibid., p. 1191.

[66]Burley 1985, p. 31.

[67]Basolo 1990.

[68]Michael J. Ryan. Personal communication, 1990. Also see Ryan 1986, 1990, and Ryan and Rand 1990.

[69]Ryan 1980.

[70]Ryan and Rand 1990, p. 306.

[71]Michael J. Ryan. Personal communication, 1990.

[72]Ibid.

215

CHAPTER 3

[1]Symons 1985, p. 143.

[2]Daly and Wilson 1988, p. 188.

[3]United Nations 1991, p. 2.

[4]Siskind 1973b, p. 233.

[5]Hartung 1982, p. 1.

[6]John Hartung. Personal communication, 1981. These observations were published in Hartung 1976.

[7]Essock-Vitale and McGuire 1988, p. 222.

[8]Bruce Ellis. Personal communication, 1990. See Ellis 1991.

[9]Irons 1979, p. 258.

[10]Trivers 1985, p. 331.

[11]Daly and Wilson 1988, p. 132.

[12]Chagnon 1979a, p. 379.

[13]Napoleon A. Chagnon. Personal communication, 1992.

[14]Dickemann 1979a, p. 175.

[15]Ibid.

[16]van Gulik 1974. Cited in Dickemann 1979a, p. 175.

[17]See Richard Dawkins's response in Vining, 1986, p. 190.

[18]See William Irons's response in Vining 1986, p. 198.

[19]See J. Hill's response in Vining 1986, p. 196. "In primitive and poor human societies, sociocultural success leads to reproductive success, but in the novel environment of surplus wealth the link is severed. Sociocultural success is no longer the proximate goal to reproductive success but becomes an ultimate goal in its own right alongside reproductive success. . . . It is the emergence of prestige as a goal in its own right that makes the difference, and that is possible only when there is more wealth than can be devoted to reproductive success, at least among the richest members of the population."

[20]For a full discussion and peer review of the decline in birthrates among the wealthy, see Vining 1986, pp. 167–216.

[21]Essock-Vitale 1984.

[22]Turke and Betzig 1985.

[23]Irons 1979, pp. 260–67.

[24]Voland and Engel 1990.

[25]Eckart Voland. Personal communication, 1989.

[26]Borgerhoff Mulder 1987.

[27]Monique Borgerhoff Mulder. Personal communication, 1990.

[28]Borgerhoff Mulder 1987, pp. 617–34.

[29]Borgerhoff Mulder 1990.

[30]Borgerhoff Mulder 1987, pp. 629–30.

[31]Borgerhoff Mulder, in press.

[32]Henry Harpending. Personal communication, 1989 and 1990.

[33]Napoleon Chagnon. Personal communication, 1990 and 1991. Reported in Chagnon 1989. Also see Chagnon 1992.

[34]George E. Marcus. Personal communication, 1982.

[35]Marcus 1979, pp. 86–87.

[36]Lee Cronk. Personal communication, 1991.

[37]Cronk 1989a, p. 227.

[38]This idea, which is speculative on Cronk's part, is supported by Monique Borgerhoff Mulder's finding that among the Kipsigis people of western Kenya, higher bridewealths were paid for fatter and earlier-maturing girls than for skinny, late-maturing ones. See Borgerhoff Mulder 1988, pp. 65–82.

[39]Cronk 1989a, p. 224.

[40]Buss 1989a.

[41]Ibid., p. 12.

[42]Ibid., p. 14.

[43]Ibid.

[44]Leonard 1980, p. 5.

[45]Quoted in United Nations 1991, p. 2.

[46]Stutsman 1990.

[47]Ellis 1992, p. 227.

[48]Fowler, H. An investigation into human breeding system strategy. Paper read to Animal Behavior Society Meeting, Pennsylvania State University, June 1977. Cited in D. Freedman. *Human Sociobiology: A Holistic Approach* (New York: Macmillan, 1979) p. 85.

[49]Townsend 1987, 1989.

[50]Watanabe 1992, p. A1.

[51]Ellis 1992.

CHAPTER 4

[1]Cosmides and Tooby 1987, p. 300.

[2]Ibid., p. 281.

[3]Buss 1989b, p. 46.

[4]Cosmides and Tooby 1987, p. 280.

[5]Symons 1985, p. 145.

[6]Ellis and Symons 1990, p. 533.

[7]Hill, Nocks, and Gardner 1987.

[8]Symons 1985, p. 147.

[9]Daly and Wilson 1983, p. 294.

[10]Betzig 1989, p. 669.

[11]Daly and Wilson 1983, p. 291.

[12]Ibid.

[13]Dickemann 1981.

[14]Ibid., p. 419.
[15]Lampert and Friedman 1992.
[16]Ellis and Symons 1990.
[17]Ibid., pp. 546–47.
[18]Ibid., p. 545.

Chapter 5

[1]Trivers 1985, p. 395.
[2]Thornhill 1979.
[3]Johansson 1976, p. 418.
[4]See Sabbah 1984.
[5]This concept was first mentioned to me by ecologist Daniel Janzen in a conversation in 1983.
[6]*The Taming of the Shrew*, act 5, scene 2.
[7]Bell 1990.
[8]Lamm 1966, p. 84.
[9]Loebenstein 1983, p. 8.
[10]Kahana 1977, p. 15.
[11]Murphy and Murphy 1974, p. 141.
[12]Angier 1991, pp. B5–8.
[13]Trivers 1985, p. 219.
[14]John Sivinski. Personal communication, 1990.
[15]Thornhill and Alcock 1983, p. 238.
[16]Alcock 1989.
[17]Stutsman 1990.
[18]Saadawi 1980, pp. 7–8. Quoted in Lionnet 1991, p. 4.
[19]Heise 1989, p. 19. Other material on this subject appears in Lightfoot-Klein 1990.
[20]Hrdy 1979.
[21]Hrdy 1981, p. 76.
[22]Hrdy 1988, p. 114.
[23]Taub 1984.
[24]Packer, Scheel, and Pusey 1990.
[25]Frederick vom Saal. Personal communication, 1991.
[26]Betzig 1986, p. 88.
[27]Ibid., pp. 2–3.
[28]Ibid., p. 79.
[29]Ibid., p. 77.
[30]Ibid., pp. 85–87.
[31]Daly and Wilson 1988, p. 128.
[32]Shields and Shields 1983, p. 127.
[33]Quoted in Schuster 1979, p. 149.
[34]"A Night of Madness," *Time*, Aug. 12, 1991, p. 43.

218

[35]Radway 1984, p. 216.
[36]Ibid.
[37]The two studies are Thornhill and Thornhill 1983, and Shields and Shields 1983.
[38]Thornhill and Thornhill 1983, pp. 143–44.
[39]See Table II in Thornhill and Thornhill 1983, p. 150.
[40]Amir 1971.
[41]Eisenhower 1969.
[42]Brownmiller 1975, chap. 3.
[43]*Num.* 31.
[44]Dawkins 1976.
[45]Shields and Shields 1983, p. 123.
[46]Ibid., p. 115.
[47]Thornhill and Thornhill, 1983, p. 139.
[48]Shields and Shields, 1983, p. 115.
[49]Ibid., p. 133.
[50]Randy Thornhill. Personal communication, 1981.
[51]Thornhill 1980a. Also see Thornhill 1981.

CHAPTER 6

[1]Hrdy 1981, p. 55.
[2]Angier 1990b, pp. B5–8.
[3]Tiger and Fox 1971, p. 117.
[4]Shepher 1978, p. 258.
[5]Wittenberger and Tilson 1980.
[6]Wilson 1975, p. 330.
[7]Hrdy 1981, p. 36.
[8]Ibid., p. 34.
[9]Ibid., p. 40.
[10]Ibid., p. 41.
[11]Ibid., p. 55.
[12]Dunbar, 1980.
[13]Hrdy 1986, p. 132.
[14]Lovejoy 1981.
[15]Owen Lovejoy. Personal communication, 1982.
[16]This theory was explored by Helen E. Fisher in Fisher 1982.
[17]Hrdy 1988c, pp. 101–36.
[18]Ibid., p. 107.
[19]Quoted in Hrdy 1988c, p. 110.
[20]Hrdy 1988c, p. 111.
[21]Ibid., p. 116.
[22]Ibid., p. 115.

[23]Small 1988, p. 82.

[24]Ibid.

[25]Eck Menning 1979.

[26]Reuben 1992.

[27]Shepher 1978, p. 262.

[28]Hrdy 1988c, p. 125.

[29]Burley 1979, p. 842.

[30]Ibid.

[31]Sadik 1990, p. 10.

[32]Burley 1979, pp. 842–43.

[33]Alexander 1979, p. 240.

[34]Stutsman, 1991, p. 3.

[35]Sub-Saharan Africa's traditions encourage high fertility, in contrast to the Eurasian pattern that predominates in most of the rest of the world. Two factors contribute to this: (1) there is no individual ownership of land; rather, it is owned by a clan or lineage; (2) women do most of the agricultural work in sub-Saharan Africa, and children help them. The more children men and women have, the greater the strength of their lineage. For more on this subject, see Caldwell and Caldwell 1990.

[36]Abcarian 1991.

[37]Henderson 1988.

[38]Joseph Shepher. Personal communication, 1982.

[39]Shepher 1978, p. 259.

[40]Ibid., pp. 259–60.

[41]Ibid., p. 260.

[42]Ibid.

[43]Joseph Shepher. Personal communication, 1982.

[44]Lampert and Friedman 1992.

CHAPTER 7

[1]Barash 1986, p. 216.

[2]Hanawalt 1986, p. 198.

[3]Friedan 1983, p. 385.

[4]Rosenblatt and Cozby 1972.

[5]Smuts 1986, p. 398.

[6]Ibid., pp. 385–99.

[7]Morris 1967, p. 33.

[8]Hamburg 1961, p. 278.

[9]Hamburg 1989, p. 17.

[10]Money 1980, p. 64.

[11]Ibid., p. 65.

[12]Shaver, Hazan, and Bradshaw 1988, p. 90.

[13]Buss 1988b, p. 100.

[14]Dorothy Tennov. Personal communication, 1990. Also see Tennov 1979.
[15]Baronne Germaine de Staël-Holstein 1796. *De l'Influence des Passions.*
[16]Rousseau 1979, p. 329.
[17]Money 1980, pp. 65–67.
[18]Sternberg 1986.
[19]Taylor 1954, p. 51.
[20]Capellanus 1982.
[21]Ibid., p. 9.
[22]Lewis [1936] 1953, p. 4.
[23]Lucka 1922, p. 139.
[24]Duby 1978, p. 14.
[25]Bogin 1976, p. 57.
[26]Fox 1980, p. 206.
[27]de Rougemont 1956, pp. 51–52, 75.
[28]Bogin 1976, p. 67.
[29]Ibid., pp. 99–101.
[30]Capellanus 1982, p. 24.
[31]Bogin 1976, p. 10.
[32]Mussell 1984, p. 6.
[33]Ibid., p. 138.
[34]Radway 1984, pp. 112–13.
[35]Ibid., p. 158.
[36]Siskind 1973a, p. 18.

CHAPTER 8

[1]Dwyer and Bruce 1988, p. 7.
[2]United Nations 1991, p. 82.
[3]Sadik 1990, p. 14.
[4]Kunstadter 1963.
[5]United Nations 1991, p. 16.
[6]Shepher 1981.
[7]Dwyer and Bruce 1988, p. 4.
[8]Mencher 1988, p. 114.
[9]Schuster 1979, p. 114.
[10]Moyers 1989.
[11]U.S. Department of Health and Human Services 1990, p. 872.
[12]Sadik 1990, pp. 12–14.
[13]Stutsman 1990.
[14]Jacobson 1987, p. 20.
[15]Ibid., p. 13.
[16]Dwyer and Bruce 1988, p. 6.
[17]Ibid., pp. 6–7.

[18]Marshall 1991, pp. 54–55.

[19]United Nations 1991, pp. 19–20.

[20]Hill and Hill 1989.

[21]Hamilton 1985, p. 50. For the world population as a whole, however, there are more men than women. According to the United Nations 1991, p. 11, "Of the world's 5.3 billion people in 1990, fewer than half (2.63 billion) were women. Indeed, in many countries there are fewer than 95 women for every 100 men." Women do outnumber men in most regions, but have higher mortality in countries where widow burning, dowry deaths, female infanticide, and the new phenomenon of abortion on the basis of male preference occur. In addition, girls and women in many areas are denied the same nutrition and health care that males receive. As a result, there are only ninety-five women for every one hundred men in Asia and the Pacific, enough to offset the world balance in favor of men.

[22]Gwynne 1981.

[23]Thornhill and Alcock 1983, pp. 443–44.

[24]Gwynne and Simmons 1990.

[25]Hamilton 1985, p. 50.

[26]Ibid.

Chapter 9

[1]Johansson 1976, p. 418.

[2]Sanger 1920, p. 1.

[3]United Nations Development Programme 1991, p. 27.

[4]Dickemann 1979a.

[5]Gargan 1991.

[6]Divale and Harris 1976, p. 527.

[7]Ibid., p. 524.

[8]Ibid., p. 530.

[9]Sanger 1920, p. 230.

[10]Hilts 1990, p. 55.

[11]United Nations Population Fund 1991, p. 2.

[12]Baker 1981, pp. 16–17.

ᖆᒧ

BIBLIOGRAPHY

Abcarian, Robin. 1991. A web of terror. *Los Angeles Times,* Oct. 6, pp. E1–12.

Alcock, John. 1984. *Animal Behavior: An Evolutionary Approach.* Sunderland, MA: Sinauer Associates.

———. 1986. Conjugal chemistry. *Natural History,* April, pp. 75–81.

———. 1989. Freedom fighters. *Natural History,* March, pp. 69–74.

———. 1990. Desert jaws. *Natural History,* April, pp. 88–92.

Alexander, Richard D. 1974. The evolution of social behavior. *Annual Review of Ecology and Systematics* 5:325–83.

Alexander, Richard D. 1979. *Darwinism and Human Affairs.* Seattle: University of Washington Press.

———. 1981. Evolution, culture, and human behavior: some general considerations. In *Natural Selection and Social Behavior,* ed. R. D. Alexander and D. W. Tinkle, pp. 509–19. New York: Chiron Press.

Amir, M. 1971. *Patterns in Forcible Rape.* Chicago: University of Chicago Press.

Anderson, Judith L. 1988. Comment, breasts, hips, and buttocks revisited. *Ethology and Sociobiology* 9:319–24.

Angier, Natalie. 1990a. Hard-to-please females may be neglected evolutionary force. *New York Times Science Times,* May 8, pp. B5–6.

———. 1990b. Mating for life? It's not for the birds or the bees. *New York Times Science Times,* Aug. 21, pp. B5–8.

———. 1990c. A male trait in fish has that certain something. *New York Times,* Nov. 9, p. A12.

———. 1991. In fish, social status goes right to the brain. *New York Times Science Times,* Nov. 12, pp. B5–8.

Baker, C. Scott, Anjanette Perry, and Louis M. Herman. 1987. Reproductive histories of female humpback whales *Megaptera novaeangliae* in the North Pacific. *Marine Ecology–Progress Series* 41:103–14.

Baker, Lynn S. 1981. *The Fertility Fallacy.* Philadelphia: Saunders Press.

Barash, David. 1977. Sociobiology of rape in mallards. *Science* 197:788–89.

———. 1978. Sexual selection in birdland. *Psychology Today,* March, pp. 82–86.

———. 1979. *The Whisperings Within.* New York: Harper & Row.

———. 1986. *The Hare and the Tortoise: Culture, Biology, and Human Nature.* New York: Penguin Books.

Barlow, George W. 1967. Social behavior of a South American leaf fish, *Polycentrus schomburgkii,* with an account of recurring pseudofemale behavior. *American Midland Naturalist* 78:215–34.

Basolo, Alexandra L. 1990. Female preference predates the evolution of the sword in swordtail fish. *Science* 250:808–10.

Bateman, A. J. 1948. Intra-sexual selection in Drosophila. *Heredity* 2:349–68.

Bateson, Patrick, ed. 1983. *Mate Choice.* Cambridge: Cambridge University Press.

Beach, Frank A. 1976. *Human Sexuality in Four Perspectives.* Baltimore: Johns Hopkins University Press.

Beecher, Michael D., and Inger Mornestam. 1979a. Promiscuity: a bitter pill for swallows. *Science News,* Oct. 6, p. 229.

———. 1979b. Bank swallows. *Science* 205:1282–85.

Beehler, Bruce M. 1983. Lek behavior of the lesser bird of paradise. *Auk* 100:992–995.

———. 1989. The birds of paradise. *Scientific American* 261(6):116–23.

Beehler, Bruce M., and M. S. Foster. 1988. Hotshots, hotspots, and female preference in the organization of lek mating systems. *American Naturalist* 131:203–19.

Bell, Amelia Rector. 1990. Separate people: speaking of Creek men and women. *American Anthropologist* 92:332–45.

Benshoof, L., and R. Thornhill. 1979. The evolution of monogamy and concealed ovulation in humans. *Journal of Social and Biological Structures* 2:95–106.

Betzig, Laura L. 1986. *Despotism and Differential Reproduction.* New York: Aldine Publishing.

———. 1989. Causes of conjugal dissolution: a cross-cultural study. *Current Anthropology* 30:654–76.

Betzig, Laura L., Monique Borgerhoff Mulder, and Paul Turke, eds. 1988. *Human Reproductive Behavior: A Darwinian Perspective.* Cambridge: Cambridge University Press.

Bleier, Ruth. 1984. *Science and Gender.* New York: Pergamon Press.

Bogin, Meg. 1976. *The Women Troubadours.* New York: Paddington Press.

Boone, James L., III. 1986. Parental investment and elite family structure in preindustrial states: a case study of late medieval–early modern Portuguese genealogies. *American Anthropologist* 88:859–78.

Borgerhoff Mulder, Monique. 1987. On cultural and reproductive success: Kipsigis evidence. *American Anthropologist* 89:617–34.

————. 1988. Kipsigis bridewealth payments. In Betzig, Borgerhoff Mulder, and Turke 1988, pp. 65–82.

————. 1990. Kipsigis women prefer wealthy men: evidence for female choice in mammals? *Behavioural Ecology and Sociobiology* 27:255–264.

————. In press. Reproductive strategies in ecological context. In *Evolutionary Ecology and Human Social Behavior*, ed. E. A. Smith and B. Winterhalder. New York: Aldine Publishing.

Bradbury, Jack W. 1972. The silent symphony: tuning in on the bat. In: *The Marvels of Animal Behavior*, ed. Thomas B. Allen, pp. 112–25. Washington, DC: National Geographic Society.

Brownell, Robert L., Jr., and Katherine Ralls. 1986. Potential for sperm competition in baleen whales. *Report of the International Whaling Commission* (special issue 8), pp. 97–112.

Brownmiller, Susan. 1975. *Against Our Will: Men, Women and Rape.* New York: Simon and Schuster.

Burley, Nancy. 1979. The evolution of concealed ovulation. *American Naturalist* 114:835–58.

————. 1981. Mate choice by multiple criteria in a monogamous species. *American Naturalist* 117:515–28.

————. 1985. The organization of behavior and the evolution of sexually selected traits. In *Avian Monogamy*, ed. P. A. Gowaty and D. W. Mock, pp. 22–44. Ornithological Monographs, no. 37. Washington, D.C.: American Ornithologists' Union.

————. 1986. Sex-ratio manipulation in color-banded populations of zebra finches. *Evolution* 40:1191–1206.

————. 1988. The differential-allocation hypothesis: an experimental test. *American Naturalist* 132:611–28.

Buss, David M. 1985. Human mate selection. *American Scientist* 73:47–51.

————. 1988a. From vigilance to violence: tactics of mate retention in American undergraduates. *Ethology and Sociobiology* 9:291–317.

————. 1988b. Love acts: the evolutionary biology of love. In *The Psychology of Love*, ed. Robert J. Sternberg and Michael L. Barnes, pp. 100–118. New Haven, CT: Yale University Press.

————. 1989a. Sex differences in human mate preferences: evolutionary hypotheses tested in 37 cultures. *Behavioral and Brain Sciences* 12:1–14.

————. 1989b. Toward an evolutionary psychology of human mating. *Behavioral and Brain Sciences* 12:39–49.

Caldwell, John C., and Pat Caldwell. 1990. High fertility in sub-Saharan Africa. *Scientific American* 262(5):118–25.

Capellanus, Andreas. 1982. *The Art of Courtly Love.* Translated by John Jay Parry. New York: Frederick Ungar Publishing.

Chagnon, Napoleon A. 1979a. Is reproductive success equal in egalitarian societies? In Chagnon and Irons 1979, pp. 374–401.

———. 1979b. Mate competition, favoring close kin, and village fissioning among the Yânomamö Indians. In Chagnon and Irons 1979, pp. 86–132.

———. 1983. *Yânomamö: The Fierce People*. 3rd ed. New York: Holt, Rinehart and Winston.

———. 1988. Life histories, blood revenge, and warfare in a tribal population. *Science* 239:985–91.

———. 1989. The Great Transformation. Paper delivered at the 1989 Human Behavior and Evolution Society conference. Northwestern University, Evanston, IL (Aug. 25–28, 1989).

———. 1992. *Yânomamö: The Fierce People*. San Diego, CA: Harcourt Brace Jovanovich.

Chagnon, Napoleon A., Mark V. Flinn, and Thomas F. Melancon. 1979. Sex-ratio variation among the Yânomamö indians. In Chagnon and Irons 1979, pp. 290–320.

Chagnon, Napoleon A., and William Irons, eds. 1979. *Evolutionary Biology and Human Social Behavior.* North Scituate, MA: Duxbury Press.

Christian, Sue Ellen. 1990. Murder rate soars for young black men. *Los Angeles Times*, Dec. 7, A3–23.

Christy, John H. 1987a. Competitive mating, mate choice and mating associations of brachyuran crabs. *Bulletin of Marine Science* 41:177–91.

———. 1987b. Female choice and the breeding behavior of the fiddler crab *Uca beebei*. *Journal of Crustacean Biology* 7:624–35.

Clarke, Margaret R., and Kenneth E. Glander. 1984. Female reproductive success in a group of free-ranging howling monkeys (*Alouatta palliata*) in Costa Rica. In Small 1984, pp. 111–26.

Clutton-Brock, T. H. 1991. Lords of the lek. *Natural History*, October, pp. 34–40.

Clutton-Brock, T. H., S. D. Albon, and F. E. Guinness. 1981. Parental investment in male and female offspring in polygynous mammals. *Nature* 289:487–89.

———. 1984. Maternal dominance, breeding success and birth sex ratios in red deer. *Nature* 308:358–60.

Cockburn, Andrew, and Anthony K. Lee. 1988. Marsupial femmes fatales. *Natural History*, March, pp. 41–47.

Cosmides, Leda, and John Tooby. 1987. From evolution to behavior: evolutionary psychology as the missing link. In Dupré 1987, pp. 277–306.

Cox, Cathleen R., and Burney Le Boeuf. 1977. Female incitation of male competition: a mechanism in sexual selection. *American Naturalist* 111:317–35.

Cronk, Lee. 1989a. From hunters to herders: subsistence change as a reproductive strategy among the Mukogodo. *Current Anthropology* 30:224–34.

———. 1989b. Low socioeconomic status and female-biased parental investment: the Mukogodo example. *American Anthropologist* 91:414–29.

———. 1991. Preferential parental investment in daughters over sons. *Human Nature* 2 (4):387–417.

Daly, Martin, and Margo Wilson. 1982. Homicide and kinship. *American Anthropologist* 84:372–78.

———. 1983. *Sex, Evolution, and Behavior.* 2nd ed. Boston: Willard Grant Press.

———. 1984. Sociobiological analysis of human infanticide. In Hausfater and Hrdy 1984, pp. 487–502.

———. 1988. *Homicide.* New York: Aldine de Gruyter.

Darwin, Charles. 1859. *The Origin of Species.* London: Murray.

———. [1871] 1981. *The Descent of Man, and Selection in Relation to Sex.* Reprint. Princeton, NJ: Princeton University Press.

Davis, Lloyd Spencer. 1991. Penguin weighting game. *Natural History,* January, pp. 46–54.

Dawkins, Richard. 1976. *The Selfish Gene.* New York: Oxford University Press.

de Rougemont, Denis. 1956. *Love in the Western World.* Translated by Montgomery Belgion. New York: Pantheon Books.

Devine, Michael C. 1975. Copulatory plugs in snakes: enforced chastity. *Science* 187:844–45.

DeVore, Irven. 1965. Male dominance and mating behavior in baboons. In *Sex and Behavior,* ed. Frank A. Beach, pp. 266–86. New York: John Wiley & Sons.

Diamond, Jared M. 1981. Birds of paradise and the theory of sexual selection. *Nature* 293:257–58.

Dickemann, Mildred. 1975. Demographic consequences of infanticide in man. *Annual Review of Ecology and Systematics* 6:107–37.

———. 1979a. The ecology of mating systems in hypergynous dowry societies. *Social Science Information* 18:163–95.

———. 1979b. Female infanticide, reproductive strategies, and social stratification: a preliminary model. In Chagnon and Irons 1979, pp. 321–67.

———. 1981. Paternal confidence and dowry competition: a biocultural analysis of purdah. In *Natural Selection and Social Behavior,* ed. R. Alexander and D. W. Tinkle, pp. 417–38. New York: Chiron Press.

———. 1985. Human sociobiology: the first decade. *New Scientist* 108:38–42.

Divale, William Tulio, and Marvin Harris. 1976. Population, warfare, and the male supremacist complex. *American Anthropologist* 78:521–38.

Downhower, Jerry F., and Luther Brown. 1980. Mate preferences of female mottled sculpins, *Cottus bairdi. Animal Behavior* 28:728–34.

Draper, Patricia, and Henry Harpending. 1988. A sociobiological perspective on the development of human reproductive strategies. In *Sociobiological Perspectives on Human Development,* ed. K. B. MacDonald, pp. 340–72. New York: Springer Verlag.

Duby, Georges. 1978. *The Chivalrous Society.* Translated by Cynthia Poston. London: Edward Arnold.

Dunbar, R. I. M. 1980. Determinants and evolutionary consequences of dominance among female gelada baboons. *Behavioral Ecology and Sociobiology* 7:253–65.

Dupré, John, ed. 1987. *The Latest on the Best: Essays on Evolution and Optimality.* A Bradford Book. Cambridge, MA: MIT Press.

227

Dwyer, Daisy, and Judith Bruce, eds. 1988. *A Home Divided: Women and Income in the Third World.* Stanford, CA: Stanford University Press.

Eberhard, William G. 1985. *Sexual Selection and Animal Genitalia.* Cambridge, MA: Harvard University Press.

———. 1990. Animal genitalia and female choice. *American Scientist* 78:134–41.

Eck Menning, B. 1978. *Infertility: A Guide for the Childless Couple.* 2nd Edition. Englewood Cliffs, NJ: Prentice-Hall.

Eckholm, Erik. 1984. New view of female primates assails stereotypes. *New York Times Science Times,* Sept. 18, pp. B17–18.

———. 1986. Is sex necessary? Evolutionists are perplexed. *New York Times Science Times,* Mar. 25, pp. B15–16.

Eisenhower, M. S. 1969. *To Establish Justice, to Insure Domestic Tranquility:* Final Report of the National Commission on Causes and Prevention of Violence. Washington, DC: U.S. Government Printing Office.

Ellis, Bruce J. 1992. The evolution of sexual attraction: evaluative mechanisms in women. In *The Adapted Mind,* ed. J. H. Barkow, L. Cosmides, and J. Tooby, pp. 221–242. New York: Oxford University Press.

Ellis, Bruce J., and Donald Symons. 1990. Sex differences in sexual fantasy: an evolutionary psychological approach. *Journal of Sex Research* 27:527–55.

Emlen, Stephen T., and Lewis W. Oring. 1977. Ecology, sexual selection, and the evolution of mating systems. *Science* 197:215–23.

Essock-Vitale, Susan M. 1984. The reproductive success of wealthy Americans. *Ethology and Sociobiology* 5:45–49.

Essock-Vitale, Susan M., and Michael T. McGuire. 1985. Women's lives viewed from an evolutionary perspective. I. Sexual histories, reproductive success, and demographic characteristics of a random sample of American women. *Ethology and Sociobiology* 6:137–54.

———. 1988. What 70 million years hath wrought: sexual histories and reproductive success of a random sample of American women. In Betzig, Mulder, and Turke 1988, pp. 221–35.

Fisher, Helen E. 1982. *The Sex Contract.* New York: William Morrow and Company.

Fisher, R. A. 1930. *The Genetic Theory of Natural Selection.* Oxford: Clarendon Press.

Flinn, Mark V. 1988. Mate guarding in a Caribbean village. *Ethology and Sociobiology* 9:1–28.

Ford, C. S., and F. A. Beach. 1951. *Patterns of Sexual Behavior.* New York: Harper & Row.

Fox, Robin. 1973. *Encounter with Anthropology.* New York: Harcourt Brace Jovanovich.

———. 1980. *The Red Lamp of Incest.* New York: E. P. Dutton.

Freedman, D. 1979. *Human Sociobiology: A Holistic Approach.* New York: The Free Press.

Friedan, Betty. 1983. *The Feminine Mystique*. 20th anniv. ed. New York: W. W. Norton & Co.

Gager, Nancy, and Cathleen Schurr. 1976. *Sexual Assault: Confronting Rape in America*. New York: Grosset and Dunlap.

Gargan, Edward A. 1991. Ultrasonic tests skew ratio of births in India. *New York Times*, Dec. 13, p. A12.

Gaulin, Steven J. C., and Lee Douglas Sailer. 1985. Are females the ecological sex? *American Anthropologist* 87:111–19.

Ghiselin, Michael T. 1974. *The Economy of Nature and the Evolution of Sex*. Berkeley: University of California Press.

Gibson, R. M., and J. W. Bradbury. 1985. Sexual selection in lekking sage grouse: phenotypic correlates of male mating success. *Behavioral Ecology and Sociobiology* 18:117–23.

Gladstone, Douglas E. 1979. Promiscuity in monogamous colonial birds. *American Naturalist* 114:545–57.

Goleman, Daniel. 1990. Women's depression rate is higher. *New York Times/Health*, Dec. 6, p. B8.

Gould, Stephen Jay. 1976. Ladders, bushes, and human evolution. *Natural History*, April, pp. 24–31.

———. 1982. The oddball human male. *Natural History*, July, pp. 14–22.

———. 1984. Only his wings remained. *Natural History*, September, pp. 10–18.

Greene, John C. 1959. *The Death of Adam*. Ames: Iowa State University Press.

Gregor, Thomas. 1973. Privacy and extra-marital affairs in a tropical forest community. In *People and Cultures of Native South America*, ed. Daniel R. Gross, pp. 242–60. Garden City, NY: Doubleday.

Guinness Book of World Records. 1988. New York: Bantam Books.

Gwynne, D. T. 1981. Sexual difference theory: Mormon crickets show role reversal in mate choice. *Science* 213:779–80.

———. 1983. Coy conquistadors of the sagebrush. *Natural History*, October, pp. 70–75.

Gwynne, D. T., and L. W. Simmons. 1990. Experimental reversal of courtship roles in an insect. *Nature* 346:172–74.

Hall, Roberta L., ed. 1985. *Male-Female Differences: A Bio-Cultural Perspective*. New York: Praeger.

Hamburg, David. 1961. The relevance of recent evolutionary changes to human stress biology. In *Social Life of Early Man*, ed. S. Washburn, pp. 278–88. Chicago: Aldine Publishing Co.

———. 1989. Confronting a violent past to chart future peace: interview with the author. *Calypso Log*, December, pp. 14–17. Los Angeles: The Cousteau Society.

Hamilton, Margaret E. 1984. Revising evolutionary narrative: a consideration of alternative assumptions about sexual selection and competition for mates. *American Anthropologist* 86:651–62.

229

_____. 1985. Sociobiology and the evolutionary history of relations between males and females. In Hall 1985, pp. 1–50.

Hamilton, W. D. 1964. The genetical evolution of social behavior. *Journal of Theoretical Biology* 7:1–51.

Hamilton, William D., and Marlene Zuk. 1982. Heritable true fitness and bright birds: a role for parasites? *Science* 218:384–87.

Hanawalt, Barbara A. 1986. *The Ties That Bound: Peasant Families in Medieval England*. New York: Oxford University Press.

Hapgood, Fred. 1979. *Why Males Exist*. New York: William Morrow & Co.

Harris, Marvin. 1977. *Cannibals and Kings: The Origins of Cultures*. New York: Random House.

Hartung, John. 1976. On natural selection and inheritance of wealth. *Current Anthropology* 17:607–22.

_____. 1981a. Genome parliaments and sex with the red queen. In *Natural Selection and Social Behavior*, ed. Richard D. Alexander and Donald W. Tinkle, pp. 382–402. New York: Chiron Press.

_____. 1981b. Paternity and inheritance of wealth. *Nature* 291:652–54.

_____. 1982. Polygyny and inheritance of wealth. *Current Anthropology* 23: 1–12.

_____. 1985a. Author's response: lineal extinction—a bridge for ecology? *Behavioral and Brain Sciences* 8:683.

_____. 1985b. Matrilineal inheritance: new theory and analysis. *Behavioral and Brain Sciences* 8:661–688.

Hausfater, Glenn, and Sarah Blaffer Hrdy, eds. 1984. *Infanticide: Comparative and Evolutionary Perspectives*. New York: Aldine Publishing.

Heise, Lori. 1989. Crimes of gender. *World Watch*, March–April, p. 19.

Henderson, Julia. 1988. Stabilizing the human family: interview with the author. *Calypso Log*, October, pp. 14–16. Los Angeles: The Cousteau Society.

Heyning, John E. 1989. Leviathan amour: the mating systems of whales and dolphins. *Terra* 23(2):39–47.

Hiatt, L. R. 1989. On cuckoldry. *Journal of Social and Biological Structures*. 12:53–72.

Hill, Elizabeth M. and M. Anne Hill. 1990. Gender differences in child care and work: an interdisciplinary perspective. *Journal of Behavioral Economics* 19:81–101.

Hill, Elizabeth M., and Bobbi S. Low. 1989. Using life-history and parental investment theories for predicting human reproductive choices. Paper presented at Human Behavior and Evolution Society conference, August 25–28. Northwestern University, Evanston, IL. Manuscript from authors.

Hill, Elizabeth M., Elaine S. Nocks, and Lucinda Gardner. 1987. Physical attractiveness: manipulation by physique and status displays. *Ethology and Sociobiology* 8:143–54.

Hilts, Philip. J. 1990. *Birth-control backlash*. New York Times Magazine, Dec. 16, pp. 41–74.

Hölldobler, Bert. 1976. Mating behavior of harvesting ants. *Behavioral Ecology* 1:423–25.

———. 1977. Mating behavior and sound production in harvesting ants. *Insectasociaux* 24:191–212.

Hrdy, Sarah Blaffer. 1976. Care and exploitation of nonhuman primate infants by conspecifics other than the mother. *Advances in the Study of Behavior* 6:101–58. New York: Academic Press.

———. 1977. Infanticide as a primate reproductive strategy. *American Scientist* 65:40–49.

———. 1979. Infanticide among animals: a review, classification, and examination of the implications for the reproductive strategies of females. *Ethology and Sociobiology* 1:13–40.

———. 1981. *The Woman That Never Evolved.* Cambridge, MA: Harvard University Press.

———. 1984. Female reproductive strategies. In Small 1984, pp. 103–9.

———. 1986. Empathy, polyandry, and the myth of the coy female. In *Feminist Approaches to Science*, ed. R. Bleier, pp. 119–46. New York: Pergamon Press.

———. 1988a. Daughters or sons. *Natural History* April, pp. 63–82.

———. 1988b. Interview. *Omni* 10:91–130.

———. 1988c. The primate origins of human sexuality. In *The Evolution of Sex*, ed. R. Bellig and G. Stevens, pp. 101–36. San Francisco: Harper & Row.

———. 1988d. Raising Darwin's consciousness: females and evolutionary theory. In *The Evolution of Sex* ed. R. Bellig and G. Stevens, pp. 161–69. San Francisco: Harper & Row.

Hrdy, Sarah Blaffer, and Daniel B. Hrdy. 1976. Hierarchical relations among female hanuman langurs (primates: colobinae, *Presbytis entellus*). *Science* 193:913–15.

Hrdy, Sarah Blaffer, and Patricia L. Whitten. 1987. Patterning of sexual activity. In *Primate Societies*, ed. B. B. Smuts, D. L. Cheney, R. M. Seyfarth, R. W. Wrangham, and T. T. Struhsaker, pp. 370–84. Chicago: University of Chicago Press.

Huck, U. William. 1984. Infanticide and the evolution of pregnancy block in rodents. In Hausfater and Hrdy 1984, pp. 349–65.

Huck, U. William, and E. M. Banks. 1982a. Male dominance status, female choice and mating success in the brown lemming *Lemmus trimucronatus. Animal Behavior* 30:665–75.

———. 1982b. Differential attraction of females to dominant males: olfactory discrimination and mating preference in the brown lemming *(Lemmus trimucronatus). Behavioral Ecology and Sociobiology* 11:217–222.

Huck, U. William, E. M. Banks, and S. C. Wang. 1981. Olfactory discrimination of social status in the brown lemming. *Behavioral and Neural Biology* 33:364–71.

Irons, William. 1979. Cultural and biological success. In Chagnon and Irons 1979, pp. 257–72.

231

Jacobson, Jodi L. 1987. *Planning the Global Family.* Worldwatch Paper no. 80. Washington, DC: Worldwatch Institute.

———. 1990. *The Global Politics of Abortion.* Worldwatch Paper no. 97. Washington, DC: Worldwatch Institute.

———. 1991. *Women's Reproductive Health: The Silent Emergency.* Worldwatch Paper no. 102. Washington, DC: Worldwatch Institute.

Jankowiak, William R., Elizabeth M. Hill, and James M. Donovan. 1992. The effects of gender and sexual orientation on attractiveness judgments: an evolutionary interpretation. *Ethology and Sociobiology.* In Press.

Johansson, Sheila Ryan. 1976. "Herstory" as history: a new field or another fad? In *Liberating Women's History,* ed. Berenice A. Carroll, pp. 400–430. Chicago: University of Illinois Press.

———. 1984. Deferred infanticide: excess female mortality during childhood. In Hausfater and Hrdy 1984, pp. 463–485.

Kahana, Kalman. 1977. *Daughter of Israel: Laws of Family Purity.* Translated by Leonard Oschry. 3rd ed. New York: Feldheim Publishers.

Kevles, Bettyann. 1986. *Females of the Species.* Cambridge, MA: Harvard University Press.

Kirkpatrick, Mark. 1987. Sexual selection by female choice in polygynous animals. *Annual Review of Ecology and Systematics* 18:43–70.

Kirkpatrick, Mark, and Michael J. Ryan. 1991. The evolution of mating preferences and the paradox of the lek. *Nature* 350:33–38.

Kodric-Brown, Astrid, and James H. Brown. 1984. Truth in advertising: the kinds of traits favored by sexual selection. *American Naturalist* 124:309–23.

Krebs, John R., and Nicholas B. Davies, eds. 1978. *Behavioural Ecology: An Evolutionary Approach.* London: Blackwell Scientific Publications.

Krebs, Robert A., and David A. West. 1988. Female mate preference and the evolution of female-limited Batesian mimicry. *Evolution* 42:1101–4.

Kristof, Kathy M. 1990. Women at the top—almost. *Los Angeles Times,* May 28, p. D1.

Kummer, Hans. 1968. *Social Organization of Hamadryas Baboons.* Basel, Switzerland: S. Karger.

Kunstadter, Peter. 1963. A survey of the consanguine or matrifocal family. *American Anthropologist* 65:56–66.

Lamm, Norman. 1966. *A Hedge of Roses.* New York: Philipp Feldheim.

Lampert, Ada, and Ariela Friedman. 1992. Sex differences in vulnerability and maladjustment as a function of parental investment: an evolutionary approach. *Social Biology* 39.

Lancaster, Jane B. 1984. Introduction. In Small 1984, pp. 1–10.

Lennington, Sarah. 1980. Female choice and polygyny in redwinged blackbirds. *Animal Behaviour* 28:347–61.

Leonard, Diana. 1980. *Sex and Generation.* London: Tavistock Publications.

Levine, Judith. 1986. *Abortion in America.* Washington, DC: Zero Population Growth.

232

Lewis, C. S. [1936] 1953. *The Allegory of Love*. Reprint. London: Oxford University Press.

Lieberman, Leonard. 1989. A discipline divided: acceptance of human sociobiological concepts in anthropology. *Current Anthropology* 30:676-82.

Lightfoot-Klein, Hanny. 1990. *Prisoners of Ritual: An Odyssey into Female Genital Circumcision in Africa*. New York: Haworth Press.

Lionnet, Françoise. 1991. Feminism, universalism and the practice of excision. In *Passages* (issue no. 1). Evanston, IL: Northwestern University Program of African Studies.

Lloyd, James E. 1979. Firefly communication. *Anima*, June, pp. 25-34.

———. 1981. Sexual selection: individuality, identification, and recognition in a bumblebee and other insects. *Florida Entomologist* 64:89-118.

———. 1984. Lights in the summer darkness. In *1984 Yearbook of Science and the Future*, pp. 188-201. Chicago: Encyclopaedia Britannica.

Loebenstein, Rabbi Yosef, trans. 1983. *Kitzur Dinei Taharah: A Summary of the Niddah Laws following the Rulings of the Rebbes of Chabad*. Brooklyn, NY: Kehot Publication Society.

Lovejoy, Owen C. 1981. The origin of man. *Science* 211:341-50.

Low, Bobbi S. 1990. Marriage systems and pathogen stress in human societies. *American Zoologist* 30:325-339.

Lucka, Emil. 1922. *The Evolution of Love*. Translated by Ellie Schleusener. London: George Allen & Unwin.

McClure, P. A. 1981. Sex-biased litter reduction in food-restricted wood rats *(Neotoma floridana). Science* 211:1058.

Marcus, George E. 1979. Elopement, kinship, and elite marriage in the contemporary kingdom of Tonga. *Journal de la Société des Océanistes* 63:83-96.

Marshall, Alex. 1991. Heifers. *Populi: Journal of the United Nations Population Fund* 18(1):52-56.

Mencher, Joan P. 1988. Women's work and poverty: women's contribution to household maintenance in South India. In Dwyer and Bruce 1988, pp. 99-119.

Milinski, Manfred, and Theo C. M. Bakker. 1990. Female sticklebacks use male coloration in mate choice and hence avoid parasitized males. *Nature* 344:330-33.

Money, John. 1980. *Love and Love Sickness: The Science of Sex, Gender Difference, and Pair-bonding*. Baltimore: Johns Hopkins University Press.

Morris, Desmond. 1967. *The Naked Ape*. New York: Dell Publishing Co.

Moyers, Bill. 1989. The vanishing family: crisis in black America. *A Second Look with Bill Moyers*. A production of Public Affairs Television. New York: Journal Graphics.

Murphy, Kim. 1990. Women drivers banned by Saudis as "portents of evil." *Los Angeles Times*, Nov. 15, pp. A1-17.

Murphy, Yolanda, and Robert F. Murphy. 1974. *Women of the Forest*. New York: Columbia University Press.

233

Mussell, Kay. 1984. *Fantasy and Reconciliation: Contemporary Formulas of Women's Romance Fiction.* Westport, CT: Greenwood Press.

Norsgaard, E. Jaediker. 1975. Connubial cannibalism. *Natural History,* Nov., pp. 58–62.

O'Donald, Peter. 1983. Sexual selection by female choice. In Bateson 1983, pp. 53–66.

Orians, Gordon H. 1969. On the evolution of mating systems in birds and mammals. *American Naturalist* 103:589–603.

Packer, D. C., and A. E. Pusey. 1983. Adaptations of female lions to infanticide by incoming males. *American Naturalist* 121:716–28.

Packer, D. C., D. Scheel, and A. E. Pusey. 1990. Why lions form groups: food is not enough. *American Naturalist* 136:1–19.

Parker, G. A. 1970. Sperm competition and its evolutionary consequences in the insects. *Biological Reviews* 45:525–67.

Pruett-Jones, S. G., and M. A. Pruett-Jones. 1990. Sexual selection through female choice in Lawes' Parotia, a lek-mating bird of paradise. *Evolution* 44:499.

Radway, Janice. 1984. *Reading the Romance: Women, Patriarchy, and Popular Literature.* Chapel Hill: University of North Carolina Press.

Raymond, Janice G. 1991. Women as wombs. *Ms* 1(6):28–33.

Reuben, Carolyn. 1992. *The Parent's Guide to Preventing Birth Defects.* Los Angeles: Jeremy P. Tarcher.

Robinson, Michael H. 1978. Marvelous and much-maligned spiders. *Smithsonian,* October, pp. 66–75.

Robinson, Michael H., and Barbara Robinson. 1979. By dawn's early light: matutinal mating and sex attractants in a neotropical mantid. *Science* 205:825–27.

Rosenblatt, Paul C., and Paul C. Cozby. 1972. Courtship patterns associated with freedom of choice of spouse. *Journal of Marriage and the Family* 34:689–95.

Rosenthal, Elisabeth. 1991. The forgotten female. *Discover,* December, pp. 22–27.

Roth, Eric Abella. 1985. Population structure and sex differences. In Hall 1985, pp. 219–98.

Rousseau, Jean-Jacques. 1979. *Emile, or on Education,* Book IV. Translated by Alan Bloom. New York: Basic Books.

Ryan, Michael J. 1980. Female mate choice in a neotropical frog. *Science* 209:523–25.

———. 1986. The Panamanian love call. *Natural History,* June, pp. 37–42.

———. 1990. Signals, species, and sexual selection. *American Scientist* 78: 46–52.

Ryan, Michael J., and A. Stanley Rand. 1990. The sensory basis of sexual selection for complex calls in the túngara frog, *Physalaemus pustulosus* (sexual selection for sensory exploitation). *Evolution* 44 (2):305–14.

el-Saadawi, Nawal. 1980. *The Hidden Face of Eve: Women in the Arab World.* London: Zed.

Sabbah, Fatna A. 1984. *Woman in the Muslim Unconscious*. Translated by Mary Jo Lakeland. New York: Pergamon Press.

Sadik, Nafis. 1990. *Investing in Women: The Focus of the '90s*. New York: United Nations Population Fund.

Sakaluk, Scott K. 1991. Sex for a song (dinner included). *Natural History*, September, pp. 67–73.

Sanger, Margaret. 1920. *Woman and the New Race*. New York: Maxwell Reprint Company.

Schaller, George B. 1963. *The Mountain Gorilla*. Chicago: University of Chicago Press.

Schlegel, Alice, and Herbert Barry III. 1986. The cultural consequences of female contribution to subsistence. *American Anthropologist* 88:142–50.

Schlegel, Alice, and Rohn Eloul. 1988. Marriage transactions: labor, property, status. *American Anthropologist* 90:291–309.

Schopenhauer, Arthur. 1942. *Complete Essays of Schopenhauer*. Translated by T. Bailey Saunders. New York: Willey Book Co.

Schuster, Ilsa M. Glazer. 1979. *New Women of Lusaka*. Mountain View, CA: Mayfield Publishing.

Shaver, Phillip, Cindy Hazan, and Donna Bradshaw. 1988. Love as attachment: the integration of three behavioral systems. In *The Psychology of Love*, ed. R. J. Sternberg and M. L. Barnes, pp. 68–99. New Haven, CT: Yale University Press.

Shepher, Joseph. 1971. *Self-Imposed Incest Avoidance and Exogamy in Second-Generation Kibbutz Adults*. Ann Arbor, MI: Xerox Microfilm Publications.

———. 1978. Reflections on the origin of the human pair-bond. *Journal of Social and Biological Structures*. 1:253–64.

———. 1981. The matrifocal family: from an anthropological curiosity to a world problem. In *Absolute Values and the Search for the Peace of Mankind*, vol. 2, pp. 999–1012. New York: International Cultural Foundation Press.

Shields, William M., and Lea M. Shields. 1983. Forcible rape: an evolutionary perspective. *Ethology and Sociobiology* 4:115–36.

Siskind, Janet. 1973a. *To Hunt in the Morning*. New York: Oxford University Press.

———. 1973b. Tropical forest hunters and the economy of sex. In *Peoples and Cultures of Native South America*, ed. D. R. Gross, pp. 226–40. Garden City, NY: Doubleday.

Small, Meredith, ed. 1984. *Female Primates: Studies by Women Primatologists*. New York: Alan R. Liss.

———. 1988. Female primate sexual behavior and conception: are there really sperm to spare? *Current Anthropology* 29:81–100.

———. 1989. Female choice in nonhuman primates. *Yearbook of Physical Anthropology* 32:103–127.

———. 1990. Promiscuity in Barbary macaques. *American Journal of Primatology* 20:267–82.

235

Smith, John Maynard. 1978. The ecology of sex. In Krebs and Davies 1978, pp. 159–79.

Smuts, Barbara B. 1983a. Special relationships between adult male and female olive baboons: selective advantages. In *Primate Social Relationships: An Integrated Approach*, ed. R. A. Hinde, pp. 262–66. Oxford: Blackwell.

———. 1983b. Dynamics of "special relationships" between adult male and female olive baboons. In *Primate Social Relationships: An Integrated Approach*, ed. R. A. Hinde, pp. 112–16. Oxford: Blackwell.

———. 1986. Sexual competition and mate choice. In *Primate Societies*, ed. Barbara B. Smuts, Dorothy L. Cheney, Robert M. Seyfarth, Richard W. Wrangham, and Thomas T. Struhsaker, pp. 385–99. Chicago: University of Chicago Press.

Sternberg, Robert J. 1986. A triangular theory of love. *Psychological Review* 93:119–35.

———. 1988. Triangulating love. In *The Psychology of Love*, ed. R. J. Sternberg and M. L. Barnes, pp. 119–38. New Haven, CT: Yale University Press.

Strum, Shirley C. 1987. *Almost Human: A Journey into the World of Baboons.* New York: Random House.

Stutsman, Rebecca. 1990. *The Invisible Woman: Improving the Status of Women Key to Stabilizing Population.* Washington, DC: Zero Population Growth.

———. 1991. *A Child's Place in an Overpopulated World.* A ZPG Backgrounder. Washington, DC: Zero Population Growth.

Symons, Donald. 1979. *The Evolution of Human Sexuality.* New York: Oxford University Press.

———. 1985. Darwinism and contemporary marriage. In *Contemporary Marriage: Comparative Perspectives on a Changing Institution*, ed. Kingsley Davis, pp. 133–55. New York: Russell Sage Foundation.

———. 1987a. An evolutionary approach: can Darwin's view of life shed light on human sexuality. In *Approaches and Paradigms in Human Sexuality*, ed. J. H. Geer and W. T. O'Donohue, pp. 91–125. New York: Plenum.

———. 1987b. Darwinism and contemporary marriage. In *Theories of Human Sexuality*, ed. James H. Geer and William T. O'Donohue, pp. 99–125. New York: Plenum.

———. 1989. A critique of Darwinian anthropology. *Ethology and Sociobiology* 10:131–44.

Tambiah, Stanley J. 1989. Bridewealth and dowry revisited: the position of women in sub-Saharan Africa and North India. *Current Anthropology* 30:413–35.

Taub, David Milton. 1984. Male caretaking behavior among wild Barbary macaques. In *Primate Paternalism*, ed. D. M. Taub, pp. 20–55. New York: Van Nostrand Reinhold.

Taylor, G. Rattray. 1954. *Sex in History.* New York: Vanguard Press.

Tennov, Dorothy. 1972. Prostitution and the enslavement of women. *Woman Speaking* 2:10–12.

236

_____. 1979. *Love and Limerence: The Experience of Being in Love.* New York: Stein and Day.

Thornhill, Randy. 1976. Sexual selection and paternal investment in insects. *American Naturalist* 110:153–63.

_____. 1979. Adaptive female-mimicking behavior in a scorpionfly. *Science* 205:412–14.

_____. 1980a. Rape in *Panorpa* scorpionflies and a general rape hypothesis. *Animal Behaviour* 28:52–59.

_____. 1980b. Sexual selection in the black-tipped hangingfly. *Scientific American* 242(6):162–71.

_____. 1981. *Panorpa (Mecoptera: Panorpidae)* scorpionflies: systems for understanding resource defense polygyny and alternative male reproductive efforts. *Annual Review of Ecology and Systematics* 12:355–86.

Thornhill, Randy, and John Alcock. 1983. *The Evolution of Insect Mating Systems.* Cambridge, MA: Harvard University Press.

Thornhill, Randy, and Nancy Wilmsen Thornhill. 1983. Human rape: an evolutionary analysis. *Ethology and Sociobiology* 4:137–73.

Tiger, Lionel. 1970. Male dominance? Yes, alas. A sexist plot? No. *New York Times Magazine*, Oct. 25, pp. 35–136.

Tiger, Lionel, and Heather T. Fowler, eds. 1978. *Female Hierarchies.* Chicago: Beresford Book Service.

Tiger, Lionel, and Robin Fox. 1971. *The Imperial Animal.* New York: Dell Publishing.

Tobach, Ethel, and Betty Rosoff, eds. 1978. *Genes and Gender: I.* New York: Gordian Press.

Townsend, J. M. 1987. Sex differences in sexuality among medical students: effects of increasing socioeconomic status. *Archives of Sexual Behavior* 16:425–41.

_____. 1989. Mate selection criteria: a pilot study. *Ethology and Sociobiology* 10:241–53.

Trivers, R. L. 1971. The evolution of reciprocal altruism. *Quarterly Review of Biology* 46:35–57.

_____. 1972. Parental investment and sexual selection. In *Sexual Selection and the Descent of Man 1871–1971*, ed. B. Campbell, pp. 136–79. Chicago: Aldine Publishing.

_____. 1974. Parent-offspring conflict. *American Zoologist* 14:249–64.

_____. 1976. Sexual selection and resource-accruing abilities in Anolis garmani. *Evolution* 30:253–69.

_____. 1985. *Social Evolution.* Menlo Park, CA: Benjamin/Cummings Publishing.

Trivers, R. L., and H. Hare. 1976. Haplodiploidy and the evolution of the social insects. *Science* 191:249–63.

Trivers, R. L., and D. E. Willard. 1973. Natural selection of parental ability to vary the sex ratio of offspring. *Science* 179:90–92.

237

Turke, Paul W. 1984. Effects of ovulatory concealment and synchrony on pro-tohominid mating systems and parental roles. *Ethology and Sociobiology* 5:33–44.

Turke, Paul W., and Laura L. Betzig. 1985. Those who can do: wealth, status, and reproductive success on Ifaluk. *Ethology and Sociobiology* 6:79–87.

United Nations. 1991. *The World's Women 1970–1990: Trends and Statistics.* New York.

United Nations Development Programme. 1991. *Human Development Report 1991.* New York: United Nations Development Programme.

United Nations Population Fund. 1991. *Population Issues Briefing Kit.* New York: United Nations Population Fund.

U.S. Department of Health and Human Services. 1990. Homicide among young black males—United States, 1978–1987. *Morbidity and Mortality Weekly Report* 39:48. Atlanta: Centers for Disease Control.

van Gulik, R. 1974. *Sexual Life in Ancient China: A Preliminary Survey of Chinese Sex and Society from ca. 1500 B.C. till 1644 A.D.* Leiden: E. J. Brill.

Verner, J. 1964. Evolution of polygamy in the long-billed marsh wren. *Evolution* 18:252–61.

Verner, J., and M. F. Willson. 1966. The influence of habitats on mating systems of North American passerine birds. *Ecology* 47:143–47.

Vining, Daniel R., Jr. 1985. Comment on J. Hartung. Matrilineal inheritance: new theory and analysis. *Behavioral and Brain Sciences* 8:680–81.

———. 1986. Social versus reproductive success: the central theoretical problem of human sociobiology. *Behavioral and Brain Sciences* 9:167–216.

Voland, Eckart, and Claudia Engel. 1990. Female choice in humans: a conditional mate selection strategy of the Krummhörn women (Germany, 1720–1874). *Ethology,* pp. 144–54.

vom Saal, Frederick S. 1983. Models of early hormonal effects on intrasex aggression in mice. In *Hormones and Aggressive Behavior,* ed., B. B. Svare, pp. 197–222. New York: Plenum Press.

———. 1984. The intrauterine position phenomenon: effects on physiology, aggressive behavior and population dynamics in house mice. In *Biological Perspectives on Aggression,* ed. K. Flannelly, R. Blanchard, and D. Blanchard, pp. 35–179. New York: Alan R. Liss.

Waage, Jonathan K. 1979. Dual function of damselfly penis: sperm removal and transfer. *Science* 203:916–17.

Walker, William F. 1980. Sperm utilization strategies in non social insects. *American Naturalist* 115:780–94.

Warner, Robert R. 1984. Mating Behavior and hermaphroditism in coral reef fishes. *American Scientist* 72:128–36.

———. 1987. Female choice of sites versus mates in a coral fish, *Thalassoma bifasciatum. Animal Behavior* 35:1470–78.

———. 1988. Traditionality of mating-site preferences in a coral reef fish. *Nature* 335:719–21.

———. 1989. Resource assessment versus traditionality in mating site determination. *American Naturalist* 135:205–17.

Watanabe, Teresa. 1992. In Japan, a "goat man" or no man. *Los Angeles Times*, Jan. 6, pp. A1–8.

Weinrich, James D. 1977. Human sociobiology: pair-bonding and resource predictability (effects of social class and race). *Behavioral Ecology and Sociobiology* 2:91–118.

West-Eberhard, Mary Jane. 1979. Sexual selection, social competition, and evolution. *Proceedings of the American Philosophical Society* 123:222–34.

———. 1983. Sexual selection, social competition, and speciation. *Quarterly Review of Biology* 58:155–83.

Wilson, Edward O. 1971. *The Insect Societies.* Cambridge, MA: Belknap/Harvard University Press.

———. 1975. *Sociobiology.* Cambridge, MA: Belknap/Harvard University Press.

Wittenberger, James F. 1981. Male quality and polygyny: the "sexy son" hypothesis revisited. *American Naturalist* 117:329–42.

Wittenberger, James F., and Ronald L. Tilson. 1980. The evolution of monogamy: hypotheses and evidence. *Annual Review of Ecology and Systematics* 11:197–232.

Wolf, Larry L. 1975. "Prostitution" behavior in a tropical hummingbird. *Condor* 77:140–44.

Wu, Chung I. 1983. Virility deficiency and the sex-ratio trait in *Drosophila pseudoobscura. Genetics* 105:651–79.

Yosef, Reuven. 1991. Females seek males with ready cache. *Natural History,* June, p. 37.

Zahavi, Amotz. 1975. Mate selection—a selection for a handicap. *Journal of Theoretical Biology* 53:205–14.

———. 1977a. The cost of honesty. *Journal of Theoretical Biology* 67:603–5.

———. 1977b. Reliability in communication systems and the evolution of altruism. In *Evolutionary Ecology,* ed. B. Stonehouse and C. Perrins, pp. 253–59. London: Macmillan Press.

———. 1981a. The lateral display of fishes: bluff or honesty in signaling? *Behaviour Analysis Letters* 1:233–35.

Zuk, Marlene, Kristine Johnson, Randy Thornhill, and J. David Ligon. 1990. Mechanisms of female choice in red jungle fowl. *Evolution* 44:477–85.

INDEX